MW01167195

WITH MURDER
YOU GET SUSHI

By Maddi Davidson

With Murder You Get Sushi

Denial of Service

Outsourcing Murder

WITH MURDER YOU GET SUSHI

A MISS-INFORMATION TECHNOLOGY MYSTERY

MADDI DAVIDSON

DEDICATION

To the people of Hawaiʻi, for the spirit of
aloha they have given to the world.
To all the Hawaiian surfers who
graciously shared their waves with us.
Aloha pumehana iā ʻoukou.

ACKNOWLEDGEMENTS

While sampling Mai Tais on Waikīkī—strictly for literary verisimilitude purposes, you understand—we have enjoyed the soul-soothing songs of many Hawaiian musicians. Special thanks go to the members of Kapala and to Eric Lee.

It takes excellent musicians with a lot of moxie (is there a Hawaiian word for that?) to take Hawaiian music and infuse it with jazz, and to create new music that will stand the test of time, as Kapala does. Their songs about a Japanese surf town and growing taro are as good as any Hawaiian songs ever written. All that, and they are super nice guys, too. Thank you, Kimo and Zanuck, for playing "Nani Hanalei" and "Raising Hāloa" for us so often. You can find more about Kapala and their *mele nani loa* (very beautiful music) at www.kapalamusic.com.

Whether Eric Lee is playing solo or with others, he is always *kamaha'o* (amazing). He plays classic and contemporary Hawaiian music and can even imitate—with respect and humor—other well-known Hawaiian musicians. Eric is always, always delightful. It seems apropos, as the Hawaiian voyaging canoe Hōkūle'a sails around the world to spread her message of *mālama o ka 'āina*, to call out Eric's rendition of "Hōkūle'a Hula," guaranteed to give you chicken skin. Check out Eric and his music at www.ericleehawaii.com.

PROLOGUE

"When ill luck begins, it does not come in
sprinkles, but in showers."
Pudd'nhead Wilson, Mark Twain

I READ SOMEPLACE that bad luck, like celebrity deaths, comes in threes. There are notably depressing exceptions, such as Dirk Hunter, a ranger for the U.S. Forest Service struck by lightning seven times. Make that lucky seven, since he lived to tell the tale and has moved to the Mojave Desert in a concerted attempt to avoid rain for the rest of his charmed life. My college classmate CeeCee Davis has worked for four different companies in the past few years, each of which has gone belly up. She swore off the private sector and went to work for the city of Stockton, just before they went bankrupt.

As for lucky lil' ol' me, what are the odds on finding three dead bodies in six months? My bad-and-rising *corpus delicti* count is a mystery to me, Emma Elizabeth Jones. I've never caught the bouquet at a wedding, I never find the last parking space let alone at rush hour, and I'm convinced shamrocks only ever have three leaves. As to winning the dead body lottery: I'm not the Angel of Death, a cop or gang member, on a search and rescue team, or in any profession that would, under normal conditions, bring me into regular contact with stiffs. I'm just a twenty-six-year-old professional nerd in the information technology (IT) industry, where the only death you routinely encounter is an expired hard drive, its unbackedup data long gone to bit heaven.

1

Until last July, my experience with death was confined to a few road-kill squirrels oh-so-tragically cut down in their nutty prime. Then I walked into my despised boss's office and discovered him stretched out on the floor with a permanent eye roll, courtesy of a vicious cricket bat to the head. A few weeks later, I peered under my inexplicably immovable car and found a 190-pound, seriously unpleasant surfer, dead from a head slam to a concrete parking block. Body number three was a committed anti-war protester in my apartment building who'd been run through with a sign emblazoned "Peace." I bet she hadn't been thinking of "Rest in Peace" when she made it.

That's all in the past. I've recently been assigned to a project in Hawai'i, my spiritual home (after heaven, of course). I'm convinced my luck has indubitably turned for the better, and that San Francisco cops will stop referring to me as Emma the Exterminator.

Hey, a girl can dream.

ONE

"If someone says expect the unexpected
slap them in the face and say 'I bet you didn't
expect that.'"
Anonymous

WHEN KAREN TAPPED me on the shoulder and announced everyone was heading out for lunch, I was knee deep in the geeky bowels of software code—about as much fun as reading cattle manifests in cuneiform. "I'm not at a good stopping point," I said. "Go on without me; I'll be ten minutes behind."

"Okay, but if you're late, you'll miss out on the papas," Karen replied.

"*Pūpūs*," I said, correcting her. "Save me a little *'ahi poke* and I'll owe you big time," I called out to her retreating back. Visualizing the fresh fish appetizer, I could almost taste the soy and *'alaea* (Hawaiian sea salt) on the yellow-fin tuna, the crushed *kukui* nut and the hint of chili pepper. My mouth watered in Pavlovian response to the promise of an *'ono* meal and I quickly combed through code.

Thirteen minutes later—long enough I was thorough, short enough there'd be *poke* left for me—I grabbed my purse and ran out to my Toyota—that is, my boyfriend's Toyota: ten years old with a new red paint job. On my advice, Keoni had left his 4Runner in Hawai'i with a friend as he departed for law school in San Francisco. I was thrilled to borrow his wheels because my status as a not-senior-enough consultant allowed me to rent nothing larger than a compact car barely spacious enough to transport a pair of swim fins for a midget instead of the surfboard I toted everywhere.

The Grant and Denholm project team had been on assignment for just over two weeks at Defense Forces Accounting Services, popularly known Dee-Fass, not Diff-Ass, as I'd unfortunately referred to it before a U.S. Army officer corrected me in an icy tone. This was GD's first government project, courtesy of David Blanchard, a new partner hired to start up a public sector practice. David was treating our team to lunch at a country club on the windward side, courtesy of reciprocity privileges with a snooty club in Marin where David was a member.

Although I knew my way around the island, having attended the University of Hawai'i several years ago, I wasn't familiar with the innumerable golf courses peppering O'ahu. However, the directions David's assistant had mailed out were straightforward and confirmed that there were signs as one neared the club. I was confident I could find it. After all, how lost can one get on an island?

Traffic on the Pali Highway was light for a change, and in no time I reached the windward side of the island. Descending the deeply clawed cliffs of the Ko'olaus, I spotted a green sign with a golfer. A few moments later, I wound along a tree-covered road fronting large homes until I passed through grandiose stone gates inset with gold lettering proclaiming The Luakini Golf Club. Capital "T," no less.

Auwē, that didn't sound right. Didn't the name of our lunch location started with a "K"? Was it Kalauao? Kapalua? Killmenow?

I drove past vibrant green grass swales and intensely manicured flower beds following the parking signs, and came to rest underneath spreading banyan trees. I pulled out my phone to call Karen and check the directions, but I had almost no signal strength. *Auwē, noho'i e.* Leaving the car, I trudged across the hot asphalt toward an area fronting the clubhouse where java sparrows were squabbling over a dropped morsel.

Suddenly, the earth reverberated with a loud explosion. Throwing my arms overhead in a panic, I crouched next to a small white car while charred objects peppered the surrounding pavement, clinking and splattering. My nostrils filled with smoke. Not volcanic: Madame Pele had vacated Oʻahu many millennia ago for the Big Island. I felt detached from reality until debris landed that didn't clink or splatter, but squished. Peering at the object, I gradually recognized its familiar form: a human hand, minus an attached arm or body. I felt nauseous and then dizzy. The dismembered hand faded into darkness and I fell through a long, dark tunnel.

SIRENS BLARING NEARBY registered first in my consciousness followed by an acrid odor. Surely heaven would be more quiet and fragrant, I thought. Opening my eyes, I saw spiky coconut palm fronds overhead against a bright blue sky. I prayed that the large coconuts clustered beneath the leaves would not be falling in the next few moments. I'd hate to live through the explosion only to croak from an errant coconut.

"How are you feeling?" a voice said.

I turned my head and realized I was not lying in a parking lot but on *mahiki*, what passes for grass in Hawaiʻi. A young man sat cross-legged on the ground next to me, his face bearing marks of concern, his slightly elongated eyelids, golden skin, and shiny black hair revealing him to be a *hapa* islander.

"Okay, I guess." I responded more out of habit than any actual inventory of the state of my body parts. I wiggled my appendages to check: all there. *Mahalo, e ke Akua* (thank God).

"Looks like you hurt your head a little when you fell. No blood, just scrapes and swelling on your forehead. I couldn't see any other injuries so I moved you onto the grass."

I put my hand to my stinging cheek, wincing as my fingers touched scratched skin, and then to the back of my head, finding no damage from the debris that had last hit me. I fingered my forehead, gingerly probing the beginning-to-ache bump. I giggled with relief. "I have a bimp on my head," I said, in my best Inspector Clouseau imitation.

The young man smiled, "A what?"

"I said, 'I have a bimp on my head.'"

"Oh, you mean a bump."

"That is what I said, you idiot. A bimp."

He joined me in laughing. "I see you're a *Pink Panther* fan. I'm Danny, Danny Estrada. When I heard the explosion I ran out to see if I could help." He waved his arm toward the clubhouse. "I work in the pro shop."

That explained the design on his aloha shirt: hula girls carrying golf bags and tiki gods teeing up. The alternating Titlist and *ti*-leaf pattern in the background made this a shirt you could wear only in a pro-shop and in the club bar, downing a G and T and lying about your golf score.

The siren blare stopped abruptly and I eased myself into a sitting position. Twenty yards away, flashing blue and yellow lights marked the presence of a fire truck, several police cars, and an ambulance. I closed my eyes and concentrated on the shimmering rustle of the trade winds tickling coconut fronds. Amidst the smoke and bitter odors I could still smell *pua melia*, plumeria, the scent of paradise.

"Are you going to faint again?"

"I don't think so. What happened? What was that explosion?"

"A car. I was told there was a charred body inside. I didn't … couldn't look." He paused for a moment and then added in a lower tone, "They say it is Greg Walker."

He said it as if the dead man had been a person of importance. Should I have known who he was? Maybe I did know, but my brain was still wobbling like the hula girl on the dashboard of Keoni's car.

A few yards away, a red-haired man with a sunburned bald spot wearing a shirt similar to Danny's walked toward us, gesticulating at the paramedics and pointing forcefully in my direction. One of the paramedics, his ultra-short hair screaming "military," hustled toward me.

"I don't need medical help," I said and tried to stand up, but Danny put his hand on my shoulder, pressing me down. "I'm just a little woozy. Coffee, that's what I need: dark roast that raises the dead. Shoot, I didn't mean to say that."

"Let him check you out, just to make sure. You really don't want to mess around with a head injury," Danny said.

"I'm okay," I said to the medic who introduced himself as Gerard—or was it Gerald? Only my head and face hurt, and I prayed the scrapes were minor; I don't consider myself a raving beauty, but no woman wants scars on her face. Not unless she has a snaggletooth, ratty hair, rides a broom, and her last name is Crone.

"We'll see," Ger-whatever said as he squatted next to me and proceeded to do a series of checks on my heart rate, dilation of eyes and status of my hands, feet, and head. Dark brown eyes under heavy black brows—the longest hair on his head—checked me out as his strong hands searched for other bruises or breaks. I did have a painful kink in my neck, which I was sure would feel better under the ministrations of those strong hands. I should also tell him about the sore spot on my shoulder—a typical surfing overuse injury. I wondered if he knew *lomilomi* massage.

"Marine Corps?" I said, noting the globe-and-anchor tattoo on his arm.

He remained silent but nodded as he continued to check me over. He certainly gave a nice pat down: much better than my recent encounter with TSA.

"Look," I said. "I wasn't hit by the blast or anything. I tend to get a little faint when encountering dead bodies ... or body parts. It's become an annoying and abhorrently frequent occurrence."

Danny regarded me strangely. "Dead bodies? Body parts? Have you been in a war zone?"

I shook my head. "Just tripped over a lot of dead people. Last thing I saw before I blacked out this time was a dismembered hand landing not five feet away."

Danny, a little green, glanced toward the parking lot, then closed his eyes slowly and shuddered.

Ger-the-Marine, still not saying anything, began cleaning my cheek and forehead with antiseptic.

"Ouch."

Danny got up and moved tentatively toward where I had fainted. He stopped for a moment, took a few more steps, bent over, picked up an object, and turned back. At a distance, the *ti*-leaf and Titlist pattern on his shirt didn't appear quite as hideous. Maybe my eyesight had been affected by the head injury.

Danny returned with the hand.

I drew back, messing up Ger-the-Marine's attempt to put a bandage on my cheek.

"Hold still, ma'am," he said in a deep voice. He didn't have to add, "That's an order," as the unspoken command was conveyed by his deep voice. I hoped he wasn't going to ask me to take the hill. I'd be lucky to manage taking ibuprofen.

I could see that Danny's gory accessory was too big to be a human hand although it was remarkably lifelike, even to the articulated fingers, the wedding ring on the third finger and hair on the back of the hands. I wondered where I could get one. I was sure I could use it in a diabolical manner to inflict payback on my brother, whose idea of a joke was to stuff realistic rubber insects in my Christmas and birthday presents.

"What is it?" I asked.

"A head cover." At my lack of response, Danny explained. "For golf clubs. Protects them from rain and from dinging each other. This was a rubber hand. Mr. Walker had his head covers made special."

"You should have left that where you found it," the medic said. "This is a crime scene."

"Huh?"

"You think cars blow up by themselves?" the medic said. "After two tours in Iraq, I recognize the aftermath of an IED when I see it."

I observed the object as Danny turned it over in his hands. Ripped in places with the little finger missing, it nevertheless was making a clear and definitively lewd gesture, all lifelike fingers curled, except for the extended middle finger. Even knowing it was rubber didn't help as long as my subconscious kept insisting it was a real hand.

"Time to play twenty questions," Ger-something said.

"Okay. Are you married?"

"I ask the questions." He didn't even crack a smile.

Geez, Mr. No-sense-of-humor.

"Do you have any of the following, headache, nausea, ringing in ears, blurred or double vision, confusion?"

"My head hurts where I fell on it so yeah, that's an ache. No to the others."

"Do you know where you are?"

"Not exactly. I was on my way to meet people for lunch at a country club and I took a wrong turn. I stopped to call for directions. Maybe you could tell me how to get another country club, nearby. 'K' something or other."

"That's easy," Danny said. The medic's stare stopped him from saying more.

The medic rattled off more questions about the date, the time, where I was working and concluded with asking me to remember three words: eight, glass, and *mahimahi*.

He grabbed his bag and got to his feet. "You'll be sore, naturally. Just take a couple ibuprofen as needed for the pain." He stretched out his hand and helped me to my feet. I felt a bit light-headed.

"Dizzy?"

"I'm good." Good enough to *hele* out of here to my lunch, if Danny would give me directions.

"Do you remember the three words I told you?"

"Eight, glass and *mahimahi*. No concussion, right?"

"No signs of one." he replied. "You can both come with me; the police are asking witnesses to gather in the restaurant for questioning." Ger-whatever turned and began walking toward the clubhouse.

"Cool," Danny said. "I've never been interviewed about a murder before." He practically bounced as he trailed Ger.

Unlike Danny, I had way too much experience with the police. The only interview I really wanted was from a waitress asking for my lunch order.

TWO

"It's déjà vu all over again."

Yogi Berra

Now WHERE WAS my phone? Tendrils of irritation invaded my thoughts as I wove in and around the parked cars; a sure sign that I needed *kaukau* (food), sooner rather than later. Nothing charred, though, and no *poke*. I wouldn't be eating any raw chunks of flesh for the foreseeable future.

I nearly stepped on a newly fallen pink plumeria blossom. Picking it up and inhaling deeply, I experienced the peaceful centeredness of being in Hawai'i. Still hungry but a smidge calmer I made a more careful search and found my purse behind the front wheel of the car I'd used as a shield. I rummaged through the purse in the off chance I'd shoved the phone inside when the explosion occurred. Yup, there it was, buried next to my makeup bag amidst a couple of old receipts, a half bar of surf wax, the car keys, and a wind-up shark I bought to add to my collection. In addition, I located a few coconut M&Ms in the bottom where they'd spilled from a half-finished bag. "Lunch is served," I muttered to nobody in particular.

I walked around, looking for a spot with good reception while keeping one eye out for Ger. I didn't want him to think I was concussed and wandering aimlessly. Finally I got four bars next to a coconut palm and called Karen.

"Emma, where are you? Are you still at the office?" Karen's voice came through clearly.

"No, there's been an accident," I replied.

"Oh, my God. Emma, are you okay?"

"Yeah, I think so; I wasn't in the one who had an accident. Technically, I mean. Although, I was kinda affected by it. Sorta." I've a tendency to babble when under pressure.

"You're stuck in traffic?"

"Not exactly. I pulled into the wrong golf course and was getting ready to call you for the directions when a car blew up. Not my car—one near me. Not too near, thank God. I mean, I'm okay but the police are here and I have to stay for questioning."

"What?"

On the other end, I could hear the hubbub in the background as Karen explained the situation to our co-workers. "Oh no, poor Emma," came through clearly along with a "boy, that sucks."

"Michael wants to speak with you," Karen said. "I'm giving him my phone."

I was stunned at the first words out of Michael's mouth. "I was afraid of something like this."

"Beg pardon?" Had his personal oracle prophesized my unfortunate involvement with a bombing?

"I vetted you GDers before consenting to taking you on this assignment." Michael's superciliousness spewed from the phone. "I didn't believe what I heard about your experiences at Zucker's. Now I know your superiors weren't exaggerating about you being a catastrophe magnet."

Michael Trang, brought in from Wilson & Kumar by David Blanchard, still referred to Grant and Denholm, or GD, as "you" or "it" rather than "we." Naturally he checked out the consultants who would be working for him, but why did Laura, my previous project manager, spill the beans on attendance issues that were not my fault? I couldn't refuse a polite (if not actually engraved) invitation from the local police to discuss the dead body I'd discovered in my apartment building. Similarly, I'd been delayed one morning when my car windows were broken and tires slashed in a senseless act in the kumbaya city by the bay. As for the day I took off,

Laura said I should take whatever time I needed after being nearly strangled by Laguna's killer.

After several months of working with Laura, had I told her I'd been abducted by aliens, I believed she'd merely ask if it would affect my ability to complete my work on time. Evidently she was not quite so blasé and felt the need to share my adventurous proclivities with future project managers.

At the conclusion of the call, I slipped the cell into my purse and took a last lingering look around the parking lot. Firemen were removing a tarp-shrouded object from the burned-out hulk of a car. I averted my gaze, but gray wisps of smoke wafted in my direction and the acrid smell I'd noticed earlier now had a hint of sweetness. Was that from tropical flowers, or burned flesh? I shuddered and my stomach roiled.

With a host of others waiting to be interviewed, it took nearly an hour before I could explain to the Honolulu Police Department that I hadn't seen anything and didn't know anything. I provided them with my name, Hawai'i address, phone number, and the three things I expected in a boyfriend—okay, made that last one up.

Despite the coconut M&Ms and a petrified gummy vitamin I'd managed to forage from a side pouch in my purse, I was starved, so on the way back to the office I stopped at a strip mall sushi place and ordered a small box of *'ahi* (yellow fin tuna) sushi to go. I thought I'd ordered sushi rolls: the *'ahi* rolled up in rice with a seaweed wrapper. When I opened the box at my desk, I found *nigiri*: slices of raw red *'ahi* on an elongated roll of rice, nicely presented on a *ti* leaf but nonetheless bearing a disturbing and nausea-inducing resemblance to five freshly cut fingers. The image recalled the fake hand in the parking lot and the acrid smell of burning flesh. I closed the box and deposited it in the kitchen refrigerator. Someone would snarf it up, I felt sure. Sliding a five-dollar bill in the vending machine, I made lunch out of cheese crackers and a Diet Dr. Pepper. Boring fare with the singular virtue of bearing no conceivable resemblance to dead body parts, hallelujah.

Michael came by the cube to reiterate his concern that I not become embroiled in another murder investigation and that last fall was a "one-time" event. Obviously no one had told him I'd actively investigated the murder of my boss last summer. I didn't enlighten him, but assured him I had no relationship to the deceased and witnessed nothing relevant to the murder.

Gunnar Sigridson, another ex-Wilson & Kumar consultant, also dropped in for a chat. His probing for details revealed a gossipy interest in the macabre scene. No, of course I hadn't taken a selfie with the destroyed vehicle, I said through curling lips, resisting the temptation to add, "and nobody with a *li'ili'i* bit of *aloha* would even think about it."

I didn't particularly like Gunnar, and for the most rational of reasons: he was too handsome. Bordering on six feet tall, blond hair sun-bleached already by the Hawai'i sun, blue eyes set off by easily bronzed and never burned skin, Gunnar could have been a male model if he had spent more time perfecting his pecs and less time doing the twelve-ounce press: *beaucoup* beers after work with his fellow consultants. His slightly longish hair that he tossed often and for effect and his readily deployed dimpled smile enabled him to successfully flirt his way to what he wanted. Did Eve feel this way about the snake? When I merely said I hadn't seen anything, the charm-drip dried up and he left.

Edvard Wouters, otherwise known as The Crazy Belgian, was my next visitor. His ears were still red from an earlier brouhaha. Edvard had been sporting his Matt Damon ears that morning (one of several pairs of prosthetic ears modeled on celebrities) as part of his ongoing preventive biometrics measures. According to Edvard, the uncategorized but all-knowing, all-seeing "They" now identified people based on physical characteristics that didn't change much over a lifetime, like the shape of ears. Michael noticed Edvard's ears slipping during a meeting with the client (not enough spirit gum) and had ordered Edvard to remove them.

Edvard was anxious to theorize about my experience, *quelle surprise*, and postulated that the explosion could have been a Marine drone experiment gone amuck or the assassination of a foreign spy. Did I recognize the car as an Audi A6, the semiofficial car of the Chinese Communist Party? All I could tell him was that it was a burned-out hulk whose hood ornament had been blown onto the eighteenth green, ruining a birdie opportunity according to one unhappy golfer.

The stream of inquiries continued in my cube, in the kitchen, and in the ladies' room all the way into the stall. Even "I gotta *go*" had not been enough to cut off questions posed by a DFAS human resources specialist. Eew.

By the twentieth request for disaster details from total strangers, I'd honed my response to: "Yes, I was there. No, I didn't see anything. No, I'm not hurt: just the scratches on my face, bump on my head, and a few hand dings. It's nothing a latte and a cookie won't fix. Are you buying?" I would follow this by dropping my head, wincing in pain—not all of which was faked—thereby discouraging further questions and eliciting caffeine and sugary sympathy.

It was after nine by the time I returned to my miniscule short-term lease apartment in Waikīkī. As it was two hours later in San Francisco, I wasn't about to phone my family about the latest in the amazing true adventures of Emma the corpse collector. My parents were always in bed by ten o'clock, and my brother Virgil, with a young daughter and a wife with another on the way (child, not wife) was also the early to bed type. If my sister Ariadne, a student at the University of California San Diego were still up, she'd be out partying and would resent the interruption.

I carefully crafted an email entitled "Exciting Times" with a link to the *Honolulu-Star Advertiser* on-line article about the explosion. I added a short sentence to the effect that I was "in the area" at the time of the explosion. All true, as far as it went. Seriously, did they need to know I'd been in the fallout, Keoni's 4Runner had a few dings that might be new, I was sporting cuts and bruises, and I was expecting to have nightmares about tomato and finger shish kabobs? *A'ole loa* (certainly not).

I copied Keoni and Stacey (my best gal pal) on the email and within a minute of sending the message, my cell phone chimed the "Hawaiian War Chant." Keoni.

"*Welina e Emma!*"

"*Aloha, e Keoni. Pehea 'oe?* I didn't expect you to be awake."

"Just finished with my study group, reviewing the cases for tomorrow. At this point the tort I am interested in is the dessert kind."

"I forgot, you're not allowed to sleep your first year in law school."

"I called because of your message. I don't believe it."

"The *Star-Advertiser* article?"

"You know what I mean; you being 'in the area' of the explosion. You were right there, weren't you?"

"Why do you say that?"

"I know you, Emma. The less you say the more there is to say. What truly happened?"

I gave him the whole story. Almost. I didn't tell him the paramedic was hot.

"Why did you not go to the hospital?" Keoni knew I hated doctors. He'd had to drag me to the local doc-in-the-box more than once with fin cuts from a surfboard.

"The medic said I was fine, *ke 'ōlelo pa'a nei au*, I promise."

He might not have believed me, but there was little Keoni could do from three thousand miles away. We moved onto safer topics. He wanted the surf report; Keoni didn't have much time or inclination for surfing the Northern California beaches and was counting the days until spring break and a return to Hawai'i. He let out a large sigh, and an even larger "*Auwē, noho'i e*" when I relayed the surf report for the next day: "solid four to six feet and perfect on the South Shore." An hour passed quickly and Keoni, claiming fatigue, ended the conversation. It was then that I realized that in all his concern for me, he hadn't even asked after his beloved 4Runner.

THREE

"I pressed down the mental accelerator. The
old lemon throbbed fiercely. I got an idea."

P.G. Wodehouse

THE NEXT MORNING, my face looked as if I'd walked through an
arbor of rose bushes right smack into a door. More like a revolving door that hit me multiple times on the way through it. Okay,
I exaggerate, but a girl has the right to be sensitive about her
face. The scratches on my cheek had scabbed over and a brilliant
purple bruise had formed around the bump on my head. A quick
surf session would help; salt water is great for aches, pains, and
wounds. The small kind that is, not open gashes with a copious
amount of blood that attracts hungry sharks within a twenty-mile radius.

I chose to surf close-in Canoes, named for the large outriggers
that traverse the waves with camera-toting tourists. As a surfer,
one soon learns to listen for the outrigger horn which means "*Ho
Brah, bettah hele on fo' you get make die dead.*"

No outriggers were out that morning, but newbie surfers
clogged the waves. I had more than one occasion to turtle—grab
the sides and roll under my surfboard—to avoid being clobbered
by surfers who hadn't learned advanced obstacle avoidance. A
kāne nui loa (extra large-sized man) nearly made me his hood
ornament. Planting my feet on the bottom and fiercely gripping
my board against the impact kept me from becoming so much

flotsam, and my right heel scraped across the coral, sowing another scar to add to my collection of inadvertent tropical tattoos.

When I surfaced, Mr. Kane-nui-loa was in the water, reeling in his board, which flopped like a large flat sturgeon at the end of his leash. I turned my back, flung myself on my board, and paddled toward the surf lineup, making a mental note to come in a bit early to bandage my heel to forestall bleeding all over the DFAS floor. Even if that meant bypassing the chance to say that I had literally shed blood on this project.

Surfing chills me out to the point that I'm happier than a golden retriever chasing a tennis ball. Neither the ineptitude of the XL surfer bothered me nor the time I spent slaloming around the many newbies thronging the waves like maggots on a fresh, tasty carcass. After all, I was surfing in a paradise of warm water, perfectly formed three-foot waves, bluer-than-blue skies, and a white sandy beach. The early morning sun cast a pinkish glow over the high-rises fronting the beach; the only sounds were the waves breaking over the reefs and the occasional, "Watch out! You almost hit me!" The scene was truly one of God's best works, except for the last part.

I arrived at work in a happy-dappy mood, well caffeinated thanks to a Kapu Coffee stop for a triple espresso with coconut syrup, whipped cream, and a chocolate-covered macadamia nut. I'd learned after the first day at DFAS to bring my own coffee. Civilians working at DFAS may vastly outnumber the military, but the military controlled the coffee, best described as Rotgut Dark Roast. A Navy lieutenant proudly proclaimed that in case of emergency, it could fuel both the F/A-18 and its pilots.

"Morning," I said as I walked by Karen's cube.

I slid into my chair just as Karen stepped into my cube.

"What?" I said as she eyed me without saying anything. Did I have a whipped cream mustache? I wiped my hand over my mouth.

"I've never seen you wear so much makeup," Karen said.

"Trying to cover yesterday's cuts and bruises."

With her chestnut brown hair and flawless skin, Karen didn't wear makeup, except the occasional subtle lip-gloss, especially noticeable today since the corners of her mouth twitched with her efforts to suppress a laugh.

"You remember we have a GD staff meeting in about ten minutes?" Karen said.

"Yup, where's the meeting?"

Karen consulted her iPhone. "Lady Golf."

"The military named a meeting room for the LPGA?"

"No. Leyte Gulf," Karen said, enunciating each syllable. "I presume it's named for a naval battle since everything else around here is. Building number five, third floor. Which way is that again?"

"*Mauka* and *'ewa*." DFAS Hawai'i occupied a series of low-rise buildings that stood watch on the hills guarding Pearl Harbor. Navigation required using the local frame of reference: *makai* or *mauka* (toward the sea and toward the mountains, respectively) and *'ewa* or Diamond Head (locations west and east of Honolulu). Of course, no matter which direction you took, you'd eventually run into the Pacific.

"I just need to check my email," I said, "and I'm ready to go."

"You'll want to sit near Edvard at the meeting and give him a careful once over." Karen didn't say more but when she turned to leave, her chignon bounced and her shoulders shook with laughter.

What was that about?

My email revealed no messages from family or friends. Home free, I believed, blissfully unaware that neither Stacey nor my mother were fooled by my message the previous evening. Knowing that I was unable to keep secrets from Keoni, they'd each called him that morning to give him the friends and family grill special.

I kept my eyes open for Edvard's departure and fell in alongside him as we traipsed the corridors. Despite Karen's intimation, I couldn't discern what if anything was different about him. Oh sure, he rambled on about one of the social media companies hoovering through emails and selling intelligence to advertisers ("Breaking up with your boyfriend? Our tissues dry more tears! Oh, and click here for a free membership in JerksNoMore Dating Service!"). But that was typical Edvard.

Arriving at the correct building and floor, we found enclosed offices stretching along the walls, providing the occupants with gorgeous views. A sea of identical cubicles filled the interior, swimming in artificial light. At the far side of the building we found the meeting room.

Michael and the other ex-Wilson & Kumar consultants sat on one side of the table. The old-guard GDers occupied the other side. To get a good view of Edvard, I sat with the ex-Wilson & Kumar team. I'd been seated for all of forty-five seconds when I gripped the edge of the table firmly, ensured both feet were on the ground, and peered into Edvard's eyes. Either I was becoming lightheaded or his eyes were off. Off being the acceptable, inclusive, diversity-embracing term for "nausea-inducing."

I glanced away quickly, took a sip of my coffee, and asked Edvard, obliquely, "Do I want to know why your eyes make the room spin?"

"Ah, those." He cleared his throat. "Special contact lenses."

"Don't tell me—they're a surveillance foil."

Unasked and without taking a breath, Edvard explained that iris scanners could be used at a distance of ten feet to identify individuals. The United States military had deployed hand-held iris scanners in Afghanistan to identify insurgents. He rattled off the various government agencies that were building databases of iris scans to the point where I began musing whether LASIK could be used to clear nearsightedness *and* foil the Department of Homeland Security.

Everyone appeared stunned. Whether from staring into Edvard's eyes or from his spiel, I couldn't be sure. Maybe both. When Michael spoke, he made it clear that however much Edvard might want to be undetectable by iris scan, his right to anonymous eyes stopped short of making clients and co-workers seasick or "iris-ill." He gave Edvard two minutes to ditch the contacts. Not a fan of Michael's dictatorial style, I was nonetheless grateful for it this time.

Michael quickly led us through the reporting of task progress versus plan. Our project included consolidating information from multiple, disparate legacy systems. Legacy is a consulting term for a bunch of software older than the tablets of Moses, written in a nearly dead programming language. We had a mountain of work to do, a mountain much bigger than Ararat.

As we were preparing to leave, Michael reminded Rafe, an old-guard GDer, that he was overdue in taking several government courses relating to ISM and PII—good names for irrational numbers, but in this case cryptic acronyms relating to security. I'd finished the courses the prior Sunday and on the boredom scale, they ranked right up there with the tutorial on using the new expense form.

"You need to get on the ball and complete the training so I can tell DFAS that everyone is up to speed; I'm spending more time generating reports on who has and hasn't taken courses than it would take you all to Just Get It Done." His eyebrows temporarily met in a fierce arch; there was no mistaking his meaning.

"I'd like to be excused from the PII training," Rafe said. "For religious reasons."

The packing up of computers and papers stopped as Rafe's request sunk in.

"What?" Michael was incredulous.

In unison, heads swiveled toward Rafe.

"Besides the fact that it is irrelevant to what I'm doing, I object to clicking on a demonic icon."

Heads swiveled toward Michael.

"What the heck are you talking about?" (In truth, his linguistic choice was a bit stronger than "heck.")

Back to Rafe.

"To start each module, one has to click on what appears to be a man holding a glass ball. It's blatant occult symbolism. I bet the course designer is a Satan worshipper."

Gunnar's vain attempt to suppress laughter came out as a snort.

"Take the course," Michael growled.

Karen clicked away on her computer. "I've got it," she said. She peered at her screen. "It is like a swami with a crystal ball. I never noticed that." She turned the screen so others could see.

Several of us crowded in to get a better view, but not Michael. "I don't give a … Take the training or you're off the project."

"Couldn't we get them to publish a new version without the symbol?" Rafe asked. "I mean, since this is being used across the U.S. Federal Government, others will have issues, too."

"If you think I'm going to ask the Feds to change their training module …" Michael was almost trembling with fury. He and Rafe stared at each other, neither willing to budge.

"How about if I click on the symbols for him?" I said, aiming to break deuce.

Rafe turned to me. "Couldn't let you do that. Galatians 6:5, 'For each one should carry his own load.'"

"I've taken the training so if there is a sin, I've already committed it."

"Now that you know the symbols are Satanic, it will be a double sin to click again."

Double sin? Is there a point system I don't know about? Like a credit score for entrance to heaven? "Rafe," I said in my sincerest tone, "I think I'm being called by the Lord to do this for you."

"Well, if that's the case, okay."

Snorting and hooting from the end of the table signaled Gunnar's abandonment of restraint. Michael's demeanor revealed no trace of amusement. "Today," he snapped.

FOUR

"I'll do what I can," I had said, immediately regretting my promise. Keoni had been so annoyingly persuasive that I wondered if his first semester in law school included a course in Pitching Legal Woo. He had told me, prior to extracting my reluctant promise of help, how much he missed me and how anxious he was to see me. All spoken in Hawaiian with his best baritone voice, which left me in a pleasantly and receptively mushy state before he made The Big Ask.

"*E kōkua mai iāia*" (help him), Keoni had pleaded. "Things look bad for Kealoha, and you might be the only one who can. He's *ʻohana*."

Use of the 'o' word was the ultimate guilt card. *ʻOhana* was family in Hawaiian culture, including both blood relations and family in spirit. Keoni's family had accepted me as *ʻohana*, which meant that technically, Kealoha was my *ʻohana*, too. There might be six degrees of separation between Kevin Bacon and the rest of the world, but in Hawaiʻi, there weren't more than two degrees of separation among *ʻohana*.

Kealoha Kanekoa had been arrested just two days after the murder of Greg Walker. The local TV stations KITV, KHNL, and KGMB had engaged in saturation coverage and I'd followed the news accounts closely, curious as to who had blown up my lunch hour and why. Half the puzzle was solved with the arrest, or so I thought until Keoni had called. Keoni had no idea why Kealoha had been arrested, just that he could not be a killer and needed my investigative skills.

I had reminded Keoni that enlightened self-interest fueled my previous sleuthing efforts. When my boss Padmanabh was murdered I became a suspect, and thus my investigatory efforts were expended to avoid living the remainder of my natural life in a heinous-shade-of-orange jumpsuit. I wouldn't have become involved in my neighbor Laguna's murder if Magda, my landlady and friend, hadn't been the prime suspect. Who would take in my mail and water my plants (not to mention, be my in-house bartender of choice) if she ended up in the slammer?

"No more Ms. Snoopypants," I'd told my mother when she called the day before, curious as to whether my proximity to a murder meant that I'd be taking up my Holmesian mantle (sans the deerstalker hat) once again. Since I'd merely experienced the explosion and wasn't fingered—pardon the expression—as a suspect, there was no earthly reason for me to fire up my forensic scientist, don my detective, parade my PI, or eye my investigator. Mother believed me. Heck, I believed me, until Keoni played the *'ohana* card.

Now I was on the hook, a reluctant catch and, if truth be told, miffed at Keoni for picking the scab of a sore spot between us. Whether he was guilty of murder or not, Kealoha was guilty of being a committed native Hawaiian rights activist. Keoni's recent passion for Hawaiian rights had ignited his interest in a law degree and a move to San Francisco, both good things. Yet his zeal left me, whose ancestors were a European goulash, feeling excluded. It was not an acceptable reason for refusing to help Kealoha, but my slow burn was crackling as I contemplated my predicament.

Reality bore no resemblance to *Hawaii Five-0* where one could zip around the island in a hot sports car, interview suspects, and trip over clues. Or be romanced by men with chiseled features and cute dimples, either. Traffic was so bad in Hawai'i that no one zipped anywhere, especially not on the H-1 at rush hour where the chronic island slowness known as *aloha* time reached new levels of torpor. Not to mention, GD Consulting would be less than thrilled if I missed my deadlines trying to get a line on the dead. Michael had made that clear. Besides, most Hawaiian men I knew didn't have dimples and, however much I might appreciate them, I wasn't currently in the market, for men or dimples.

What could I do? An Internet search, of course. At least an on-line investigation would let me listen to my favorite Hawaiian music, although given my lack of enthusiasm for this case, blues music may have been more apropos.

An hour-long online search fortified by a handy one-pound bag of coconut M&Ms brought a treasure trove of articles and a choco-late-induced high. (No, I didn't eat the whole bag.) The victim, Greg Walker, was a flashy real estate developer. He'd lived in the island for years and his projects ran the gamut from industrial parks to high-density apartments to high-end single-family homes. His profession-ally whitened teeth and combed-over hair regularly popped up in the opening of this or that new complex and in pictures of fundraising efforts that involved playing golf or otherwise drinking and hugging cute women.

Kealoha Kanekoa's Internet footprint was much smaller: two articles connected to his protest activity and a picture of his Kame-hameha high school class reunion. Whatever overlap existed between the Walker and Kanekoa orbits wasn't obvious.

"I'VE HAD A few words with Woutters," Michael said. "His weird behavior has to stop. Immediately. If the client gets wind of his oddi-ties, we may lose all credibility and a chance at follow-on work."

I had to agree with him, but why was he telling us about his problems with Edvard? I'd barely made it in the door that morning when Karen and I had been summoned to an audience with His Grimness.

No "good morning," "please, sit down," "nice day, isn't it," or anything approaching a pleasant preamble. Michael launched right into his diatribe about Edvard, concluding with "I expect you two to manage Woutters."

"Why us and manage how?" Karen said.

"I'm aware you've worked with him before," Michael said to Karen. "He said you were a friend, too." Michael turned to me.

"He called me a friend?"

"He said you understood him."

How on earth had I given that impression, besides entirely and emphatically unintentionally and now, regretfully?

"As for managing him, I want you both to keep an eye on him. Check his appearance daily. I don't want a repeat of the lunatic contact lenses or the elf ears. Ensure one of you is with him in every meeting. In the event he starts in on one of his conspiracy theories, you can shut him down ASAP: change the subject, kick him under the table, whatever you have to do."

"We're to baby-sit him?" Karen was incredulous.

"Exactly. Edvard Woutters is half crazy and 100 percent brilliant. We need him on this project. Managing him is as important as your other work assignments. Just get it done."

Jeez. Not even an offer of a cup of coffee. I can be enticed much more readily over a frothy caffeine concoction than over frothy rhetoric.

Returning to our cubes, Karen mumbled about needing to impress Michael no matter the cost while I pondered which would be more difficult, solving a murder or being Edvard's minder.

The subject of our thoughts arrived moments later sporting a wool Rat Pack fedora. My conspiracy antennae were suddenly on the alert. In Hawai'i, the normal hat is never anything heavier than the canvas of a baseball hat or *lau hala*—woven pandanus leaves. Karen and I both saw the sunlight flash off the inside of Edvard's hat when he took it off.

The inquisition regarding Edvard's odd sartorial choice was held in abeyance when he loudly announced he'd brought six KopeManias: Kona coffee, macadamia nut and sugar cane syrups topped with whipped cream and a dark chocolate-covered coffee bean. Yum.

Gunnar and Rafe emerged from their cubicles to tank up and we stood around for a few minutes, enjoying the coffee and gossiping.

"Why can't people just talk instead of putting it all on slides?" Rafe said. Just over a week into our assignment it had become painfully obvious that DFAS was managed through PowerPoint. "I mean, if they want me to read it, just hand me the deck instead of making me sit for an hour while they flip through fifty slides."

"Fifty is nothing," Gunnar said. "I was on a project at right pat when a bird colonel started shitting bricks over a visit from DC brass who'd heard he had an IBM. He had us help him prepare a humongous PowerPoint presentation: a hundred and eighty-four slides!"

"What is right pat?" Karen asked as she reached into her cube for a pen and a scrap of paper.

Gunnar looked surprised. "Wright-Patterson Air Force Base."

Karen jotted down a note. "And bird colonel?"

"A full colonel, higher than a lieutenant colonel."

"Got it," Karen said as she took more notes. "Why was the bird colonel upset about IBM? Were you supposed to be using Hewlett-Packard or Apple? Or do you mean IBM the big missile?"

"IBM stands for Internal Bloody Mess." Gunnar said. "Did you think I meant Intercontinental Ballistic Missile? That's ICBM." He shook his head in an "everybody knows that" fashion.

Karen signaled for Gunnar to proceed.

"Where was I?" he said. "Oh yes, the slides. They never saw the light of day. Snowpocalypse came through the day of the planned visit and dropped sixteen inches of the white stuff. The brass, er, Air Force officers rescheduled their visit for the following week. ABD, another big dump, came through with ten inches of new snow and high winds. Long story short, the visit didn't take place until that summer, by which time the bird, er, colonel had orders and was on his way to another billet."

"A toilet?" Karen asked.

"Not bidet, billet. A military assignment." More "everybody knows that" headshaking by Gunnar. Apparently, everybody didn't know that.

"Telling your Wright-Pat story again?" Linda Sun, another former Wilson & Kumar consultant, strolled into the office. Edvard handed her the last coffee.

"Absolutely," Gunnar responded. "I love having fresh meat for my war stories." He flashed a big smile at Karen. "If you're willing to listen to more tales from the annals of government malpractice, I'll teach you a few more useful acronyms."

The gossip group dispersed leaving Karen and me to converge on Edvard's cube.

Karen spoke first. "Why does your hat have a silver lining?"

Yup, let Karen handle this one. I took another gulp of my concoction. Deelish. I wish he'd gotten the *nui loa* (very big) size.

"Foil," Edvard responded. "Protects against mind reading. I'm wearing my George Clooney ears, too; realistic, aren't they? I'd add eyebrows except they don't stay put in the heat. If I keep my head down, surveillance cameras can't make me."

A discussion of Edvard's concern about mind reading would inevitably lead to la-la land, so Karen chose to ignore it. "Surveillance cameras may not pick you out, but your position can be triangulated through the GPS system in your cell phone," she said.

"I thought of that, too." Edvard opened his messenger bag and dropped a small rectangle on Karen's desk with a thud. "My case shields the phone from cellular signals, WiFi and GPS."

"Meaning you can't use the phone?"

"It has a fast release mechanism—I can make a call, then cover it up again to prevent 'Them' from tracking me. The case is an electric field-blocking Faraday cage."

"Does it turn into a light saber?" Karen asked.

"Joke all you want—'They' will know exactly where you are when 'They' come to pick you up."

"Would that be our government or the NSA as in the National Society of Aliens?" Karen's irritation was palpable.

I reluctantly entered the conversation. "Did you use enough spirit gum on your ears today? Michael won't be happy if they fall into the coffee pot again."

Edvard nodded. "I got a new tube; I'm all set."

Melia, one of the DFAS IT managers, chose that moment to sashay in for a meeting with Edvard, greeting him warmly. She wore a form-fitting dress with a flared skirt, red, with white hibiscus, and was that a hint of perfume? I sniffed again. Tuberose, and quite heavenly.

"What are you meeting about?" I inquired.

"Determining which is the system of record for the information we're consolidating."

Karen and I exchanged meaningful glances. She broke first. "I think I need to be in on that," she said.

Was I imagining it, or did Melia's face fall in disappointment?

Karen grabbed her laptop and moved into Edvard's cube. No smugness on my part at winning round one with Karen, as I knew my babysitting at-bat would come.

With Karen out of her cube and out of hearing range, I took the opportunity to call Keoni's Uncle Kimo. A lawyer by trade, Uncle Kimo practiced civil law relating to native Hawaiian issues. It was he who had encouraged Keoni's interest in native rights, informed Keoni of Kealoha's arrest, and found Kealoha a good defense lawyer.

After pleasantries, Uncle mentioned that Keoni had called and told him that I could help prove Kealoha's innocence. "Keoni has great faith in your abilities," he said.

It was clear from the stress on "Keoni" that Uncle did not share that faith. Nevertheless, he agreed we should meet to discuss the case. Uncle suggested I join him after work at KJ Chan. Not to be confused with PF Chang, KJ's was a well-known local watering hole on the edge of Chinatown, its sole commonality with PF being an offering of chicken lettuce wraps; KJ's was *much mo' bettah da kine.*

FIVE

"The people to whom your fathers told of
the living God, and taught to call 'Father,'
and whom the sons now seek to despoil and
destroy, are crying aloud to Him in their time
of trouble; and He will keep His promise,
and will listen to the voices of His Hawaiian
children lamenting for their homes."

Queen Liliuokalani

"If you see the Aloha Tower, you've gone too far," Uncle Kimo had said when giving me directions. The Aloha Tower, once the tallest structure in Hawaiʻi, had long since been dwarfed by several forty-story skyscrapers in downtown Honolulu. Nevertheless, it is still a convenient reference point along Nimitz Highway/Ala Moana Boulevard and a beacon of nostalgia for the days when a glamorous trip to Hawaiʻi was on a Matson ocean liner.

As Uncle predicted, I missed the turn for KJ's. Just past the aforementioned Aloha Tower I whipped a U-turn on a slightly pink light in front of a sign prohibiting U-turns. Two cars behind me executed the same maneuver. Traffic moved slowly—one of the virtues of rush hour—and I was able to spot KJ's in a not-yet-redeveloped strip mall, which included a paint store, a UPS store, and of all things, a combination martial arts/yoga studio. Do you say "namáste" before or after kicking your opponent's *ʻōkole*?

A wall of sound, indicative of an active bar scene, greeted me as I strolled in. KJ's offered a sit-down restaurant, but the bar was clearly the profit center, occupying just one-third of the floor space but nearly all the clientele. A typical *pau hana* (after work) Hawaiian gathering, the patrons reflected the island mix of ethnicities. Males resembled *pīkake* (peacocks) in their colorful aloha shirts, and the women dressed in everything from a *muʻumuʻu* to jeans.

"Emma. Emma Jones, over here."

Uncle Kimo beckoned from a table near the front window. If he hadn't augmented his five-foot-five stature by standing on a chair, I never would have spotted him.

I returned his wave and began to corkscrew my way through the packed bodies. When I reached him, Uncle carefully stepped off the chair and gave me a warm hug.

"Emma, it's been too many years. *He nohea ʻoe i kuʻu maka* (you are lovely indeed). Let me introduce you to John Morimoto and Tashi Uyeda. John, Tashi, this is Emma."

The two men sitting at the table stood and shook my hand. Both were of similar stature to Uncle, making me feel positively Amazonian. Politely, they waited until I sat down before resuming their seats. Uncle Kimo explained to John and Tashi that I was a friend of Keoni's, U. of H. grad, *ʻohana*, and in Hawaiʻi on a consulting gig. In turn, he told me that Tashi, a state legislator, had been his neighbor for over twenty years and John was a childhood friend.

"John plays with Keoni," he said, turning to me.

It took me a moment to realize he meant with Keoni's music group.

"What instrument?" I managed to blurt out.

"Alto uke and slack key guitar."

"*Mea hoʻokani pila akamai*, a skillful musician," Uncle said.

John laughed and his eyes twinkled. "*Kahiko wale nō*, merely an old musician."

"I remember when you first learned 'Mary had a Little Lamb,'" Uncle said. "It was dreadful."

That led to a conversation about how life was different when they were boys. Mostly they spoke among themselves, seemingly replaying a conversation they'd had many times about the old Hawai'i versus the new Hawai'i. Occasionally they'd ask me to provide "a young person's point of view" on some matter. Clearly preferring many aspects of the old Hawai'i, they nevertheless agreed the new Hawai'i had its pluses, like the availability of *poi* and *lomilomi* salmon in a convenient combo-pack at the grocery store.

When the waitress emerged from the crowd, I asked for a white wine. Tashi urged me to order the *'ahi poke*. "*Fresh here, ya? 'Ono.*" I didn't need convincing.

John began speaking of the disruption occurring by the construction of the new Honolulu rail system when Uncle Kimo shook his head. "No, no, no. We'll be here for hours if we start in on that mess, and Emma and I have business to discuss. That goes double for any discussion of Kaka'ako," he said.

John and Tashi got the not-so-subtle hint, excused themselves, grabbed their drinks and headed for the bar. Their chairs were still warm when a heavy-set man at a nearby table swooped in like a hungry gull and snatched them for his flock of eight open-mouthed relatives standing at a table for four.

"What's Kaka'ako?" I asked before Uncle could speak.

"Another in a long line of developments." Uncle waved his hand dismissively. "We have a more important matter to discuss."

Uncle moved his chair closer to mine so I could hear him more easily above the noise. "I must be honest with you, I don't understand why my nephew chose to involve you in this killing. He said that *ke Akua* works in mysterious ways and that you have developed a talent for solving murders."

"Whether it is a blessing or a curse from *ke Akua*, I don't know, but I expect you want to hear about the bodies and killers I've encountered." Uncle nodded and I proceeded to acquaint him with the murders of Padmanabh and Laguna, pausing merely to sip wine and scarf down the *poke*. Clearly not a trial lawyer, Uncle's face registered his disbelief as I told of bugging apartments, having my car vandalized and fighting off killers with Hawaiian war instruments. Hey, if I hadn't lived through it, I'd have a hard time believing it, too.

I concluded my tale by explaining that I was in the parking lot when Greg Walker's car exploded. "Maybe that's God's way of involving me, whether I want to be or not."

"Who am I to question *ke Akua*?" Uncle said. He didn't even crack a smile. "It's clear that you have a gift for investigation and have been fortunate. However, I do not feel that you should actively search for Greg Walker's killer."

Maybe Uncle had sensed I'd grudgingly agreed to Keoni's request. "I can live with that. You'll tell Keoni, right?" *Maika'i nō* (great), I was off the fishhook.

Uncle held up his hand. "Not actively search for the killer," he repeated, "but use your skills to surface other motives or suspects. You do not need to prove their guilt, but simply assess who might have set off the bomb and why."

"But I don't know any of the people involved. In my prior ... experiences, I was on home turf. Wouldn't a local PI be better?" Having experienced a brief respite, I was eager to be free of my promise.

"Not being locally connected is a positive. You will be able to assess evidence without the prejudices of those of us who are too close to see clearly. *He 'ike ana hou*. A fresh viewpoint."

Rats. There went my "Get Out of Investigation Free" card.

Uncle launched into an overview of the case against Kealoha. As he talked about Greg Walker, I sensed he was struggling to remain non-judgmental. Nevertheless, the Greg Walker that emerged from his narrative was not Mr. Congeniality. More like Mr. Contentious. Walker had been divorced twice and had been living with a young woman twenty years his junior. He had five children from the two marriages and some said he had fathered the daughter of his current girlfriend, Joline Smutz, a former Lentil Queen from Colfax, Washington.

Was there actually a place called Colfax and who would want to be a sovereign of a legume?

Walker came to Hawai'i in his late twenties. Within six months he had married Marla Matsumoto, a young woman from a wealthy *kamaʻāina* (long-term resident) family, and was developing residential real estate. He became a well-known and even notorious developer across the islands due to his high profile and often-fractious developments. He'd gone through several booms and busts, making and losing fortunes along the way. Rumor was that he had recently lost significant amounts of money, despite the generally positive real estate climate.

The case against Kealoha stemmed from an investment by Walker in a research and development facility, the Loʻi Kalo Labs, whose goal was to bio-engineer taro to improve yields. Although the lab claimed it was experimenting with Tahitian taro, local environmental and native Hawaiian groups were upset that the lab's work might contaminate Hawaiian taro, a staple crop of old for the *kānaka Hawaiʻi* (people of Hawaiʻi). Kealoha was the leader of the protest movement, Kūlohelohe.

"Which means?" I didn't recognize the Hawaiian word.

"Natural, not contaminated by human hands."

"With two ex-wives and a trail of disappointed investors in Mr. Walker, why do the cops think Kealoha did it?"

"First of all, the lab had received threatening letters from someone purporting to be from Kūlohelohe. There have been incidents: spray painting of the buildings, fences cut, and for some odd reason *lūʻau* left on cars in the parking lot. You know *lūʻau* in this case means 'taro tops,' ya?"

I nodded, although I'd not heard that usage before.

"Secondly, a preliminary report on the chemical signature of the explosive indicates a possible match with the explosives being used in the construction of HART, the Honolulu Rail Transit project, where Kealoha's company is working. Finally, Kealoha was seen at the country club near the time of the explosion. It's hardly conclusive evidence, but my friends in the district attorney's office think they can build a strong case. Kealoha is in deep *kimchi*."

"Do the police have any other serious suspects?"

"That I don't know."

We sat in silence for a few moments, each deep in thought. Mine included wondering if I should order *kālua* pork potstickers since I was still *pōloli loa* (very hungry).

"John, whom you just met, is giving a *lū'au* this Sunday; it's the one-year birthday of his grandson. Kealoha will be there. You must come and meet him in an informal setting."

How could I say no to that? I nodded my assent.

"Is there anything else I can do to help you?"

I shook my head. "Not until after I've interviewed a few of the suspects."

"Where are you going to start?"

"At the beginning, of course. *Wid numbah one wahine.*" As I got up to leave Uncle touched my hand softly.

"*One moah ting*: I'd like your promise that you will share with me everything that you discover and you'll take no risks."

I duly gave Uncle my promise. At the time, I meant it, too. Unfortunately, neither of us knew that in paradise, my danger-ometer didn't work worth a darn.

SIX

"More than one in ten Americans would
rather get a colonoscopy than spend time
cleaning up their computer."
PCTools Survey

FRIDAY PASSED UNEVENTFULLY, thank God: no dead bodies, no new conspiracy theories from Edvard, and no PowerPoint-marathon meetings. Okay, someone accidentally hit the fire alarm and we had to evacuate, but I wasn't going to complain about a fifteen-minute recess on a glorious, warm afternoon. Especially when I'd grabbed the last almond croissant from the kitchen before leaving the building. I thought sure the announcement was "all pastries must evacuate immediately."

The day passed quickly and I left work at seven to meet up with a few college friends.

"Hey girl! *Howzit?*"

Noelani beckoned me into the tiled foyer of her apartment and gave me a big hug; we hadn't seen each other in over two years.

"*Mahalo no ka lei lani,*" I said in appreciation for the *ti* and *pīkake lei* she placed on my shoulders. "Mmm, smells lovely."

Noelani stepped back and gave me the once over. "*You looking keʻokeʻo, sistah.*"

"Hey, I'm working on my tan; I don't have your natural advantages." Noelani, a mixed island plate like many of my Hawai'i friends, sported a naturally golden skin courtesy of her *kānaka maoli* (native) roots, whereas her long black and very glossy hair was a testament to her Chinese great-grandfather.

"Is that the *haole* girl?" a voice called from inside the apartment.

"C'mon back. Clarissa and Maryn are here," Noelani said.

I kicked off my shoes reflexively by the door—nobody in Hawai'i wears shoes in the house—and followed Noelani down the short hallway to a white-carpeted living area.

Screams of recognition and more hugs greeted my arrival. Clarissa Kawakami was Noelani's cousin and a fellow surfer—she'd taken me out at Laniakea for my first North Shore experience. Maryn Paniagua had been a suitemate freshman year. These three friends had seen me through my college years and sine wave (up-down-up) romance with Keoni without ever once telling me I was *hūpō loa* (very stupid).

The view from Noelani's thirty-second floor apartment was killer: a panorama of the hundred-acre Ala Moana Beach Park, Magic Island, and the ocean. Before I could ask, Noelani confessed that her mother, a long-time real estate agent, had purchased the condo as an investment and Noelani was renting from her parents at a below-market rate.

I was still admiring the vista when Noelani thrust a wine glass in my hand. "Here, try this, it's *'ōkolehao*. Rissa brought a bottle."

I dubiously eyed the splash of liquid swirling in the glass. *'Ōkolehao* was a native Hawaiian alcoholic drink based on the root of the *ti* plant. The name, *'ōkolehao*, meant "iron-bottom" for the pots used in the still, although I'd heard it also described the way one felt after drinking too much of it.

A hesitant sip revealed an indeterminate tropical flavor and a surfeit of alcohol.

My face must have revealed my reaction because without saying anything Noelani took my glass and handed me a white wine.

"Thanks," I said. "A little strong for my taste."

"Me too," she said, "Just thought you might want to try it; as I recall you were willing to try almost anything."

"Gastronomically, yes, except for the fried crickets."

Noelani laughed. "You'll be happy to know insects are not on the menu tonight." She led me to a small alcove housing the *pūpū* table. Vulture like, I hovered over the table while she pointed out the choices: *pipikaula* (Hawaiian beef jerky), Korean-style short ribs, Portuguese sausage, coconut-battered shrimp with spicy orange sauce, a cream cheese/yogurt dip with fresh strawberries, pineapple, and papaya, and Portuguese sausage formed into finger-size links. At the sight of the links the memory of the pungent smell of the wreckage overtook me, inducing an ever-so-brief spell of nausea. Quickly I filled my plate, ignoring the sausages and loading up on the coconut shrimp.

I trod carefully into the living area, concerned lest I spill food on Noelani's pristine-white carpet. Taking a seat on a rattan sofa that I recognized from college, I dove into the food. A few moments later I sensed a lull in the conversation and raised my head to find my friends staring at me.

"What? Do I have coconut on my cheek?"

Rissa nodded at my plate. "Got enough there?"

"We'll see."

Noelani grinned. "Same old Emma. Don't get between her and the food when she want *grindz*."

"If you can take a breath or two while you're eating, tell us what you're doing in Hawai'i," Maryn said. "Noelani wouldn't tell us."

"Not wouldn't but couldn't," Noelani said, "I don't understand tech-speak. Go ahead, Emma, tell them what you told me."

I licked the orange sauce off my fingers. "If you must know, I'm working on a project to apply non-traditional database management tools to capture, store, search, and analyze a large, complex data set, synthesizing data currently residing in multiple, disparate systems to identify correlations that may indicate potential duplication in the procurement of goods and services across DoD with the intent to reduce DoD expenditures in line with the Fiscal Responsibility Act of 2008."

"If you don't want to talk about work, just say so." Noelani said.

"I don't want to talk about work."

"Then let's talk about when you're moving back," Clarissa said.

"Who said I was moving back?"

"C'mon. You know you miss it here in *Hawai'i nei*. Besides, I understand you and Keoni are hot and heavy again."

"Where did you hear that?"

"The coconut wireless, *sistah*," she said. "Keoni's Auntie Elikapeka's cousin Momi is the hairdresser of my *makuahine*. Naturally, I know everything about what he's up to. If you decide to get hitched, let me know *wha kine ring you like. Fastah dat way*."

"I do miss Hawai'i. Keoni and I are seeing each other, naturally, since he's in San Francisco. That doesn't mean I'm going to move back to Hawai'i."

"So you and Keoni are going to break up again?" Noelani said. "Because you know he'll come back here when he's done with school. I thought after a couple years of the career thing—you know, the work you don't want to talk about with *kau mau hoa maika'i*, your good friends—you'd realize that there is more to life."

"It's not just about career opportunities," I said and explained that the gulf between Keoni and me regarding native Hawaiian rights loomed large. It was if I had netted a shark, engaging in a thrashing dance to avoid bloodshed. Noelani and Maryn were adamant in their support of the native Hawaiian rights movement. Rissa pointed out that neither of them were more than 1/8th Hawaiian and that some of the rights activists were thinly disguised racists, which led to an argument about who were the "real Hawaiians." The depth of feeling on both sides took me aback. We were saved by the bell from further acrimony. Literally. Jenny, Sara, and Patricia, the other members of our "Seven Sistahs" band in college arrived. They blamed their tardiness on a tattoo party.

"What is a tat party?" I said. "If it's a show and tell for tattoos, I hope the hostess vetted the guest list; I've heard of people getting inked in, well, embarrassing places."

Patricia elucidated. "It's a group tattoo session. If you can get five or more guests to sign up, a guy from Tatty-Tat will bring his equipment and do the tats in your own home, at a 30 percent discount."

"You all got new tats?" Noelani asked.

Patricia shook her head. "Most of us enjoyed the food, drink and entertainment."

"I got two." Sara Hokuikekai took off her shawl, to reveal the bandages on her shoulder. "I have to keep them covered for a couple hours. One is a Hawaiian tribal tat to honor my *kupuna*," she said, smiling brightly. "The other is a star formation including *Ke Ali'i o Kona i ka Lewa*, one of the stars followed by my ancestors sailing from *Kahiki* to Hawai'i."

"Emma, you still tat-less?" Patricia said.

I nodded. "My ancestors, Vikings, were sailors who explored new worlds, too. But I think a tribal tat to honor them would include a bearded Norseman in a horned helmet."

Everyone agreed I should find another way to honor my ancestors.

During the remainder of the evening we chatted about the usual subjects on the minds of twenty-something females: boyfriends, fashion, careers, boyfriends, eating, recipes, and boyfriends. Rissa and long-time boyfriend Tomas, whom she'd been with as long as I had been dating Keoni, had split up a few months earlier because of his gambling addiction. Small-time gambling being prevalent on the islands, Rissa did not realized the extent of his problem until Tomas invited her to a party in the country which turned out to be a cock fighting event. Tomas hit her up for some money so he could place a few bets; he was low on cash because he'd "had a few losses, lately." Disgusted with the sport and the man, Rissa left and bummed a ride to the nearest bus stop.

I was sorry, of course, for Rissa, but in some small way I felt better; Keoni and I may not be on the same side of every issue, but we shared and enjoyed our addictions: caffeine and surfing.

SEVEN

"I never killed anybody, but I often read an
obituary notice with great satisfaction."
Clarence Darrow

I WAS IN the office on Saturday before seven o'clock. GD is not a
company that expects its consultants to work every weekend. However, there is an implied target of a certain numbers of hours each
week (hint: it's north of forty). If I wanted to continue my early
morning surfing and add on evening sleuthing, I needed to spend
a few hours working on the weekends, and that was fine with me.
Without interruptions for staff meetings, conspiracy theories, or
Edvard babysitting duties, I got a lot accomplished in a few hours.

Later than morning I delighted in the drive to Marla Matsumoto's home on Round Top Drive. Balanced on the hills above
Honolulu, Tantalus and Round Top Drives swept back and forth
up the mountain like dark brushstrokes on a botanical watercolor.
Rounding each S-turn propelled me further into the cool air and
thick tropical smells of the rainforest. Virtually untouched since
World War II, the roads were unencumbered by traffic lights,
guardrails, and tour buses. Occasional *ʻokina* (breaks) in the dense
forest revealed vistas of Honolulu, Waikīkī or Mānoa Valley. Narrow driveways punctuated the sinuous road, the multi-million dollar homes at their end crouching invisibly behind the tangle of
trees, hibiscus, *maile*, and other vegetation.

I found the Matsumoto home by the number on a battered red
mailbox and I eased the Toyota down the steep but blissfully short

drive to a paved area fronting a pale blue two-story home with a semi-detached garage. Two large banyan trees provided shade for the yard and four small stone Easter Island-like statues graced the front lawn. No sign of human sacrifices, although several dead roaches lay beneath the unseeing glare of the *moai*. Small sacrifices to small gods.

The door was answered almost immediately by a diminutive woman dressed with more glamour than I usually effected for the hottest of hot dates. A white tunic with a gold-embroidered anthurium pattern was complemented by dangling black oyster shell earrings, gold slacks, and black stilettos with a gold chain ankle strap. Probably not the maid.

"Ms. Matsumoto?" I said.

"Yes?"

"I'm Emma Jones. I'd like to ask you a few questions, if I may."

"Regarding what?" Her eyes narrowed behind her red-rimmed spectacles.

"Greg Walker."

"You're not police. Who are you? A private investigator?"

"I've been asked by the family of Kealoha Kanekoa to find out who murdered Mr. Walker." Hey, it was just a little lie. Keoni was *ʻohana*, right?

"Kanekoa. The man who blew up Greg." A statement, not a question. A small, dirty, animated mop raced out and ferociously barked at me, teeth bared, eyes wild and darting.

"Mr. Kanekoa didn't kill Mr. Walker and I'm trying to help find out who did." I tried sidestepping mini-Cujo, doing my best squeaky-voice rendition of "*He ʻilio nohea! He ʻilio akamai*," to fend off his slavering jaws. It always worked with Gorgon, my parents' mop-with-an-underbite.

"Poi, where are your manners?" Ms. Matsumoto said. "*Pau*." At that, Poi rolled over and yipped for a belly rub, acting less like a ferocious beast than one who would lick an intruder to death.

"I'm glad someone finally did," she said as she stooped to scratch Poi's belly.

"Glad someone started investigating?" I was confused.

"No, glad that someone finally offed that scumbag Greg." She stood up. "Since you obviously aren't the police, I can say that without incriminating myself. Not that I did it: I'd be taking a bow if I had. No, Poi, she isn't going to play with your gecko." Poi had retrieved a stuffed toy from the house and was shaking it at my feet, growling with faux ferocity. Stuffing flew over the doormat.

"I take it you didn't like the deceased?" Watching endless TV police procedurals had impressed upon me that real professionals didn't use terms like "stiff" and "guy who kicked the bucket."

"I despised every molecule in Greg Walker's body. I so hope he didn't die instantly but felt the agony as the blood ebbed from the crater in his chest and flames seared his legs." Ms. Matsumoto's eyes glinted as she imagined his last moments. She saw my shock and laughed. "Oh please, dearie, absolutely everyone knows how I felt about Greg. Honestly, I've been threatening to kill that snake for years, but I wasn't willing to go to jail just to get rid of him. And before you ask, I've already told the police that I was here at home during the time Greg was being charbroiled. If I'd know what was happening to him, I would have been at the country club, camera at the ready."

I admit to making insensitive comments about the death of my odious boss Padmanabh, like intimating Satan might be his next of kin. I'd like to think insensitivity was my way of dealing with the shock of finding Pad's body. His ex-wife's comments were cruel and a bit frightening.

"Where are my manners? It is so rude of me to keep you standing here," she said. "Please come in and we'll chat. Call me Marla … and you've already met Poi." Poi obliged by scuttling toward the ankle he'd just tried to bite less than five minutes ago and giving it a gentle lick as his entire rear end wagged in greeting.

I hesitated. Had I remembered to move my mace to this purse? I wasn't sure. At least I had my pepper spray key chain if needed … for Marla. I drew the line at spraying dogs, unless they were bigger than a breadbox and within three seconds of treating a body part the way Poi had just treated his gecko.

Marla steered me through a small marble foyer into a glassed-in porch. Steps led down to a terrace flanked by taro planted in urns fashioned from black lava. From there the land dropped away precipitously to reveal a distant Diamond Head and the Moloka'i Channel beyond.

"Stunning."

She smiled. "It strikes everyone that way. Most of my guests like the night view better, but I prefer days when I can admire the brilliant blues of the sea." She pointed me to a rattan chair upholstered in a monstera leaf pattern.

"Please have a seat. Can I get you anything? Coffee? Tea?"

"Whatever you're having."

"White wine, then."

White wine on top of the double mocha latte I'd just finished. Terrific.

Marla tottered off to get the drinks. In the interim, I watched an *'apapane* (Hawaiian honey creeper) flit between two *'ulu* (breadfruit). Through the open sliding glass windows, I could hear the birds calling and I drank in the thick scent of *pua melia* (plumeria) and *pīkake*.

In no time, Marla returned and handed me a humongous glass of white wine. No way was I going to drink all that and suffer the headache that would undoubtedly follow. Marla placed her equally large glass and the remainder of the bottle on a table before settling on the rattan couch.

"Marla, I'd like to talk with you about Mr. Walker and some of his enemies," I said. "As I told you, I'm trying to help prove that Kealoha is not a murderer."

Marla shrugged. "If he's innocent, I'd hate to see him jailed, but don't you think the police should handle this?"

"The family thinks the police can use the help."

Marla took a sip of her white wine. "Ask away, dearie."

"I've been told that you were married to Greg Walker for ten years and had two children. Your divorce was … ah … not amicable."

Marla let out a whoop. "'Not amicable!' Nice of you to be tactful, but no one who knows me would put it that way." She laughed uncontrollably, tears streaming from her eyes, occasionally repeating the phrase "not amicable" and shaking her head.

First the glee at Greg's death, now the hysterical laughter over a messy divorce. Was Marla seriously unbalanced or just smashed?

"I was perfectly charming," she said after wiping the tears from her eyes, "when I told Greg that I planned to cut up his $3,000 suits, paid for with my money, and set fire to the Lamborghini, also purchased with my money. He didn't believe me. You should have seen his face when I doused the Lamborghini with gasoline. He tried to stop me so I whacked him with the can. Dented the can and sent him to the emergency room."

I must have appeared shocked.

"Don't worry darling, I didn't burn the car. I donated it to a homeless shelter for auction." Marla took a swig of her wine. "I did cut up his suits, though. Sent them to him in pieces. Would have liked to see his face then, too, but a judge had issued a restraining order against me." Marla laughed so hard that she slopped wine on the carpet.

I admit it, I liked Marla's ideas of getting even, but the professional me tried not to giggle as I buried my face in my wine glass, taking slow sips. Poi took the opportunity to jump into my chair and edge onto my lap. He pawed my non-wine glass hand, insistently seeking scritching.

Marla's mirth passed and she continued. "Greg married me for my money and my looks; I was a Miss Hawai'i runner up. After ten years together, he still wanted my money—to spend with a younger model. We divorced and he married Miss Coconuts."

"His second wife was also a beauty queen?"

Marla snorted. "A waitress at Greg's golf club. Married Greg for the money she thought he had. I expect her boobs, big as coconuts, were paid for by Greg using my money."

For the next few minutes, Marla heaped insults upon Greg and Coconuts punctuated by pauses to gulp wine. Somewhere in her diatribe, I learned that Coconuts' real name was Carmen and that "she got her due" years later when Greg divorced her for the Lentil Queen or as Marla called her, Peabrain. Marla had little to say about Peabrain, saving her invective for Coconuts.

"Greg was a conniving bastard." Marla reached for her wine again. At this, Poi jumped off my lap, trotted to the couch and jumped up next to Marla. He shook his stuffed gecko—a little less stuffed than before as the piles of white filling decorating the room attested to—and stared expectantly at Marla.

"Poi, did you disembowel Greg again? Good doggie!" At this, Poi woofed, shook Gecko, er, Greg repeatedly, and growled.

"Conniving in what way?" I asked.

Marla seemed startled, as if she'd forgotten I was there. Taking a small dish from the coffee table, she poured a few drops of wine in the dish and put it on the floor. Poi jumped down and immediately began lapping at the Chardonnay. I wonder how he felt about Pinot Grigio.

Marla refilled her now empty glass and took a large swallow before speaking.

"Greg made a few good deals and a lot of bad ones. Even on the bad ones, he sometimes made money by getting someone else to pay for them. Like Akakoui."

According to Marla, Greg had purchased land near Akakoui State Park five years ago and then ran into financial difficulty. It was rumored he had gambling debts. Greg couldn't afford to develop the parcel. Consequently, he persuaded the county government to expand Akakoui State Park by purchasing half of his parcel at the same price he'd paid for the entire acreage. Within two years, he needed money again, and got the county to purchase the remainder of the land for ball fields, at twice its assessed value. A local journalist wrote an exposé of the deals, which upset no one. At least, no one in authority.

"Everyone knows developers and politicians are tight. Greg, always after more money, sued the journalist and the newspaper. They settled out of court. Greg made a bundle for developing nothing."

"I was told that Walker had a proclivity to sue," I said.

"Honey, his attorney was on speed dial. He's personally responsible for a six-month backlog in the courts. Didn't you read the newspaper this morning? When he died, Greg was involved in fifty-four outstanding suits in the courts, the bastard!"

"Could one of the people he was suing be the killer?"

Marla shook her head. "It's Coconuts."

When pressed, Marla admitted she had no evidence. She just knew Coconuts was guilty.

I changed the subject to Greg's investment in Lo'i Kalo Labs. Marla knew nothing about it. She was more interested in vilifying Coconuts as a slut, ranting about Greg's neglect of their twins and elaborating upon Greg's loathsome character. The more Marla drank, the less she laughed and the coarser her language.

It was time to extract myself from the melodrama. I made a lame excuse about another appointment, evaded Marla's attempts to pour more wine into my glass (not that there was much left in the bottle) and weaved my way out of the house. Poi didn't follow; he was conked out on the floor, snoring loudly.

Despite my vow, I had overindulged. I plucked an old granola bar from the bottom of my purse and scarfed it down in two bites, hoping it would soak up the alcohol sloshing around in my stomach. I oh-so-carefully maneuvered down the mountain, avoiding all temptation to admire the view, and headed for King Street and a small shop that sold *manapua*, a large steamed bun filled with *char siu* (sweet pork) nicknamed "meat donuts" by the locals. Twenty minutes, two *manapua*, and a cold Coke mitigated the alcohol-induced dizziness, although I still had a raging headache. When I got back to my apartment, I fell into bed for what turned out to be a two-hour nap and too many dreams of angry ex-wives throwing coconuts at very expensive cars.

EIGHT

"Gather round there's something you should
know about two finger poi
Mahiʻai kalo in the loʻi, it's their pride and joy.
Jump right in muddy feet, working through
the morning heat, oʻopu beside ya, watch out
for the cane spider …"

"Raising Hāloa," Lopaka Hoʻopiʻi, Zanuck Lindsey, and
Adj Larioza

THE *LŪʻAU* WAS well underway when I arrived; cars and trucks were parked nose-to-tail alongside the road leading to the house, narrowing the passable roadway to a lane, or lane-and-one-half, tops. I left Keoni's 4Runner half-on, half-off the road behind a rusty red truck covered with surf stickers and trudged along the narrow road flanked by modest homes on tiny lots, most of which were fronted by lava-rock walls. At the end of the road squatted a small *hale* (house) in the perfect shade of *ti*-leaf green with white trim. Wide, overhanging eaves typical of the plantation style covered a veranda that wrapped around the house.

Music and the aroma of cooking food beckoned so I wandered around back without bothering to knock on the door. Four men with *ʻukuleles* and guitars perched on the back *lānai*, plucking and tuning their instruments, amidst laughter and low voices comparing play lists of *nā mele* Hawaiʻi. The host, John Morimota, was among them and I gave him a wave when I caught his eye.

Sixty to eighty guests milled around the yard, spilling onto the beach. A half-dozen women ferrying large trays of food bustled in and out of the house. A small crowd surrounded an older woman cradling a fussy baby. The raison d'être of the *lūʻau*, I deduced. Children of all ages ran around with abandon, screaming and laughing. While I was observing the activity, a large woman in a red, flower-print *muʻumuʻu* broke away from the baby group and approached me. She introduced herself as Nellie, aunt of the birthday boy, and I told her I was a friend of Kimo. She welcomed me, told me to *hoʻomāʻona* (eat up) and pointed me toward picnic tables buried in *pūpūs*.

"Emma! *Aloha ahiahi*! I was beginning to think you wouldn't make it." Wearing a bright red aloha shirt, scruffy cargo shorts, and flip-flops, Uncle greeted me with a plate of food in one hand and a beer in the other.

"Sorry, I had a few things to attend to."

"Your timing is good: the pig is nearly ready to come out of the *imu*." Uncle gestured toward several men removing banana leaves from a pit in the ground. The husky mouth-watering scent of *kālua* pig caressed my taste buds. The *manapua* were forgotten and I was famished.

"Grab a drink and we'll have a quick chat with Kealoha before we eat."

I followed his advice and grabbed a Longboard Lager, a locally brewed beer. To salve my hunger pains, I snagged a few sushi and a paper towel.

I inhaled one of the sushi as Uncle Kimo led me onto the beach and over to a large man, long dark hair in a ponytail, wearing an antique aloha shirt, a fishhook necklace made of *koa* and rimmed with shark's teeth, khaki shorts, and *slippahs*.

"Kealoha, this is Emma Jones. Emma, Kealoha Kanekoa."

I stuffed the paper towel and uneaten sushi in my pocket and wiped my sticky fingers on my shorts before putting out my hand. Kealoha gave me a big smile and gazed into my eyes as he firmly shook my hand. Reflexively, my polite smile turned into a sincere grin.

"I am very happy to meet you." Kealoha's voice was level and strong. "Let me introduce you to my family. This is my wife Pikake." He turned and put his arm around a large, dark-skinned woman in a pretty yellow *mu'umu'u*. Pikake flashed me a smile, but her anxious, dark eyes betrayed her true feelings.

"And those are our *keiki*, Maile and Keoki." Kealoha gestured toward two school-age children dancing along the beach and playing tag with the waves.

Soon Uncle Kimo, Kealoha, and I were walking along the beach, having left Pikake in charge of the children. Nothing was said for a few minutes as we pushed through the soft sand, creating distance between the celebration and ourselves.

The sound of the crashing waves and wind overpowered the music from the *lū'au*, leaving it a faint whisper in the distance. I picked up a beautiful piece of coral, faintly pink, and shoved it in my pocket. Too late I remembered the sushi, now crushed and creating a damp spot on my shorts. Way to go, Emma.

Kealoha spoke first. "Pikake cries when we speak of my situation, and the children sense something is wrong. When Kimo told me, Emma, of your gift for solving murders and that you have agreed to help … well, you have given us hope."

I felt uneasy and surprised that Uncle Kimo had given me such a glowing recommendation. I hoped he hadn't oversold my abilities; I had a long way to go to be in the league of hard-boiled detectives. Or even over-easy detectives.

"I'm happy to try to help *'ohana*." Was there a term for *'ohana* of *'ohana*? "Though Kimo gives me too much credit. I've been fortunate in my little investigations." Fortunate in both cases not to have been killed by those intent on perpetrating another murder. Now here I was involved in yet another murder, through no fault of my own, I might add.

"What can I tell you that will help?" Kealoha asked.

"Ah, well …" I was having trouble organizing my thoughts amidst my sudden apprehension that this man, his wife and adorable children were relying on me. "I'd like to know a little more about your protests against the taro lab," I finally blurted out. "Background on issues, who's involved, that sort of thing." Hey, that was almost coherent.

Kealoha gazed toward Kailua Bay. A few windsurfers were out and in the distance sailboats sped over the bay in a cluster, as if in a race. When Kealoha began speaking, it was to tell me the story of *kalo*, taro, in the Hawaiian culture.

I knew the story, of course, but Kealoha related the tale with dignity and reverence.

Wakea, the sky father, and Hoʻohokukalani, the star mother, were the parents of Hāloa, born prematurely in the shape of a bulb. They buried the stillborn child in the ground. Eventually, a *kalo* plant emerged and grew strong. Wakea and Hoʻohokukalani conceived and bore a second child, also named Hāloa; he was the first man. The brothers were foreordained to care for each other. If the younger Hāloa would respect and care for the elder Hāloa, then the elder, the *kalo*, would sustain young Hāloa and his descendants until the end of time.

"*Kalo* represents our obligation to *mālama*, to care for the land and all living things of Hawaiʻi. We've allowed foreigners to come to this land with their stories and cultures, and our land has suffered. Overdevelopment, new pests, and diseases have hurt the *kalo*, the land, the animals, and our people."

I nodded in understanding.

He continued. "Crop yields have been declining for a long time. Scientists tell us they can rescue *kalo* through genetic modification." Kealoha shook his head. "What should be changed is the environment; we must take better care of the land. We Hawaiians believe the taro is sacred and should not be altered under any circumstances. That is why we protest the laboratory."

"Isn't there a moratorium on genetically modifying Hawaiian taro?" I said.

"The Loʻi Kalo Labs are working with a Tahitian cultivar related to the Mana Opelu and Mana KeoKeo *kalos*. There's a risk this cultivar will flower naturally, spreading pollen and transferring genes to the Hawaiian varieties, corrupting them."

"Doesn't the state require certain processes and procedures to prevent such contamination?" I said. I knew Hawai'i was protective of the native taro; I couldn't believe one would be able to operate a lab unfettered by rules and regulations.

"Yes, there are precautions, but what if they are not followed? What if someone deliberately contaminates our *kalo*?" Kealoha's voice rose in anger as he spoke. "The owners of the lab were outsiders and we do not trust those who are not of these islands."

Then why are you asking an outsider to help you?

With difficulty, I kept my mouth shut.

Uncle Kimo must have sensed my discomfort and sought to change the subject. "Tell Emma about meeting Walker at his country club."

"Mr. Tam refused to end his work, or to let us inspect the lab."

"Who is Tam?" I inquired.

"Raymond Tam. The scientist who started the lab and was sole owner before Walker invested," Kimo said.

Kealoha continued. "I thought perhaps Mr. Walker would listen and I tried to meet with him, but he refused. That's why I was at The Luakini Golf Club. A friend at the club called and told me Walker was golfing, and that he'd be off the course by 11:30 a.m. His habit was to have a quick beer with friends before leaving."

"Did you speak with Mr. Walker?"

"Yes, for a moment at the bar. He told me he was a passive investor, that Mr. Tam made all the decisions, and that he would not interfere with the work of the lab."

"Is that true?"

"As far as we know," Uncle said.

"I told him for the good of Hawai'i he should close the lab. We argued and I left." Kealoha denied he'd threatened Walker.

When I asked Kealoha about access to the HALO explosives, he laughed ruefully. He declared Hawai'i's grand plan for developing a rail system on O'ahu was a train wreck—so to speak. Despite paying off state inspectors, the project was in disarray and already falling behind schedule. Unexpected problems and low productivity were triggering budget overruns and shortcuts were being taken to save money, including site security. The loss of material was rampant: compressors, rebar, tools, and yes, explosives were disappearing.

"You're telling me that anyone on the island could have stolen the explosives?"

Kealoha nodded. "Even Kimo. No one checks IDs or locks up material."

I made a mental note to avoid riding HALO—if it were ever completed.

"What about the other members of Kūlohelohe," I asked. "Is anyone passionate enough about the cause to kill Greg Walker?"

Kealoha stiffened and crossed his arms. There was an uncomfortable standoff as we all stared at each other. Kealoha gave a half smile and softened his stance, letting his arms fall to his sides. "I am grateful for your help and I do not want to treat you like an enemy, but I do not know what is in the hearts of others."

For a man facing a murder charge, Kealoha was singularly unhelpful.

"If we want food, we'd better move," Uncle Kimo said. "Why don't you go on ahead, Emma. Kealoha and I need to talk."

Amen. I *hele*-ed toward the house at a quick clip, my companions trailing behind. As I neared the celebration, I noticed the music had stopped and a hoard had gathered near the food tables. Driven crazy by the mouth-watering smell of *kālua* pork and not willing to wait for food, I opted for the now deserted appetizer table to take the edge off my hunger. I was working my way through a fruit kabob when Pikake approached.

"He didn't tell you anything, did he?" she said without preamble and then waited for my reply as I swallowed the fresh pineapple I'd been enjoying.

"Not much," I said.

She sighed. "He told me you were bound to ask about other suspects and he wasn't going to give you names." She glanced nervously over her shoulder and, seeing Kealoha and Uncle entering the yard from the beach, furtively slipped me a piece of paper and sidled away to fill a plate with fingers and blood ... make that Vienna sausages and ketchup; food for the *keiki*, no doubt. That was enough for me. Time for *kālua* pork and all the fixings.

Uncle Kimo and I sat together, eating, drinking—I was still working on my now-warm beer—and listening to the music. My thoughts frequently turned to Kealoha's words and attitude. I believed that he was sincere in his gratitude for my help, but the sudden shut down and protection of friends was an attitude I'd encountered before. Hawaiians, generally open and friendly, often displayed an unwillingness to allow outsiders into their world. Perhaps a trait not uncommon among other groups, but it was a clear reminder that even as *'ohana* I was not *kanaka maoli* (one of the people).

"I'm sorry your afternoon was wasted," Uncle Kimo said. "At least you got a meal out of it."

"A little more than that." I reached into my pocket and pulled out Pikake's note, the piece of coral I'd found, and the sushi. Uncle's eyes crinkled in amusement as I dumped the sodden mess on my plate.

I unfolded the note. It read: "Kevin Ortiz and Samuel Abbott work with Kealoha and are part of Kūlohelohe."

I passed the paper to Uncle to read. "Can you find some information on these two men?"

He nodded and I sat back to let the music wash over me, a song about the sea breeze.

NINE

"E lauhoe mai na wa'a; i ke ka, i ka hoe; i
ka hoe, i ke ka; pae aku i ka 'aina." (Paddle
together, bail, paddle; paddle, bail; paddle
toward the land.)
Hawaiian Proverb

GRANT AND DENHOLM corporate went berserk that week, bombarding employees with a host of corporate notices about required password changes that read like an alphabet soup: VPN (Virtual Private Network), CCN (Conference Calling Number)—not to be confused with CRN—Conference Room Number, SSO (single sign-on) and WRR (women's rest room)—okay, I made that one up. Don't get me started on why we needed a separate password to book conference rooms. Was GD worried that a hacker would book all the conference rooms, thereby bringing us to a screeching halt as nobody could HYABM (Hold Yet Another Boring Meeting)? Not surprisingly, each system required a distinct password that hadn't been used before. Hence, I was pressed into creating such memorable sign-ins like #%&mKD4**8lTz. Since our corporate policy forbade us writing down passwords, that left me with few choices. Perhaps %&^$#@You, except I didn't use language like that, however tempted I might be due to incessant password changes.

It was no surprise that GD's quarterly password change-a-thon engendered yet another binge of Edvard-anoia. I was standing at the vending machine, deliberating which cold drink had more caffeine, when Edvard entered the kitchenette. He was sporting his Matt Damon ears, but appeared free of strange apparel. Over the coffee pot, he announced that it was just a matter of time before we all got digital tattoos for security purposes. Edvard proceeded, in between adding three containers of hazelnut cream and two of fake sugar to his coffee, to describe flexible electronic circuits that could be attached to a wearer's skin using a rubber stamp.

"Medical teams use the bio-tat to measure the health of their patients remotely, but the manufacturer is already planning on using them for authentication, especially with tablets and—"

"If I go swimming, does my password get fried?" I interrupted. "Or do I just not shower, ever, and stink to high heaven? Oh, and will the circuit capture my perfume and report back to the manufacturer? I demand perfume privacy!"

Edward ignored my comments. "We're also close to taking pills that can be used to identify you remotely. You know this means 'They' can track you anywhere. Unless you get good at throwing up or cut open your own—"

"Please, I haven't finished my Danish yet. Can't a girl get a sugar high in peace?" said a short red-haired lieutenant whose khaki uniform was already strained at the seams. She stuffed the remaining half pastry in her mouth, grabbed her coffee so quickly it sloshed on the floor, and huffily dripped and crumbed her way back to her office.

Edvard and I returned to the office area, Edvard still monologing on digital tattoos. He was certain the tats would be exploited to gather more personal information and was fretting over how to avoid being tracked if he was forced to get one. He asked me whether I thought there was a market for metallic long underwear that could block the electronic signal.

"You must resist," said an ethereal voice, rising from one of the cubes.

Edvard stopped in mid-rant.

"Your soul is in danger," the voice repeated. Rafe popped up from a nearby cube, his frowning face slowly panning the room like Moses surveying a golden calf-worshipping convention.

"'Both small and great, both rich and poor, both free and slave, will be marked on the right hand or the forehead, so that no one can buy or sell unless he has the mark, that is, the name of the beast or the number of its name,'" Rafe said. "It's from the Book of Revelation. If you take the mark of the beast, you will burn in hell. 'And the smoke of their torment goes up forever and ever, and they have no rest, day or night.'"

Mouth agape, Edvard stared at Rafe.

Karen stood up in her cube, threw Rafe a withering look, and pointedly inserted a pair of ear buds before sitting down.

I found my voice before Edvard. "I think we're all on the same page that we don't like the idea of digital tattoos, even to improve security."

Linda's head became visible above her cube, her face registering her surprise at the unfolding tableau. Maybe she hadn't been blessed with this kind of entertainment at Wilson & Kumar.

"What else does the Bible say about technology?" Edvard was still staring at Rafe as if he were a creature from Mars.

"The advent of the Internet and sharing of information has increased our knowledge, many times over. Just like the Book of Daniel, chapter twelve, verse four, that tells us, 'to the time of the end: many shall run to and fro, and knowledge shall be increased,'" Rafe said.

"Or it could be people with digestive problems reading while on the can," I said, shooting my mouth off before thinking. "That covers 'shall run to and fro' and 'time of the end.' Literally."

Rafe was scandalized. "You equate the Book of Daniel with, with diarrhea? That's—"

"Why are you working in technology if it is helping to bring an end to the world?" Edvard said.

By this time, everybody in the immediate area not wearing headphones had popped up to watch the floor show. Never one who enjoyed being the center of attention (I failed kindergarten Show and Tell) I slipped past Edvard and unobtrusively returned to my cubicle.

"I've been asked that before," Rafe responded. "While technology advances are harbingers of the end times, they are not the cause, nor do they in and of themselves cause men to sin."

Except for taking the Lord's name in vain every time there is an upgrade.

"As a Christian, why shouldn't I welcome the end times? I know where I am going. Do you, Edvard?"

Cue dramatic pause as we all waited for Edvard's response.

"I'm going to my cube, to finish my coffee."

Amen.

The coffee pot must have been laced with Conspiracy Kona—or was it Backlash Blend?—because when I went back to hit up the vending machine for a snack, I got an earful from Melia. Although she was spending a lot of time with Edvard, I'd not been more than a minute or two in her company as Karen had been the babysitter, or more correctly, chaperone. Karen was convinced Melia was the latest in Edvard's female admirers.

Melia bemoaned the travails her team was having with a major at Kadena Air Force Base on Okinawa. The Air Base tenants were foot-dragging about providing raw data to enable our analytics. Because they were based outside the United States, they felt they should be exempt from the DFAS analysis.

"They're concerned that DFAS will fail to appreciate the unique nature of their command's expenditure in furtherance of their core mission, which will negatively impact their budget projections," Melia said. "And that's why they don't want to give us the goods."

"Beg pardon?"

"They are afraid of losing budget if we find cost savings."

"Can't they spend the savings for other needs?"

Melia shook her head. "It doesn't work like that. The worst government accounting sin is not spending all of one's appropriated funds. If it isn't spent, the government will cut the budget for the next fiscal year. Redirecting savings is a no-no. The money is appropriated for a specific purpose."

"There is no incentive to find savings?" I said.

"Not for those spending it," Melia replied.

Haruto, a DFAS analyst, joined the conversation. "You do have to wonder when you see mountains of duplication. Why do we need a Navy store and an Army store when the bases are next to one another? Do the Army and Navy require different pencils, too? Isn't the Marine Corps part of the Navy? Why do they even need their own anything?"

"Part of the Navy? The Marines are *affiliated* with the Navy." A Marine Corps officer whom I didn't know had just entered the kitchen area. "We are 'first to fight,' and …" As she poured herself a cup of coffee, black, she continued to expound on the virtues of the Marine Corps. Eventually, she ran out of superlatives and marched out of the kitchen.

"Poor Harry Truman tried to eliminate the Marine Corps after World War II," Haruto said. "Couldn't do it. Too much pressure from ex-Marines."

"*Former* Marines," Melia hissed, glancing over her shoulder lest the Marine officer was nearby. "There are no *ex*-Marines—"

"Only former Marines, I know," Haruto said.

"Besides," Melia said, "even when the military wants to change, it's typically the civilians who are the problem. They just outlast the military, stonewalling until an officer is transferred to a new assignment. If you can't beat 'em, stall 'em."

When I returned to my cube, Melia walked with me. "I need to speak with Edvard," she said. "Soooo, how long have you known him?"

That evening, I drove to Coconut's, er, Carmen's house. I'd called her several times that week and been routed to voicemail, so I decided on the direct approach. I parked in her driveway, marched up to the front door, and punched the doorbell. The peals of church bells echoed through the walls, eventually bringing a scantily clad, petite woman to the door. Her long black hair was heavily permed, she had three earrings in her right ear, and she wore jeans that were cut off as far as they could possibly be without becoming a denim pocket protector. Her bikini top barely held her—Marla was right, they did appear artificial—boobs. Visible on her right breast was, as my Grandmother Swenson put it, a "tramp stamp." I didn't stare enough to make out what it was, though it wouldn't have surprised me if it read "for a good time, call" followed by her phone number. Meow.

Marla's epithets about Carmen being a slut were, no doubt, coloring my judgment. After all, she could be shy and demure; maybe I just caught her wearing her ratty clothes to scrub the kitchen floor.

"Yes?" A half smile was pasted on her face. Who over the age of fifteen uses glitter eye shadow and what's with the black eyeliner with the upward flourish at the outer edge of her eyes? Is she emulating Catwoman? Hosting a costume party?

"Good evening. I'm Emma Jones. I've left you—"

"I know who you are," she snapped. "I got your messages. I've absolutely nothing to say to you." She stepped back from the door, preparing to close it. Ah, gold platform sandals with stiletto heels—a nice touch with the cutoffs. Maybe she wasn't scrubbing floors after all.

"I don't see why you won't—"

"Marla told me all about you, Miss High and Mighty Consultant to the San Francisco Police Department. Leave. Now." She ended with an exclamation point by slamming the door.

Dang! That was unfortunate. The surfeit of wine was to blame for my lack of discretion with Marla. I'd revealed a tad too much about my investigative triumphs in San Francisco, which weren't all that triumphant, it pained me to admit. Why Marla had felt compelled to share the information with the detested Coconuts, particularly if she thought Carmen was the killer, was a mystery to me, and I didn't need another mystery. My cup runneth over, and my cup was a modest B, not a EEE like Carmen.

Walking back to the 4Runner, I sensed someone watching me. Turning around suddenly I caught Carmen peering out the front window. I gave her a cheerful wave, which was not returned.

Before I'd even backed out of Carmen's driveway, I had Marla on the phone, asking why she'd alerted Carmen to my activities.

"I want her to squirm," Marla said. "It gives me pleasure to ruin her day."

Mental eye roll. "That's it? You just wanted to torment her?"

"Of course." Her cackle could have given the Wicked Witch of the West a run for the money, or perhaps a broom ride for the money.

"And what's this about my being a consultant to the San Francisco police? I never said that."

"I exaggerated a bit."

"I would have thought you wanted me to be successful. This isn't helping."

"Don't worry, dearie. Coconuts is guilty. I'm sure you'll figure it out without that little golddigger's help. She's bound to have made a mistake, somewhere; she only *thinks* her IQ is bigger than her chest size."

TEN

"Nānā ka maka; ho'olohe ka pepeiao; pa'a
ka waha."
(Observe with the eyes; listen with the ears;
shut the mouth.)
Hawaiian Proverb

"Everything okay?"

"Fine and dandy," Karen replied crisply.

Karen could face the computerization of an archaic accounting system kept on clay tablets with unruffled composure, but her rigid expression and the four packets of sugar I'd seen her dump in her coffee earlier were signs that all was not right in Karenville. Walking back to our cubes with our drinks she had dropped a file folder—I couldn't quite decipher her mutterings, but I suspected they included a few epithets—and nearly tripped over a power cord snaking between cubes; enough mishaps to tell me her id was acting like an idiot. Clearly she'd lost her aplomb.

Had I irritated her? A quick breath check and underarm sniff confirmed I was innocent of bodily odor offenses. Maybe I said something offensive, but if so, I'd no clue what it was. There was one way to find out for sure.

"Have I done anything wrong?" Working with the military was reinforcing my tendency to use the direct, frontal assault mode of communication.

"No." Karen didn't even glance my way as she stepped into her cube.

Maybe it was that time of the month. Bothered by the fact that steady-as-she-goes Karen did not typically exhibit mood swings, I stopped outside her cube and gave it one last shot.

"If you need to talk about anything at all, like better living through appropriation accounting, for example, let me know. Lunch might be a good venue for that if one happened to eat at mid-day and if one would like an excellent island plate."

Karen stepped out of her cube, swept the area with her eyes and even peeked over the neighboring cubicles. Seeing no one, she turned to me and whispered, "Do you know someplace we could meet after work? Local, but not too close to the base, so, ah, we won't see anyone who works here? Preferably a place with a generous pour."

I proposed the bar at Sam Wong's, a high-end celebrity chef restaurant just off the Nimitz Highway. It was pricy enough and far enough away that I doubted we'd run into anybody from work.

Karen agreed and suggested we leave around five. I returned to my cube and she disappeared into hers like a box turtle into its shell.

Karen's evening work schedule was legendary; prying her out of the office before six in the evening was a singular accomplishment and a reflection upon the gravity of whatever was bothering her. Her long hours had nothing to do with impressing the client, particularly at DFAS where most employees, military and civilian, kept *aloha* hours. The four o'clock stampede of workers fleeing the premises rivaled the Pamplona running of the bulls.

DESPITE THE FOODIE fan following, Sam Wong's was a modest building in an industrial park. The already close-to-strip-club-full parking lot gave the game away that this was a much-in-demand restaurant. The bar was full-on tiki, complete with bamboo chairs and tables, tiki torches, and a reasonably ferocious facsimile of the god Kū with a Mai Tai-induced hangover. Pacific island music played in the background.

Karen and I grabbed two bar stools and she let me do the ordering: *liliko'i* daiquiris and *pūpūs*. For one moment I wondered if I should check the area to ensure it was secure—doubtless a side effect of being around Edvard. As I didn't have the proper equipment for a sweep, I contented myself with a visual survey of the bar area for cameras, a surreptitious peek under the bar itself for any bugs and a sneak peek into the restaurant proper to ensure no DFASers were hiding behind an umbrella drink wearing earphones.

We didn't talk much until the barkeep deposited two daiquiris. Several times during our desultory conversation Karen shook her head back and forth as if she were either listening to hip hop or had a huge knot in her neck. Was there a difference?

"Thanks, Emma," Karen said after the drinks arrived and she took a long slurp.

"No problem. I've been meaning to try this place."

"I meant, thanks for meeting with me."

The *'ahi poke* and the coconut shrimp came out, together with a basket of fresh taro chips. The bartender gave me a conspiratorial wink and a borderline leer when I pointed out we hadn't ordered the taro chips. He'd get a good tip for the chips, but not my phone number.

I stuffed a couple chips in my mouth. Yum. "These are great," I said. "Try them; they're still warm."

I dropped a few more handfuls on my plate telling myself they were vegetables. Taro was a staple food as well as a centerpiece of Hawaiian culture; therefore, I was just celebrating indigenous cuisine, like having a second margarita on Cinco de Mayo.

"So, what's up? Clearly you are upset about work. Just don't tell me it has anything to do with finding dead bodies; I've already exceeded my lifetime corpse quota."

Karen swallowed her mouthful of taro chips before answering. "There aren't any dead bodies unless I elect to run over Gunnar. Though that would leave too much forensic evidence, wouldn't it? Not that I'd know: you're the expert on these matters."

"What's he done?" I picked up a large piece of *'ahi* with my chopsticks and popped it in my mouth. Sam Wong was known for using super fresh *'ahi* and his own special *kukui* nut oil.

"He's putting the moves on me and it's really uncomfortable. No, it's sick, is what it is."

Wow. I hadn't seen that coming. It had never occurred to me that near-male-model Gunnar would be interested in Karen. Don't get me wrong. Karen was pretty in her own way; she just didn't strike me as the kind of arm candy that would attract Gunnar.

"Not to doubt your word, or anything, but what exactly did he do?"

"It started out with the usual touching: putting his hand on my shoulder while leaning over my computer, brushing his hand on my lower back when I go through a door."

Hand on lower back was a clear come-on. Karen wasn't imagining things.

"I tried to tell him politely to knock it off."

"And?" I said.

She shook her head and took a long pull at her daiquiri. "Boy, these are delicious. *Liliko'i* is what?"

"Passion fruit."

"Passion is what I do not need—at least, not at work. If Gunnar had stopped when I asked him, we wouldn't be here. His behavior got worse."

The waiter refilled our water glasses and I took another long swig. I didn't drink that many mixed drinks and when I did, I made it a rule to drink a glass of water for every drink to dilute the alcohol. Of course, food was a must. I helped myself to one of the large coconut shrimp.

Karen took another swig of her daiquiri. "I could get used to these."

"Gunnar? Worse behavior?"

"A few days ago, I was working late. Gunnar walked in, started massaging my shoulders and telling me how he'd be happy to teach me a few new acronyms … at my apartment. The acronym I felt like using was FYSLF."

"Beg pardon?"

"Eff you, strong letter follows. Anyway, I asked him to stop."

"Maybe you should have dropped a few swear words. Asking a sexual harasser to please cease and desist is like telling a mugger 'have a nice day' after he robs you."

"Emma, I'm not naïve; I have dealt with harassment before. The message was clear that I would report the harassment if it didn't stop immediately."

"Good. You're going to report him to Michael and HR."

"I don't think so. The situation is complicated."

I helped myself to yet another shrimp, waiting for Karen to explain.

"You might have guessed that I'm interested in moving to the government practice," she said. "Gunnar has made it abundantly clear that he's a friend and golf buddy of Michael and David. He said if I did a few favors for him, he'd put in a good word for me and my move to the new practice would be assured. Subtext: if I rat him out, he'll torpedo my chances."

"What a …" I'd been raised not to use words like the one I was thinking, so I settled for "horse's behind," with apologies to the Equine Anti-Defamation League, who doubtless would protest being compared to a scum sucker like Gunnar.

"I know he's not lying about the golf; he and Michael played last weekend, both Saturday and Sunday."

"Is being part of David's group that important to you?"

For the next few minutes Karen expounded on the opportunities in the new group and the thrill of learning about government accounting, which was "totally different than the private sector and hugely interesting." Did I mention Karen was a finance systems geek? I know that sounds like the kiss of death, but in Karen's case, it's a compliment. I find working on accounting systems to be about as exciting as alphabetizing my household cleaners. Karen's enthusiasm made the work almost interesting for non-accounting types.

When the bartender walked by Karen held up her empty glass, signaling for another. If she kept going at this rate, I might have to pour her into a taxi.

"What do you want me to do?" I said, interrupting her soliloquy on the fun of fund accounting.

"I'm not sure. It's just that, well, you seem to have some success at solving murders …"

"You said there were no dead bodies." I realized after I said it that my voice had risen in volume.

"Shh." Karen eyes frantically swept over the nearby tables. "There aren't. It's just that I thought you might have an idea about how to prove Gunnar's harassment."

"You don't need proof; you're a long-term GD employee and your complaint will be taken seriously."

"You don't understand. I want proof of his harassment so there is no doubt about his guilt." Karen's rationale was that, faced with proof, Gunnar would back off for fear of losing his job. She also could hold it over his head to forestall any interference with her move to the government practice. In other words, enjoying better living through blackmail.

"Do you have any intention of pursuing legal action?" I asked.

Karen shook her head more vigorously than a bobble-headed doll in a pickup traversing a minefield.

"Fine, then our methods don't have to be legit; we can consider secret recordings, entrapment, fabricating evidence, breaking and entering, and—"

"Emma!" Karen clearly was shocked. Had I been rubbing my hands together and cackling?

"Right. Need to be practical. Give me a day or two and I'll have a plan."

"Awesome." Karen slumped back in her chair and smiled broadly. Whether it was the prospect of my help or the effects of the alcohol, I couldn't be sure. She held up a fresh daiquiri and said, "What's a good Hawaiian toast? In honor of Gunnar becoming toast in Hawai'i."

"*Imua*," I said, clinking her glass. "Forward!"

I MEANT TO work on Karen's problem that evening, but was side-tracked by calls from Uncle Kimo and Noelani.

On Sunday, Noelani and I had surfed Ala Moana. While bobbing around in the line-up, I'd asked Noelani if she would solicit her mother's opinion of Greg Walker. I tried to play it cool, or as cool as I could given the water temperature was 78°F. I pretended I'd been reading about his murder and had heard conflicting stories about him. I was just curious, I said.

I fooled Noelani not one iota; she knew me too well. At the end of three hours, we'd caught several good waves and Noelani had uncovered most of my investigative activities.

"You ought to put this in the Alumni Notes," she said. "It would make a nice change from Caitlyn and Justin getting married or Ashley finishing a Ph.D. in aromatherapy."

"Which Caitlyn and Justin?"

"Who cares, there were about fifteen of each in our class."

"What do you suggest I say, keeping within the two-sentence limit, of course? 'Emma Jones currently on a roll in discovering dead bodies. If you've lost one, please contact her.'"

"How about three dead bodies, two murd'ring men, and a disembodied hand in a *hau* tree?"

"Technically, that's a stanza, not a sentence," I said.

"You can always add more bodies, like twelve corpses rotting."

"I'll pass, Noe. I'd prefer to stop at three."

"Isn't it four? What about the surfer stiff under your car?"

"I keep forgetting about him, although my friend Harrison took up a collection to help convince me to investigate. Maybe when I finish this GD assignment and get back to the mainland I will, just so Harrison stops talking my ear off about Shamu every time I see him in the lineup. Back to Greg Walker. Could you be my designated snooper and talk to your mother?"

Noelani was reporting in. "'Plenty *pilikia*' was Mom's description of his dealings," she said without preamble.

Six years ago Noelani's mother had put down a deposit on a condo, hoping to flip it. Because Walker and the contractor fought constantly about change orders, the amenities (pool, common room, picnic area) weren't even near to completion when the units became available for occupancy. With an uncertain timeline—it took three additional years to finish them—Noelani's mother had to sell the unit for less than what she paid. Never again did she invest in a Walker project. "Too many fish in the sea to play with a tiger shark."

A short time later, Uncle called about the names Pikake passed on at the *lū'au*. Kevin Puanini Ortiz had minor trouble with the law before joining the military at eighteen. Apparently, the military had straightened him out: Ortiz had received a Purple Heart and a Meritorious Service Medal and been honorably discharged. For the past five years he'd worked for HuliHuli Construction, the company that employed Kealoha.

Uncle turned up very little on Samuel Abbott. Other than a few speeding tickets, Abbott had no contact with the law. Like Ortiz, he worked for HuliHuli.

Presumably, the police were aware that Abbott and Ortiz were members of the protest movement and as employees of HuliHuli, had access to the HART explosives. Unlike Kealoha, they had not been seen at The Luakini Golf Club near the time of the blast.

Kealoha had said security was so poor that anyone could have taken explosives from the work site. I expect that's true, but with explosives in hand, just how easy was it to make a bomb? I spent the evening on the Internet answering that question, and was left shaken by the experience.

I knew intellectually that one could learn how to do just about anything on the Internet: restring your *'ukulele*, tie a Windsor knot, master a reduction sauce, and find true love and happiness (on TrueLoveAndHappiness.com, no less). Making an IED appeared to be easier than any of those activities, though not as tasty as a good reduction sauce or as satisfying as finding true love and happiness.

I wasn't totally surprised to find instructions for making a standard wireless-controlled improvised explosive device (IED) online.

Nevertheless, I was shocked at the plethora of sites providing "easy to assemble" instructions for would-be bombers; anyone from angry adolescents to cantankerous centenarians could do it. Several sites provided videos that demonstrated the impact on a car using varying sizes of bombs. Alexander Pope was correct: "a little learning is a dangerous thing."

ELEVEN

"The only man she'll go out with is one who
is tall, dark, and has some."
Anonymous

JOLINE WAS A babe; there was no other way to describe her. Whether God or the plastic surgeon had given her a cup size that seriously runneth over didn't seem to matter to the men whose eyes latched onto her as she strutted across the lobby of the Aloha Waves Hotel in a "runway indifference meets come hither hula hips" mien. I expect that they were hoping for more than just June to bust out all over, a prospect enhanced by the low-cut sequined and more-spandex-than-cotton T-shirt she wore.

Not until I rose to shake her hand did I notice that she had a face, and a stunning one at that: soft blond hair surrounded pale peach skin that was sheltered by a large brimmed, floppy black hat. Her large green eyes were framed by kohl eyeliner and her lips benefited from collagen as much as from the becoming lip-gloss in the precise shade of pink plumeria.

"Thanks for coming," I said.

We took our seats in worn wicker chairs flanked by plastic palms in faux-rattan containers. It wasn't that hard to grow the real thing in Hawai'i, where you could drop a raspberry on the ground at breakfast and by the time you got home for dinner, you'd have an entire bush, such was the fecundity of Hawaiian soil.

When I had called Joline to explain what I wanted—almost calling her Peabrain after hearing Marla repeatedly use that term—

I told her I was staying in Waikīkī and she suggested we meet at the Aloha Waves Hotel. Blocks from the beach and decades from its heyday, if it ever had one, the property's clientele appeared to be Japanese tour groups and last hurrah golden oldsters.

"I'm sorry to be late," Joline said before I could launch into my spiel. "But parking is like, super difficult in this area."

"I know what you mean about the parking; my apartment is two blocks from here and if I'm not home by seven, it can take me thirty minutes or more to find a space big enough for my 4Runner. I certainly appreciate your willingness to meet with me." I gave Joline my most sympathetic and sincere smile. Was I overdoing it?

As I was speaking, Joline reached into her tiny purse, barely big enough to hold a cell phone, and pulled out a tissue. She gently dabbed around her eyes. The nails on her right hand were ebony black with silver letters that spelled "alker." I didn't even have to look to know the other hand spelled out "GregW." The silver tips were a nice touch even if the effect was Lady Vampire meets Fashion Week. Especially since her toes were polished in the same format.

"As I said on the phone, I'm happy to help any way that I can." Joline paused to wipe away incipient tears and sigh deeply. "I want the person who killed my Greggers, like, caught and locked up. Forever." That last accompanied by a resolute squaring of her shoulders and a jiggle. Not of her shoulders.

Out of the corner of my eye, I caught a young Japanese man watching us and frowning. Was he blaming me for the tears? Couldn't he see that Joline was over-acting? And was he squinting at her or her heaving breasts? Another big sigh and she'd be popping sequins.

"You can help by telling me about anyone who had a motive to kill Greggers … ah … Greg."

With eyes cast down and her lower lip trembling, Joline carefully folded her hands together. Praying for Greg's soul?

I leaned forward in my chair: one of the woven sticks had broken and was digging into my back. "Maybe someone he worked with or someone in the family who had a grudge?"

Still gazing at her hands, Joline shrugged, occasioning another jiggle.

"Can you tell me about his ex-wives?"

Suddenly garrulous, Joline gave me her own version, or should I say, Greg's version, of the family dynamics, painting Marla as an over-controlling shrew who turned her kids against Greg, without any first-hand evidence but with many a "Greggy said," or occasionally, a "poor Greggy said." Moving along to wife number two, she described Carmen as an ungrateful spendthrift who drove "darling Greggers" to the brink of bankruptcy. Joline and her four-year-old daughter Chloe—the most talented, sweetest, smartest, and adorable child ever—were the font of Greg's eternal happiness.

I wondered if she ever called him "Greg" or "Gregory." Thank heavens, I only heard one "Greggums." Eew.

"Carmen made Greggy's life a living hell, even after the divorce. Six months ago, she, like, threatened to take him to court over visiting rights with the kids. Greggy adored those girls and Carmen knew he'd like do anything to see them as often as he could."

A continuing pain in the back of my right thigh from more broken wicker caused me to shift my weight to the left, where like, a sharp stick stabbed me in the butt. I mean, a sharp stick did stab me in the butt. Now Peabrain had me using "like" as an adverb.

Joline continued in a consistent rhythm of eye dab, vitriol, and hand wringing. Several men were now watching us, perhaps hoping to be the first to the rescue should Joline burst into a flood of tears in need of consoling.

"Carmen wanted money from Greggy to keep up her lifestyle. He was paying her more than the courts had awarded because he wanted the best for his kids, but last year, he stopped the extra payments because her boyfriend was, like, such a bad influence on the girls."

"Who is this boyfriend?"

"Was. She dumped him for the money. An Italian name. Tony … what was it? Barilla?"

"Barilla like the pasta sauce?"

"No, that's not right. Maybe Pirelli?"

"As in the tire company."

"Let me think." Joline bit her lower lip again. I had to get the name of her lipstick brand, which seemed impervious to being bitten off. She frowned in concentration, which I suspected was indeed a strain for her. Marla was right: Peabrain indeed. "Perello! That's it. His name is Tony Perello."

No motorcycle company or reality TV star came to mind. "Why did Greggy, er, Greg, think Mr. Perello was a bad influence?"

"He said Perello was low-life and a criminal. Greggers punched him once. He told Carmen, I think it was in June, no, July, early July, cuz I'm like, that's when he paid for my butt tat, or was it late June?"

Why would anyone want needles in their butt? I shifted my weight again; now both my rear end and leg hurt.

"What did he tell Carmen?" I may have been snappish.

"Huh? Oh, like, he was no way going to pay her anything until she got rid of Perello. So she totally dumped him, super big-time."

"Did Carmen resent Greg for that?"

Joline shrugged. "She wanted the money, honey, not a honey with no money."

I pressed. "Could Carmen have been angry enough to kill Greg?"

"With a bomb, and cut off papa pay day?" She shook her head. With her, it manifested as a hair toss.

Time to try a different tack.

"How about you and Greg? You said you were working; is it because you need the money?"

"I work part time in a nail bar because I like it and I get a discount on all the latest colors and tools for to-die-for manicures. You can tell a lady by her hands, my mom always says. And anyone who's not matching their scent to their nail color is so not cool. Like my favorite is orchid."

"So you didn't need the money?" I was anxious to get her back on track, finish this interview, and escape from the torture of bad grammar and a broken chair.

Another shake of the shag-cut hair. She should be careful: any more vigorous head-shaking and she'd damage her few working neurons. "Greggy provided e-everything we needed." As if remembering her role, Joline dabbed her eyes with a fresh tissue and her lower lip resumed its tremolo. Joline was fashion forward: I had no idea that kohl came in cry-proof formulations. "He always took such good care of me and Chloe. That's why I didn't mind when he'd spend weekends with his daughters."

"Chloe wasn't his daughter?"

"He treated her like a daughter," she snapped. "He was going to adopt her."

I noted the vanished tremolo. "But you and Greg never married."

"We were going to, just as soon as his older kids got off child support, which they did last October when they turned eighteen and inherited money from Marla's parents. But then Greggers said he needed to work out a few business issues first, because he wanted to give me a really big wedding and buy me a new house. Greggy was going to rent a yacht for the wedding, and we'd sail out of Lahaina just before sunset, and—"

"Work out a few business issues? What kind of business issues?"

"Huh? Oh, I don't know. We never talked about his business."

"Not even when his business problems were delaying the wedding?"

"I trusted Greggy. He loved me and anyone who says different is just being mean!" Joline was clearly angry.

Hmm. What was under that sore spot? "Just being mean, huh?" I dripped with sarcasm.

"Greggy was under a lot of strain so he maybe drank too much and … he only stayed out all night a few times. Like, less than five. I think. I'm like, so he blew up and stormed out when I asked him about it. It didn't mean anything. He would have come back, I know it."

"So he was cheating on you."

"That is so not nice," Joline said, her voice rising. "Why are you attacking my poor Greggy?"

Already the center of attention, Joline's loud protestations attracted even more of the lobby residents to stare unabashedly at us. Correction, at Joline.

"It wasn't Greggers' fault. Other women were always throwing themselves at him. Sluts."

Dang, I'd pushed her too far; I needed to calm her down if I expected more information. "I'm sorry." I said, doing my best imitation of contrition. "Poor choice of words. I didn't mean to imply anything. I'm just trying to find out what kind of person he was. Mostly, I want to find out who did this dreadful thing to poor Greggy." I tried to work up a single tear in one eye, hoping it would trickle down my cheek slowly.

Joline was past listening. She railed at me, her voice now carrying to the outdoors, causing passers-by to pause and glance into the lobby. If a fire had broken out at that point, I doubt anyone would flee; all eyes and ears were tuned to Joline and her audition for *Who Wants To Be a Drama Queen?*

"You said you needed my help to catch my Greggers's killer but all you do is insult his memory. He was a wonderful man—a great man. I didn't have to come here. I skipped my Pilates class to be here." That last accompanied by a long stretch. Funny, I didn't recall a Pilates move that involved throwing your chest out.

It was obvious the interview was over and I was prickly—literally—from the being poked in all sorts of places by the wicker chair. That's my excuse, anyway, for what I said next.

"By all means, please go to your class. Maybe it will help the sagging skin under your arms." Joline gasped and pulled her arms close to her chest. Using just her forearm and hand, she snatched her purse off the chair. She shot out of the chair, turned her back to me, and flounced out. I don't think I ever understood the meaning of flounce until I saw her do it, buttocks—and breasts presumably as I couldn't see them—bouncing up and down with every stride, nose tilted in the air, gaze traveling over the heads of her audience. A sea of dark heads swiveled, following her exit. I had to hand it to her, everything bounced in perfect rhythm.

Time to pick up my own purse and leave—without the flounce. I imagined hostile stares following me as I had driven away the eye candy and floorshow.

I marched down the street, annoyed that the interview had gone poorly, that I'd lost my temper. I was even angrier that I was digging up the sordid details of a murdered man's life instead of enjoying my free time in paradise. In the midst of my pity party, I barged through a family of tourists—why do they always block the entire sidewalk posing for pictures—and made such a disagreeable face at a man trying to hand me coupons for an indoor gun range that he immediately snatched the coupon back, presumably aware that a person in my state of mind shouldn't be anywhere near a firearm. Not even a squirt gun.

I headed for the beach, keeping an eye out for security cameras and blowing a raspberry at each one I passed. I'd have to ask Edvard if scrunching up the face or sticking out the tongue made one unrecognizable to facial recognition systems. He would know.

Seeing the waves and feeling the warmth radiating from the soft sand, calmness seeped into my soul. My hands unclenched and my shoulders de-tensed. I watched surfers waltz with the waves while the sun sailed below the horizon, leaving a golden trail in its wake. Sigh. For the past week, I might as well have been in my childhood home in Minnesota for the time I'd spent enjoying the perfect weather and waves. Not that there was anything wrong with Minnesota, if you liked snow and mosquitoes. Not at the same time. Usually.

I needed to get off my *'ōkole* and get back in the water. Tomorrow morning. Definitely tomorrow morning, because tomorrow night I was headed back to San Francisco, land of fifty-degree water and the great white shark capital of the world. An ocean without *aloha*.

TWELVE

"All hope abandon, ye who enter here."
The Divine Comedy, Dante Alighieri

I HAD TAKEN advantage of GD's policy of transport home every three weeks to visit cold, foggy San Francisco for what I thought would be a romantic weekend with Keoni. Until, that is, my friend Jennifer called to remind me that she had scheduled a practice of the wedding party dance routine for Saturday morning. Instead of a romantic brunch with Keoni at a cozy Russian Hill bistro, I found my jet-lagged, extremely irked, and two-left-footed self in a cramped, Sumatra-temperature dance studio where Jennifer's wedding consultant had booked our rehearsal.

"No, no, no! You're crowding in too much. Keep your spacing. You should be keying off Meghann." One by one, Jennifer guided the dancers to her idea of perfect floor spacing. Perfect as in your EEE shoe width is disruptive to the dance aesthetic; move it over three millimeters. Yeesh.

I wanted to scream at yet another delay in an already tedious dance practice-athon, but held my tongue. "Now, Emma," I said to myself. "She's your friend. This is a stressful time. Be supportive. Worst case, you can get her back when you get married. A first dance involving synchronized pole dancing might make us even."

Jennifer's Gothic-themed over-the-top wedding and reception included a choreographed dance performed by the entire wedding party—except Madison the family labradoodle who was, naturally, the designated if slightly slobbery ring-bearer—to Michael Jackson's

"Thriller." The grand total was twelve bridesmaids, a large enough number that I was surprised there wasn't a special term for it. A brace of bridesmaids? A plump, clutter or rhumba of bridesmaids?

Jennifer continued repositioning her dance troupe, finally reaching me. She stood for a moment, moving her head back and forth like a dog investigating a slow moving and about-to-be-*pūpū* cricket before she grabbed my arm and pushed me back several feet and further to the left. Then to the right. Then forward by the width of a decomposing body part. A finger, God forbid.

"Sorry," I said as a slight apology for straying—staying in the absolutely perfect spot was rather taxing—and gave her a small smile.

"Another thing," she said, her voiced rose to address the group. "Remember not to smile. We're supposed to be ghouls."

For the eleventh time that morning, I wished I were surfing, even in the middle of a surf camp of twenty newbies, in sub-fifty degree, shark-infested waters. Which, arguably, could hasten my journey to becoming a real ghoul. Preferably one with better dance steps.

Moments later Jennifer restarted the music and for two minutes and forty-five seconds, I was totally absorbed in remembering the appropriate times to wiggle, throw hands to the left, give a neck twitch to the right, put hands on legs, pivot around one leg, rip the arm off of the person next to me. Okay, I made that last one up, though it would have added a certain evil undead verisimilitude to the entire shebang. Vincent Price's maniacal laugh cued us to throw our hands in the air, signaling the end. Thank God.

As we left, Jennifer announced she would post a video on You-Tube so we could practice on our own. If we'd tape our practices, Madison would critique our performances. No, not Madison the labradoodle nor even Madison the bridesmaid, but Madison, her choreography consultant. Sheesh. Couldn't parents of 1980s' children have named them for another state capital, say, Honolulu or Boise?

The rest of the weekend was a whirlwind. Keoni and I spent the remainder of a blissfully unchoreographed Saturday afternoon together and I related the highlights, in only two minutes, of my investigation. He didn't seem concerned that I hadn't done more but reiterated confidence that I'd unearth key information that would help Kealoha.

Keoni and I were having a pleasant dinner that evening with my parents when Mother threw me a curve ball.

"Your father and I were thinking of coming over to visit you," she said.

"Your mother wants to go," Dad corrected her.

"What? Why? You see me here." Okay, that didn't come out well.

"I haven't been to Hawai'i since your junior year, dear," she said. "I'd like to go again, maybe for a week while you're there."

Just great. All I needed was Mother hanging around while I pursued a mad bomber. "Did you have a date in mind?"

"How about next week?"

"Stacey's visiting. The week after that, we have deliverables due, so it will be crunch mode and I won't have much time for visitors. After that is Keoni's spring break and on the weekend I'll be visiting his parents on the Big Island. After that, I'm back here for Jennifer's wedding."

Mother gave me a funny look as if she sensed I was trying to put her off. "Will you be free the following week? That's about as late as I can go. My students will be pleading for extensions on their final papers and panic if I'm not around to grant them. It has to be that week, unless you'd rather I not visit."

Mother should have been a drama professor: that pause between "week" and "unless you'd rather I not visit" was perfectly timed to elicit the maximum amount of pity. Was it my imagination, or were her eyes starting to water? Outstanding performance by a mother in a guilt trip goes to Professor Catherine Jones! Normally I'd never think of my mother and Joline in the same breath but both seemed to have mastered the art of teary-eyed drama on demand.

"Sure, that will be great!" I said with false enthusiasm. "I mean, of course not, I'd love to have you."

Mother flashed me a grateful smile and for that one moment, I forgot about the murder and believed that we'd have a great time together.

MONDAY MORNING I was back in Honolulu and barely functioning. I'd put my shirt on backward and my pants were unzipped when I walked out to the car. A flyer was stuck under the windshield wiper. Since I wasn't close to a trashcan I tossed the flyer onto the seat where it landed face up: "HAOLE GO HOME DON'T MESS WID DA LOCAL BUSNESS." The message was handwritten in block letters. Although I admired the alliterative appeal of "*Haole* Go Home," the penmanship and spelling left much to be desired.

A neuron or two fired. Windshields of other cars parked along the street were clear of flyers. More neurons fired. Someone had delivered a special message to me. I could have been singled out because I was not native Hawaiian, but even in my fogged state I knew that, despite the spelling, the note was not about leaving trash in The Bus, aka the local transit system. Someone was warning me off the murder investigation, and that's as far as my neurons could take me without more caffeine.

The grande macadamia nut vanilla latte I wolfed on the way to work barely made a dent in my morning muddle. Hence, when I arrived at work I headed for the kitchen for a large cup of the local rotgut. Desperate times call for desperate drinks. I was not so desperate that I didn't check my face in the rearview mirror first to make sure I hadn't used lipstick as eye shadow. (Once, and only once, I was so exhausted I used analgesic muscle rub as toothpaste. My teeth weren't any whiter but they did tingle all day.)

Being mixed up on time zones was only part of my problem. Sunday after church and a sermon by Pastor Larry Lucifer—that was the unfortunate man's real name—Stacey and I went surfing. Keoni, having a bazillion pages to read, begged off. My arms hurt with every stroke: I was out of the habit of paddling through neoprene, which reminded me of trying to run a marathon in one-size-fits all pantyhose. As a consequence, my whole upper body still ached, despite my having mainlined ibuprofen for the past twenty-four hours.

I kept my head down in between gulps of rotgut, focused on work; I wasn't going to think about the note until I was sure my head was clear.

"Stupid and stupider." Gunnar's voice, loud and penetrating, broke my concentration.

A woman murmured a response.

"I knew they'd screw it up." Gunnar again, slightly less vociferous.

Did I need another coffee? My stomach roiled. Nope, but I could use a cold drink and the path to the vending machine led conveniently by Gunnar's cube.

Linda, her back to me, was chatting with Gunnar.

"How's it going?" I slowed as I approached. Out of the corner of my eye I caught a flash of movement: Rafe standing and stretching in his cube.

"Hi, Emma." Linda nodded. "We were discussing the three types of Big Data."

"Four types." Gunnar corrected. "Sensible, Scary, Stupid, and Stupider. Linda's just been the victim of all four."

"What happened?"

Linda shrugged. "I'm a casualty of my own partial success. At Wilson & Kumar, I worked on a small project for a large state government."

"Count me retrospectively happy I was not on the team," Gunnar said.

"The state wanted to consolidate information from several databases to better serve its citizens," Linda said. "So, when you search for help on the state web pages, you can put in your address and the answers retrieved will be specific for your situation, such as the hours of the nearest DMV, or property tax rate information specifically for seniors. Not Big Brother so much as helpful brother."

"It sounds reasonable to me," said Rafe, who had left his cubicle to join me. At the mention of "Big Brother," I expected Edvard to make an appearance. The fact that he hadn't meant he must be at a meeting. Karen's cube was empty, which I hoped meant she was keeping an eye on him.

Linda continued speaking. "To run tests on the completed system, I set up several dummy records using different addresses, but all tying back to my email account. Naturally, I erased the dummy records at the completion of the project. Unfortunately, it seems that IT has resurrected the data and as part of the state's effort to get more revenue, I received an inquiry from the Department of Motor Vehicles in November and then again in January about why I don't have a state driver's license. I responded both times. Today I got a notice from a city assessor that I've not paid my property tax and the municipality plans to begin proceedings to collect." Linda gave a short, high-pealed laugh. "As I recall, the State House was one of my fake residences. I can hardly wait to see my tax bill. Maybe I should agree to pay them on the condition I'm named a state senator. Seems fair."

"You could write and tell them you are dead," I offered. "Or better yet, update your status online. Send them a tweet from the hereafter. What's the hash tag for heaven?"

Rafe protested that God didn't need a hashtag and anyone who thought He did could start using #infidels in their tweets.

Gunnar was not nearly as amused. "Sensible for the government to use location data to help citizens. Scary they would resurrect deleted data without validating it. Stupid for the municipality to not have vetted the address was residential. Stupider that, despite two emails and two months, the record still hasn't been deleted. All four types of Big Data. This is the future, except it will be worse when the federal government starts earnestly sharing data across systems and wants to monitor your every move."

I departed to get a cold drink, leaving Linda, Gunnar, and Rafe still discussing the subject. It occurred to me that Gunnar sounded a lot like Edvard. Not literally; Edvard still had a Flemish accent.

But Gunnar had expressed similar paranoia about government intrusion. There was just one conclusion: "They" had planted the same microchips in Gunnar as in Edvard. Yes, indeedy.

THIRTEEN

"Three can keep a secret if two are dead."
Benjamin Franklin

MY COLD CAFFEINE-LADEN drink did the trick. Or maybe it was the sugar-rush from the bag of Coconut M&Ms. In any case, I finally felt clear-headed enough to Sherlock my earlier personalized mail delivery.

The scrap of paper appeared to have been torn from copy paper. No help there. The block letters in black pen revealed a person without a high degree of fine motor control. Or a TV addict who knew threatening notes are always written in capital letters. Lastly, the writer couldn't spell his or her way out of the first round of a spelling bee, unless the misspelling was deliberate to throw me off the track.

Sherlock Holmes would have deduced the author's name, address, educational history, hand size and favorite cocktail from the note. Being more like Dr. Watson, I tossed the note aside and did my best to deduce its implications.

Would a killer send a warning before killing again? Could the note be from someone who had a secret I might uncover during the investigation? A matter unrelated to the murder? Was it meaningful that the note didn't threaten any specific violence, e.g., car vandalized, extremities broken, really unflattering picture in a bathing suit posted on Instagram?

All in all, I was bothered less by the contents of the note than the idea that someone made the effort to track down my vehicle in Waikīkī and, by extension, had a good idea where I lived.

Since I didn't know what to do about the note, I took action on another front; I asked Karen to join me for lunch in 'Aiea. A local I'd met in the lineup, Manoa Cunha, had recommended Kekoa's Kitchen, praising their *kālua* pork plate with ginger coconut rice and fresh pineapple-cabbage slaw. A local *hale'aina* (restaurant), it would be an ideal location to talk about Karen's issue without fear of being overheard by other GD consultants. Except that a GD consultant happened to see us leaving for lunch and invited himself along, tone deaf to hints that lunch was for girls only. Let's see, who would be that oblivious?

Stepping out of the DFAS building into the piercingly bright sunshine, Karen and I whipped out our sunglasses. At the same time, Edvard pulled out ski goggles rimmed in Christmas tree lights. After adjusting the goggles, he reached into his man-bag and pulled out a bright blue burqa-like wrap, which he used to cover his head, face, and shoulders. Swathed in such odd garb, Edvard could have been a member of the Rebel Alliance ready to jump on a Tauntaun to do battle with the Empire. I was 95 percent sure his bizarre outfit was to keep "Them" from tracking him—the other 5 percent I gave to a skin condition—but I had to ask, just for the entertainment value of his explanation.

"Is that a new designer line of extraterrestrial wear?"

"Cool, huh?" Edvard responded. "Anti-surveillance tech-nology." He took the goggles off and handed them to me. "See, they're lined with small lights that emit rays pretty close to infrared."

"Which does what exactly; tans people sitting next to you?"

"You're talking about UV light, plenty of it in Hawai'i. The infrared is to confuse surveillance cameras so 'They' can't identify your face. These glasses are used a lot in Japan. I got a friend to send me a pair."

"The purpose of the burqa?"

"Masks body heat from drones," he said.

"In this climate you might die from heat stroke first," Karen observed.

Before Edvard could launch into a spiel about the increasing use of drones, I cut him off and offered him a deal: lose the burqa and goggles and I'd drop him off at the front of the restaurant. Figuring he could put his head down for the two seconds it took to get in the door, he agreed. Thank goodness.

As I drove, Edvard pointed out the locations of surveillance cameras: parks, critical intersections, bank ATMs, liquor stores, pawnshops, and military installations. Who needed to take selfies when you were being photographed every time you turned around? The quality of surveillance videos wouldn't make a splash on YouTube, but when was the last time a selfie won a photo contest? As a revenue-raising opportunity the local government could, for a small fee, let you purchase surveillance videos of yourself, with an airbrush option to erase extra chins, touch up your roots, and eliminate those extra pounds. For a hefty payment, they could even excise the videos of you with your finger up your nose at traffic stops. Just think of it: no government need operate at a deficit once they explored the revenue potential of surveillance blackmail.

Edvard continued to babble about Hawai'i's plans to install more cameras and I was torn between driving faster in order to cut short his narrative, or slowing down to avoid a ticket from the ever-present speed cameras. None too soon we arrived at the restaurant, a hole-in-the-wall in a light industrial park, and I dropped Edvard and Karen at the entrance.

Kekoa's took the humble plate lunch up a notch, most definitely. Their *kālua* pork plate was as good as Manoa had promised. Edvard and Karen skipped the island plate, each opting for the cold chicken salad with fresh macadamia-nut/ginger pesto served on Portuguese sweet bread. A taste of Karen's meal convinced me I should give it a try on a future visit.

Edvard launched into a description of the latest 3-D superheroes-saving-the-world-from-prehistoric-monsters flick and described it in such excruciating detail I had no interest in seeing it. The butler always kills the T-rex: everyone knows that. Karen, much to my surprise, had also seen the film, but confessed she much preferred foreign films; her all time favorite was *Amores Perros*, a Mexican film staring Gael Garcia Bernal. Before I could put in a word for my love of romantic comedies, Edvard and Karen were enthusiastically trading opinions on the best foreign films.

"German thriller *M*," Edvard said.

"Too much social commentary," Karen responded. "*Y Tu Mamá También.*"

"Just okay. Since Bernal is your idol, what do you think about *The Motorcycle Diaries*?" Edvard countered.

"Not a fan of Che Guevara," she replied.

As the ping-pong continued, I realized that I knew very little about Karen outside of the office. Heck, she worked such long hours that I couldn't imagine her having a life. Then again, maybe I'd allowed too much of my personal life to intrude into the office since my coworkers and managers saw me as a part time private investigator, and in Michael's case, a disaster waiting to happen.

Edvard, too, reveal new depths to his interests; he could carry on a conversation without mentioning "Them."

That afternoon, Michael enlisted Gunnar and me to pull together a presentation—PowerPoint, of course—that he could share with DFAS management on our progress. Rather than the standard GD template, Michael directed that we use the DFAS format: a large department seal and DFAS logo as headers and a footer that warned the reader not to share this information with the Chinese, Russians or CNN. This left one-third of the page available for real information, which was to be conveyed in Oh-So-Pedestrian Palatino.

By four o'clock, Gunnar and I had completed the presentation. Michael was pleased with the result and I deflected most of the credit to Gunnar, where it belonged. Gunnar had wielded a red pen like a rapier, turning our first draft of twenty rambling pages into a crisp and positive six-page summary. I was impressed with Gunnar's ability to hone in on key points, put GD accomplishments in a good light and respond to a short deadline. It was clear why Dave Blanchard had recruited Gunnar and why Karen needed to tread carefully. "Carefully" meaning, "handicap or kneecap the SOB without losing her job."

KAREN AND I rescheduled our tête-à-tête and rendezvoused after work at Ala Moana Park. I had suggested the locale as a good place to unwind. We strolled leisurely around Magic Island as we talked.

Karen listened quietly as I recounted my not-so-vast experience with hidden recording devices.

During an investigation several months earlier, I'd consulted a private investigator friend of my gal pal Stacey. He rudely disabused me of the belief that spy gadgets were cheap, easily obtainable, foolproof, and legal. After a nice Greek dinner and primer on bugs (the listening device type, not the six-legged scream-inducing type), I'd spent a hundred dollars to obtain a "listening device perfect for the nursery" off the Internet with a battery life of less than three days. It wasn't ideal—the limited transmission range meant I had to sit in my car in a sketchy neighborhood to hear anything—but it fit my budget.

Needless to say, I wasn't listening for babies crying but for proof-of-guilt utterances. Instead I overheard roommate squabbles, *Law and Order* reruns, and bathroom sounds of personal hygiene and dietary distress. Eew.

"In general," I said as I danced a few steps to avoid darting children pursuing floating orbs generated by a bubble mower, "the smaller the recording device, the more you pay. For instance, a smoke detector recorder costs less than seventy dollars, but a less in-your-face device, like a watch, will cost you nearly double that."

"I can't see hanging a smoke detector in my cube."

"Or wearing it around your neck. Realistically, you have only a few options. The watch, which I mentioned, is expensive and not without problems; you'd likely have to contort your arm to ensure you could capture Gunnar's actions."

"Or put it in his face."

"Might work, if you could pretend you had an odd muscle spasm. Another possibility is fake eyeglasses although I'd recommend against them; thick black frames are unattractive except to librarians and electrical engineering majors."

"Maybe they'd put Gunnar off and he'd stop harassing me."

I ignored her remark. "You could use a pendant. The positives are that it would be discreet and capture both audio and video. The negatives: you have to keep your chest focused right on the subject for the video. If you and Gunnar are sitting across from each other, it should work. If he's striding around the office, you'll either appear to be flaunting your chest or you'll miss most of the action."

Karen's face fell. "As I told you, he likes to touch my back when I'm at the computer; I couldn't capture any of that."

"Not with the pendant. Another option is a pen. Like the pendant, it contains a flashing LED when recording, which can't be seen if you wear it against your chest." I held up my hand as Karen was about to protest. "I know, it looks silly to clip a pen to your blouse or top. There's a way around that."

I grabbed Karen by the elbow to steer her off the path and away from a malodorous group of homeless clustered in a nearby grove of banyans. "This way," I said guiding her toward a walkway that took us to the tip of Magic Island, and the best view of the sunset. The orange orb now hung pregnant in the sky, casting its last rays across the darkening water.

"The pen," Karen said, breaking my reverie.

"Right. I pulled a pen out of my purse to illustrate. On one side of the barrel, there will be a flashing LED light. On the other side is the pinhole camera. To operate, you click the top of the pen twice. When Gunnar's harassing you, pretend to fiddle with the pen, keeping one finger over the LED light. As long as the pinhole on the other side faces him, you'll get a video. Audio too."

"And the downside is?"

"It's $120, but with free shipping."

We stopped walking and stared at the sunset.

"It never gets old, does it?" Karen said, breaking our silence.

I shook my head. Always beautiful, yet always different.

A few minutes later, the golden path on the ocean surface disappeared. The park was suddenly shadowed as the afterglow dimmed. "Time to go," I said. "Not the safest place after dark."

On the walk back Karen spoke animatedly about her conversation with Michael about joining the public sector group. Michael was convinced Blanchard would land more DFAS Hawai'i work and that Karen should talk with Blanchard when he was next in Hawai'i. "You should too," she said. "That is, if you like it here, all that surfing, Hawaiian food, and such."

Of course I was interested. One of the reasons I'd left Hawai'i after college was the dearth of career opportunities in the islands. A job that could bring me back regularly was appealing. I told Karen I'd wait to see what kind of contracts Blanchard could land before I decided; one DFAS contract on O'ahu doth not a trend make.

"I'll try the pen," Karen said, dropping the non sequitur as we reached her car. "It's pricey, but if it works, the cost doesn't matter. Maybe I can make Gunnar pay for the recording device as part of my blackmail terms."

"I think you mean, 'as part of your joint discussion of how he can help you self-actualize in the workplace.'"

"Exactly."

FOURTEEN

"When I die, bury me on the golf course so
my husband will visit."
Unknown

THE NEXT DAY I used my lunch hour to drive to The Luakini Golf
Club. Strolling toward the clubhouse, I inhaled deeply, searching
for a remnant of the acrid scent of just a few weeks ago. Thankfully,
there was no trace of it, nor signs of the explosion, except for a new
section of asphalt and curb where the burned hulk of Walker's car
had been. Despite its proximity to the clubhouse and the crowded
lot, the space was empty except for a fresh *lei* where the car had
been. Greg had been remembered, but by whom?

Standing in the center of the new pavement, I turned my back
to the clubhouse and began to stride purposefully across the lot,
counting my steps. According to Uncle Kimo, the police explosives report stated that the triggering device had been within one
hundred meters of Walker's car. At ninety strides, about eighty-two
meters, I reached a fence, beyond which lay a road and beyond
that, nothing but trees and underbrush. Thinking of Edvard, I
checked the area for a traffic camera, but just my luck, or Walker's
luck, there wasn't one.

I returned to the infamous parking spot and several times paced
out one hundred meters, or as many as I could, estimating the rest.
I walked toward the looming Koʻolaus, across the lot in several directions, through the clubhouse, and more. The area I covered was
huge; the killer could have been hiding in a car, or across the street

fronting the course, on a green or one of two tees, as well as in the clubhouse or restaurant. Heck, he could have been perched in a tree somewhere: there were plenty of those, and they were mostly old and tall. Nowhere did I find a single video camera. The Luakini Golf Club was well behind the times when it came to spying on its members (the next frontier for golf: high-tech ways to ensure nobody cheats on his golf score).

I stood on the edge of the practice green, the place I would have chosen to hide; it had a good view of the parking lot and one could inconspicuously putter around (no pun intended) waiting for Walker to leave. I stood for a few moments, absorbing the sweet smell of plumeria and the quiet taps as golfers urged little white balls toward tiny pockets. Had a cold-blooded murderer worked on his golf game whilst awaiting his victim?

A touch on my shoulder sent me jumping out of my skin. It was Danny Estrada.

"Sorry to startle you, but I said your name a couple times. You didn't respond."

"I was deep in thought."

"Checking out our magnificent golf course or hunting for me?"

Caught flatfooted, I searched for a plausible answer.

"Don't be embarrassed," Danny said. "I know I'm a stud; women try to pick me up all the time. I get off work at five. Do you want to buy me a drink and dinner? I could show you a great place to watch the sunset."

Before I could respond, Danny started laughing. "I bet you're checking the place out, wondering where Walker's killer was when the bomb exploded."

"How did you—"

"Kealoha Kanekoa is a cousin of my auntie's husband."

"Of course he is," I said.

Like me, Danny was on his lunch break, twenty minutes long in his case, and suggested we grab sandwiches and chat. He had a few things to tell me about Greg Walker. Over a BC&P sandwich (bacon, cheese, and pineapple) Danny divulged the tale of an infamous catfight involving Walker's women.

About a month before Walker's death, Joline, staking out the club before dawn, caught Walker dropping Samantha off for her morning shift as a waitress. Barely twenty, Samantha already knew (in the biblical sense) several members of the club, Greg being among them.

Joline did not confine her displeasure to verbal abuse. The ensuing fight left Samantha with a scratched face and a black eye as Joline, having broken her freshly enameled nail early in the brawl, escalated to a closed-fist punch. Greg had been heavily bruised when he had inserted himself between the combatants. Only with the aid of an iron-wielding golfer and the club manager was further damage averted. Joline, still steamed, slammed her car into Greg's silver Lexus on the way out, leaving his taillights toasted and his bumper bruised. At least, that was how Danny first heard it. By the fifth time he'd heard the tale, Samantha's face was permanently scarred and Greg's car was on the way to the scrap metal recycler.

Purportedly, Joline had not returned and Greg and Samantha were splitski. However, Danny had seen Greg chatting up—or maybe it was feeling up—the club's female tennis pro before his death. Once an eel, always an eel.

At my prompting, Danny disclosed that Greg had a plenty of friends among club members, but had lost more than a few golfing buddies over the years because of sour business deals. If the scale of his misdeeds were to be believed, his foursome may have included the last three *mea hūpō* (fools) who hadn't lost money or marriages to Greg's predations.

I pressed Danny about Marla and Coconuts, er, Carmen. Danny had been at the club for two years and therefore knew a mere smidgen about Marla, who was not a member of the club. However, Greg paid for Carmen's membership even after the divorce. An avid golfer, she played Thursdays in a women's league and every other Tuesday at a reserved tee time. More noteworthy in Danny's book were Carmen's golf clubs and car, both purchased new each year.

The envy was unmistakable when he relayed this bit of news, but whether he coveted her golf clubs or her Audi A5 Convertible, I couldn't say.

I'd shared with Danny what I knew about the effective radius of the bomb's trigger device and the places I had sussed out where one could loiter unobtrusively, waiting for the ideal moment to set off an explosion. Set off a bomb, I mean, not one of Joline's tantrums. The former list was manageable; the second, as numerous as the stars in the Milky Way.

"The police interviewed everyone who was here," Danny said. "They even came back, and again asked the staff about vehicles that left the lot near the time the bomb went off. I'm not sure how anyone could have been at the club and not be seen unless it was the Invisible Man."

I pointed out that golfers on the putting green were immersed in their own little worlds. Additionally, a hundred-meter radius included the street in front of the club. "The killer could have parked across the street, detonated the device and melted away virtually unnoticed, except for the satisfied smile on his face."

"True, but he still would have had to walk by the Lexus and throw the bomb on the seat."

"Is that where it was?" I'd never thought to ask where the bomb had been planted. Miss Marple would have been mortified.

Danny nodded, his mouth full of sandwich. "That's the rumor; back seat behind the driver. Like everyone else, Walker left his windows open. Which is another reason why Kealoha shouldn't be a suspect."

"An open window?"

"No, because Kealoha knew that day that Walker would be here."

"Because you told him."

"Yes, because he wanted to talk to Walker. Why would he bring a bomb along and then plant it in the car after making a scene with Walker? Wouldn't it make more sense to plant the bomb at a time when it would be harder to tie him to the murder?"

AFTER DINNER THAT evening, I strolled down Kalākaua Avenue. The noise on the street was deafening: street musicians on ukes played *hapa-haole* tunes; a saxophonist wallowed through blues music; another enterprising artist banged away on steel drums; and the cars and buses roared incessantly. I headed for the beach, keeping an eye out for security cameras and blowing a raspberry at each one I passed. Just because I was in that kind of mood.

The ocean was black, except for the traces of white from the waves crashing on the reef, the reflected lights from hotels on Waikīkī, and the occasional tourist-laden catamaran coming in from a late sail. The whisper of the waves and the warmth of the soft sand were comforting. I picked up a snowy piece of branched coral that hadn't yet been smoothed into an amorphous, stony shape.

Danny's story about Greg Walker and Peabrain explained Joline's blow up when I'd challenged her about not yet being married. I wondered if I needed to chat with Samantha or the club's tennis pro, but decided against it. Traipsing after Greg's conquests would be like chasing a libidinous rat down a hole, and I didn't have the time or inclination for that. It was time to step away from Walker's personal life and check out his business dealings.

Walker may have lost golf buddies over a few bad deals, but he must have done well personally, or his ex-wife wouldn't be stripping the gears on a new car every year. And inasmuch as he had over fifty suits in the court system, Greg had angered more than just golf buddies. I had a feeling that Walker's business ventures, or misadventures, might be behind his murder.

FIFTEEN

"… my people, about forty thousand in
number, have in no way been consulted
by those, three thousand in number,
who claim the right to destroy the
independence of Hawaiʻi."
Queen Liliʻuokalani

DURING MY YEARS in Hawaiʻi, I'd lived in overcrowded old homes close to the university—typical student housing. Life on a corporate expense account was different. I'd stayed in high-class hotels or corporate housing on my assignments and had become a select member of frequent flophouse clubs for all the major hotel chains. Even on a government contract, the housing that GD had arranged for us in Hawaiʻi was way above what I'd had as a student. Literally way above: I was staying in a one-bedroom apartment on the twenty-fifth floor of a building in Waikīkī. Located on Kūhiō Avenue, I was one block from the ocean and restaurants; shopping and music were just out the front door and a saunter away. I even had a partial ocean view. "Partial" meaning I could see a slice of water between two other tall buildings. The apartment had a small *lānai* where I could enjoy the fresh air if I was too lazy to go out. For those bored by the beach, poor souls, the building offered a recreation deck with a large swimming pool, hot tub, small multi-sport court, and a putting green.

One would think there was nothing more a body could desire. One would be wrong; I needed a dance studio. Jennifer was out of control over the dance routine for her wedding. Actually, she was out of control on her wedding, period, but the dance routine was an especial thorn in my side-steps. She had uploaded a video of "Thriller" to mydreamwedding.com for her undead wedding wanna-bes to commit to muscle memory. Jennifer's emails—one every second day—to the wedding party urged each of us to practice with the video and mimic Meghann, who had "nailed it" and was the star of the video. Thank *ke Akua* that I hadn't been at that particular rehearsal; who wants to be recorded staggering to synchronized eye rolls?

Not wanting to lurch around the dance floor banging into everyone and everything—think dancing hippos in "Fantasia"—I needed a space where I could practice my grapevine á la ghoul and dead body box step. My apartment was totally inadequate, as I found out when I twitched into a table and lurched into a floor lamp during a brief run-through.

Hence, one Saturday morning I found myself traipsing to Kapiʻolani Park. Why Kapiʻolani Park? Because everything goes on at Kapiʻolani: festivals, picnics, kite flying, early morning Tai Chi Chuan, hula, polo, pre-dawn civilian boot camp, ghostly voices, UFO sightings, jamming musicians, and joggers (barefoot and otherwise). Amidst all that, who is going to notice a *wahine pupule e hula ai* (crazy woman who dances)?

I arrived at the park just after seven wearing dark glasses, my hair pulled back in a short ponytail and a beach hat pulled over my ears. I had my iPhone strapped to my arm—to listen to the music, not to watch the video—and was wearing running attire. If, God forbid, a friend or colleague should recognize me, I'd tell them that I was out for a run and the routine was the latest fashion in warming up for a half marathon. Hey, it was no stranger than yoga on a surfboard or pole dancing fitness classes.

I chose the *mauka* (mountain) side of the Park along Kalākaua Avenue; the *makai* (sea) side would be populated with the still-sleeping homeless. Passing the *lei*-bedecked statue of Queen Kapiʻolani—such a small statue, was it life-sized?—I headed for a shaded area adjacent to the Victorian-era bandstand where a large contingent of older women were engrossed in their morning Tai Chi.

The first time through "Thriller," I messed up after just seventeen seconds and had to start over. The second time, I nearly made it to the forty-five second mark. None of which meant that I would be termed a graceful ghoul. Could one be graceful when losing body parts?

"Emma! Emma Jones!" The call came just as I'd set up for "third time's a charm." Karen approached me at a trot and waved her hand.

What was she doing here?

"I thought that was you," she said as she came closer. "Out for a morning run?"

"Absolutely. How 'bout you? Soccer?" She was attired in shorts, long socks, and cleats.

"Yup. I found a women's team that scrimmages here Saturday mornings. It's great fun. Want to join us?"

"No, thanks, soccer is not my thing."

"How about the brunch afterward, if you're done with your run?"

"Thanks for the invite, but a girlfriend is arriving today and I have to get my apartment ready." That would be stocking up on chips, white wine, and an extra-large pizza.

"Maybe another time, then. Gotta go."

I watched Karen trot off toward the far fields where several soccer games were in process. After she was on the far side of the fields I restarted the music and took another unsuccessful whirl, or stagger, at the routine. A few more tries and I decided to hang up my body bag. At the wedding, Jennifer would have her back to me, without a clue as to how I was doing until she saw the wedding video. I neither expected nor sought a nomination for "Best Supporting Performance by a Stiff."

I sat on the grass with my now-lukewarm vanilla macadamia nut coffee and fat-pill—a chocolate donut—and watched the sun-kissed morning unfurl around me. Mynah birds hidden in the tree above screeched and flew away when young men with Frisbees took the place of the Tai Chi group. Joggers of all shapes and sizes occasionally ran past. Two rugby teams commandeered a nearby field and began their strange race between large goal posts, stopping periodically for a big man hug. A scum. No, that's not right. A scrum. Scum is a guy like Greg Walker.

My surroundings faded from my consciousness as I replayed interviews, making mental notes and thinking about next steps—the investigation kind, not the dance-of-the-dead kind. I might still be there but for an orange Nerf football that hit me in the chest. Hard. A boy of twelve or thirteen, if I had to guess, stared at me from fifteen yards away. Beneath that deep tan, I expect he was flushed to his hairline.

"I'm sorry," he squeaked. His companions behind me laughed nervously.

I stood up, smiled, and tossed him the ball. "That's my signal to leave." Sure enough, my watch read three minutes to nine. Time to pick up Stacey.

SEVERAL HOURS LATER, Stacey and I were happily ensconced in the lineup at Populars, sitting a short distance from Manoa, the surfer who had recommended Kekoa's Kitchen. A big Hawaiian, Manoa rode a ten-foot board that could catch anything that rippled (except six-pack abs, and there were a lot of those at Pops). Manoa's *niho mano* (shark teeth) tattoo covered his abs, crept up his pectorals, and marched over his highly muscled shoulder. He also had a stretch of *niho mano* entwining his thigh. With his six-foot-four-inch frame and the dignity of his bearing and *mana* (presence), Manoa evoked the spirit of King Kamehameha's warriors.

Stacey and I espied a four-foot set wave come through and waited to see if anyone was going for it. Manoa caught it at the peak, dropped down the face, bottom turned into the slot, and cross-stepped to the end of his board. Five toes on the nose. I hooted at him and added a "*kupaianaha*" (amazing) for emphasis.

When the next wave came through, Stacey turned to catch it, angling her board down the face, when a *haole* guy paddled just inside of her, blocking her drop. She pulled out of the wave: "collision at sea can ruin your entire day" as Thucydides famously did not say (but any number of sailors and a whole lot of surfers with dinged-up boards have).

Manoa paddled out to where we were sitting and nodded his head at me. "*Howzit, sistah?*"

Haole-boy paddled back out to "way to go, Brandon" from another *haole*. They appeared to be twenty-somethings, definitely from the mainland (no tans), and surfing on boards too short for the conditions in typical-young-male-tourist cases of misplaced machismo. You surf long boards here or you don't get any waves, unless you rudely cut in front of another surfer to grab one.

Another set wave feathered on the horizon. Manoa didn't seem to be going for it so I turned around to paddle, moving slightly to the left to ensure I was over the shallower part of the reef where the wave would break first.

"*E paddle mo bettah, sistah,*" I heard over my shoulder from Manoa. Meanwhile, Brandon-the-haole had seen me move over and he did too, lining up exactly inside me so that I couldn't catch the wave without running over him. Clearly Stacey and I were facing *'o Brandon he'e nalu pua'a nui loa* (Brandon the seriously big wave hog). Rather than get angry, I signaled to Stacey and we paddled to the next break over where there were fewer surfers and none of them were Brandon.

That is, until Brandon and his friend paddled over and sat right in front of us. Stacey and I exchanged long looks. Although I had plenty of days to surf Waikīkī, Stacey didn't and she shouldn't have to put up with wave hogs on her vacation. I decided to run Brandon and friend over on the next wave and provide the sharks with a little *kaukau*. I only hoped I wouldn't damage my surfboard.

Before I could put Brandon in my sights, Manoa paddled over and sat right next to him.

"*E brah, how 'bout let da wahine catch da wave? She maika'i nō, you malahini 'ino.*"

"How about speaking English?"

Manoa lowered his head and spoke in a low voice. I missed the exchange, but I didn't miss seeing Brandon paddle off with his friend, headed to the next break over, glancing over his shoulder nervously as he left.

"I use *li'ili'i* (small) words *fo haole-boy,*" Manoa said. "*He decide go find uddah wave, poa ting. Wave come fo you and friend wikiwiki. E luana 'oe, sistah!*"

Suddenly there it was, a beautiful wave, coming our way, with nobody on it. I signaled to Stacey that it was hers. Two strokes and she popped up, took off to the left, then swung the board around and went right, a perfect fade. "*E Manoa, mahalo nui loa fo da kine wave!*" I called to him as I watched Stacey, every fiber of her being radiating happiness.

SIXTEEN

"No canoe is defiant on a stormy day."
Hawaiian Proverb

IN THE MIDST of dinner at Lulu's, Stacey and I enjoyed a few minutes of relative quiet while the band took a break. The remainder of our surf session had been pure gold. I'd even heard Stacey humming to herself as we floated on our boards; a sure sign of her contentment. We'd stayed out long enough to watch the sunset and then dragged our rental boards and wrecked bodies back to my apartment. Hunger drove us to Lulu's, with its proximity, massive portions of good food, and free music. The open-air seats with a view of the ocean were an added inducement.

I chased the last of the guacamole around my plate with a huge wedge of *kālua* pork quesadilla thinking this might be a good time to mention my latest investigative activity and request Stacey's help. She'd been my sidekick in my first two cases, adeptly drawing people out who wouldn't otherwise give me the time of day but succumbed readily to Stacey's double dip of down-home drawl and charm. No doubt, had she done the interview with Peabrain, they'd be best buddies by now and having facials together.

"Stacey, I—"

A dark haired, very-tanned guy garbed in jeans and a shirt open to the navel appeared behind Stacey's chair and tapped her on the shoulder. He flashed her an oily smile when she turned around. "I noticed you from across the room. We should get together, soon. Give me a call." He dropped a red business card on the table and swaggered off.

Did I mention Stacey was a guy magnet? Long blond hair and with curves in all the right places, she was regularly hit on by complete strangers, from pimply teens to octogenarians in walkers and everything male in between. This guy was middle aged and in a reptilian branch of taxonomy. Eew.

"A red business card?" I said. "That's a new one. What is he, a pimp?"

Stacey picked up the card, quickly read the front and tossed it back on the table. "He's a Honker."

"He's a goose?"

"A Honker. You haven't heard about them?"

I shook my head and picked up the business card. In large white letters it proclaimed "I Am So Right For You," and listed a web address.

"Honk is a subscription service," Stacey explained. "It offers a selection of business cards with pickup lines. The cards you drop on your prey, so to speak, include the website address for your profile. Charmed by your pickup line, the prey visits your profile, learns how wonderful you are, and contacts you."

"I can't believe guys pay to use this service," I said.

"Men and women both use it."

"Dare I ask why it's named Honk?"

"It's from the bumper sticker. You know, 'Honk If You Love Jesus,' or whatever. The giver of the card is a Honker."

"Indeed. I take it you've been honked before."

"A few times. The guys have been cute, but the messages on the cards … ugh."

Stacy and Shaun, the body-pierced barista at our local coffee haunt, had taken in a several free concerts in the past month, Shaun being quite knowledgeable about the local music scene. Shaun had been enamored with Stacey for many months and she, coming off two less-than-satisfactory relationships, had agreed to go out him "as a friend." They had been getting a bite to eat when a random guy honked Stacey with a card that read: "I'm better than that guy you're with In Every Way."

"Crude and insulting. Besides, Shaun was so much cuter than honk-man," she said.

"I wonder if there is a market for Honk-retort cards? I can think of a bunch of them."

"I'm afraid to ask."

"'*No habla* Honk.' Or, 'Sorry, I am busy. For the next 4398 evenings.' Or 'Thanks for inspiring me; I'm joining a convent.' Or—"

"I get the picture," Stacey said.

At that moment the band, Mānoa DNA, launched into the second set with "Love the One You're With."

"Nice sentiment," Stacey said, tapping her foot to the music, "but I still don't want to date. Busting up with Darrell and then with Jake was enough; I've sworn off men for the next six months. Maybe six years."

Most women would be loath to dump an NFL All-Pro cornerback, but Stacey had grown tired of Darrell's big ego. On the rebound, she'd landed Jake, a handsome and very successful entrepreneur. When Jake had suggested some of her contacts might be helpful to his business and he'd be glad to pay her a finder's fee, she had decided business-centeredness was no better than Darrell's self-centeredness and told Jake to go IPO himself.

"Enough about men," she said. "What are we doing this week? Besides surfing, of course."

The waitress arrived to clear our plates and take dessert orders. We agreed to split the macadamia mango lime cheesecake. "Split" meaning Stacey got the first and last bites and I got everything in between.

While we waited for the cheesecake, I described a few things Stacey could do while I was working, including visiting Pearl Harbor and the Punchbowl, aka the War Memorial of the Pacific. Since these would require a vehicle, she could drive me to and from work. Stacey said that she'd also relish the opportunity to surf in warm water for an entire day, with breaks only for food. I could relate: it was my favorite way to spend a weekend, or had been until I'd been drawn into yet another murder investigation.

"Got anything else planned?" Stacey said as the waitress brought our cheesecake and two forks.

"Oh, the usual," I said, taking a large forkful. "Free music, good food, and I could use your help with a murder investigation."

Stacey's fork fell out of her hand and clattered to the floor. I took another bite. Cheesecake helps alleviate stress. Everyone knows this.

Our alert waitress brought another fork while Stacey sat stone-faced through my explanation. I'd sent her the email about the explosion, but she hadn't thought more about it.

"Sugah, you've crossed over to the dark side." Stacey waved her empty fork as if conducting a chorus of aggrieved harpies. "You have nothing to do with this killing, yet you've involved yourself in it," she said. "Do you find murderers attractive? You know, the bad boy *personae*?"

"*Personae*. First declension plural. More than one murderer. It is also *personae* for the genitive case." My father, a professor of classics at Berkeley, was insistent that I learn Latin. It came back to me at inappropriate times, like correcting people's use of alumni (plural) when they meant to say alumnus (singular).

"Or maybe it's the danger. Surfing too tame for you?" Stacey said. "No near death experiences on the highways lately? What is it? Why are you involved? I don't for one minute believe it's just because of Keoni."

"Well, it is," I said defensively. "Kealoha is *'ohana*, family to Keoni, and that's why Keoni asked me to investigate."

"Well then, Keoni's gone off the deep end. Maybe it's law school. You know all lawyers are brain damaged. He had no right to involve you and I plan to tell him that." Stacey stabbed her fork into the cheesecake and left it there. Not that I would have minded, but her fork was blocking my attempt to snag a big bite of cheesecake plus crust plus a nice big dab of whipped cream.

"Is this the same Stacey who was eager to join my first two forays into investigative work? What happened? Why the sudden aversion to snooping in a good cause?"

"About a month ago I had a long talk with Huw about your near-death experience during your last investigation. The fact that you'd almost been killed didn't penetrate until Huw gave me a graphic description of the damage to you and your apartment before he rescued you."

Ratfink. To think that I had believed Huw was trustworthy. A surfing companion and a never-quite boyfriend, Huw had found me just after I'd fought with a killer bent on his second murder.

"He said you were the very picture of a losing cage fighter: bruises on your neck from attempted strangulation, torn clothing, bloody knees, and God-knows-what-else. Not to mention your apartment! Huw said a tornado would have done less damage. I don't understand why you would put yourself in that position again."

"Since I am investigating a murder in Hawai'i, I don't have to worry about my San Francisco apartment being trashed," I said.

"A mere technicality."

We fell silent for a few moments. Stacey retrieved her fork and stabbed off several large bites. I didn't feel like eating anymore.

Finally I spoke. "Try to understand, Stace. I know I'm not Nancy Drew or Amelia Peabody, discovering crooks and narrowly escaping danger by my wits or a fortuitous turn of events, in 250 pages or less. Yet in the past year I've encountered murder victims four times. I can't help but think that God put me in those positions for a reason."

"The reason is to understand your own mortality, appreciate the time you have on earth and not put that time in jeopardy by engaging in foolishly dangerous behavior," Stacey countered.

"Possibly," I said, "but at least I feel I'm doing something worthwhile. Let's face it, my recent work assignments haven't been providing a lot of psychic satisfaction. If I kick the bucket tomorrow, what am I going to say to St. Peter? 'I obeyed the commandments for compliance with FISMA?'"

When Stacey spoke, her voice was low and thick with earnestness. "Okay, hon. I'll buy that, for now. But let me pray about this and think about it for the next day or two. It took me a long time to break you in as my BFF and I don't want a DFF."

"'DFF' means?"

"A dead forever friend."

SEVENTEEN

"'O ka noe a ka ua li'ili'i, I ka uka o Kā'ilikahi,
Ho'okahi pua nani o ka liko, Ka'onohi wai
ānuenue." (The mist and fine rain, in the hills
of Kā'ilikahi, the most beautiful flower bud, a
patch of rainbow water.)
"Wai O Ke Aniani," Traditional

"DID YOU HEAR that?"

I nodded.

"What should we do?" Stacey whispered.

"We have to keep going forward," I said in a hushed voice. "This has to lead somewhere." I wondered for the fifteenth time that morning why I wasn't hearing creepy music signaling danger like the kind played in slasher movies. Life should imitate art, especially when it came to warning young, pretty, unsuspecting women of a mysterious menace with a machete.

Stacey and I were hiking the Kahiko Trail, which I was beginning to think should be renamed *Ala Mahea Kāua* (Where-are-we Way.) The good news was that on an island, there aren't many places to get irrecoverably lost. You hit water eventually. Streams go to the sea and the sea is a good place to quit hiking. Although, there were hikers who'd been lost in the Nāpali on Kaua'i, never to be seen again. Not a pleasant thought, but I comforted myself with the fact that Stacey and I each had cell phones with four bars and I had brought a battery charger, which was in my backpack right next to the one-pound bag of peanut M&Ms that would keep us from starving should it take us two days to hike out.

We'd dragged ourselves out of bed early that morning and, slathered with insect repellent and wired to our caffeinated gills, were on the trail by nine. We'd set a leisurely pace, stopping frequently for Stacey to take photos or inquire about the names of various plants. My botanical knowledge had been fostered by plants that were mentioned in Hawaiian songs such as *niu* (coconut) and *hala* (pandanus, whose fronds were woven into mats and hats), but I was compelled to categorize 80% of what we saw into the genus "Noideawhatsoever-iensis." Eventually, Stacey stopped asking and just took photos so she could identify the plants on the Internet.

After several stream crossings amidst gentle slopes, we forged up a steep section to a ridgeline where stupendous views amazed us for the next half-mile. There were no ugly vistas in Hawai'i, and the views atop the Ko'olaus to the windward side were ones that had inspired many songs, one of which I hummed as we hiked. Other hikers passed us as we stopped for more photos. I yearned to get pictures of the birds I could hear singing and rustling about in the brush, but the vegetation was dense and the flitting birds left few opportunities for meaningful photos. I was lucky to catch a glimpse of a common mynah, a cardinal, and a Japanese white-eye. Like much of Hawai'i, there were countless biological *malahini* (newcomers), fauna that had shoved the locals out. Many native birds could now be seen only at higher elevations, in remote places on Kaua'i and the Big Island.

"There must be a thousand shades of green," Stacey said as she gazed out at the ridgeline falling steeply to the verdant rain forest below. The cliffs folded upon themselves, as if a giant had clawed deep valleys a million millennia ago. "It doesn't even look real."

"The most beautiful places I have ever seen have all been in Hawai'i," I said.

"I half expect to see dragons swooping along the cliffs," she replied, shaking her head. "It almost beats surfing."

"Yup," I said. "And my arms are just about as tired." Even wearing sneakers, it was difficult footing and we had made good use of tree roots and pre-hung ropes to haul ourselves up the steeper sections.

"Not everyone is tired." Stacey nodded at the other hikers on the summit. Most were busy with their cameras, but three children under the age of ten were bounding around with an energy level I'd last seen in my landlady's dachshund puppy, except the *keiki* weren't stopping to mark their territory by "watering" every plant.

After taking the requisite number of photos, upwards of forty each, Stacey and I headed back down. We did break open the M&Ms to ensure they hadn't gone bad, washing handfuls down with a sports drink.

"I was worried about going down, but these ropes are a godsend," Stacey said some time later.

"Right. Can you go a little faster?"

"Sure, but why? I didn't think we wanted to go surfing until much later. The tide is too high now."

I explained my problem to Stacey.

"You drank two bottles of Gatorade?"

"I was thirsty. I thought I was sweating more." Obviously, not enough. I needed to go. Thinking about territory marking had clearly been a mistake.

I held out until we got past the steepest section, then searched for a place I could modestly step off the path to admire the view in private.

"How about here?" Stacey pointed out an opening in the vegetation, which extended into the trees for about twenty feet.

"Perfect."

Five relief-filled minutes later, I had a discovery to share with Stacey. "I saw another path. It's kind of faint, but we ought to check it out."

"Do you think that's a good idea? I mean, if one of us gets hurt, and it's not well traveled—"

"We'll be fine. Besides, I think it's a locals-only path. Sometimes there are unmarked trails that lead to neat places. Keoni took me on one that led to a waterfall." We'd had a nice swim in the pool at the foot of the waterfall, scrambled up the rock wall, and engaged in serious *honi*-ing (kissing).

Stacey shrugged and followed.

We'd been on the path about ten minutes when I heard someone behind us: fronds rustling, but not from the wind, and the bounce and rattle of displaced stones. Strange that the other hiker didn't overtake us. I signaled for Stacey to halt so I could explain about our follower. We listened and a few moments later, the noise ceased. We continued on our way and shortly afterwards heard the hiker again, louder now. Whether because he was closer or because he was making no effort to hide his presence, I knew not. In either case, I feared he had more on his mind than a nice walk through the Ko'olaus.

Stupid, Emma. Stupid, stupid, stupid. I was sure the path led somewhere, but hadn't thought that it might lead to a dead end, where we'd be trapped, unless there was a nice waterfall to hide behind, which happened only in monster movies. I had carelessly left my mace and pepper spray key chain in the apartment. What I wouldn't give now for my *lei o mano*, the shark-tooth rimmed club Keoni had made for me. As we half-trotted down the path, I hunted for a rock or a big stick we could use for self-defense. I could have used a sword, even one I had to pull out of a stone. Why weren't there any surveillance cameras around when you needed them? Bad word, bad word, bad word.

We were moving quickly and I almost missed the fork in the trail. Well, not genuinely a fork, just an opening in the wall of green. It might have been a path, or a narrow gully from a wash out. I pointed it out to Stacey.

I couldn't see our pursuer, but I was sure he was still there. The fainter track plunged nearly straight down and appeared dangerous. Yet, if we could edge down it, our stalker might continue on the main trail and miss us. Signaling Stacey to follow, I started picking my way down the steep slope. Two steps in, my feet slipped on a loose rock and I fell backward, slid fifteen feet down the slope, and plowed into dense vegetation. A tree stopped my slide, but not the string of bad words I muttered.

I lay there stunned for just a few moments before Stacey appeared. The relief on her face was evident, but she didn't say anything. Stacey told me later that she was just happy to find me conscious and, as it turned out, still in one piece.

We remained motionless as we listened for our pursuer. After a few minutes, Stacey bent down and whispered in my ear that she thought she had heard him go by and was going to take a peek.

While she crawled up the hill, I gingerly moved various extremities and determined that the luck of the Irish was with me—Mother's grandmother was a Flynn and *her* mother was a Hennessey. Nothing was broken; my backpack had cushioned my fall. Still, I was merely one-quarter Irish; I had a long scrape down my calf that salt-water immersion would take care of and my ankle was twisted. My shorts, covered in Hawaiian red dirt, were ruined, unless I planned on dying them red.

Stacey returned. "No sign of him," she whispered. "Can you move?"

I nodded, although I wasn't quite sure.

Stacey took the backpack and scrambled up the slope. I followed slowly, pulling myself up the path by hanging onto the vegetation. I remembered the Hawaiians used plants for healing; was there such a thing as a *ku'eku'e wāwae wahī* (ankle wrap) plant? Or a Mai Tai plant, in case I wanted to go straight to a liquid anesthetic?

Still whispering, Stacey called out encouragement. That is, if "I think he's coming back," and "we'll be trapped if you don't move your rear, shugah," could be considered encouragement.

No sooner had I crawled over the edge than Stacey grabbed me by the arm, lifted me to my feet, and pushed me along the trail.

I moved as quickly I could with a step-hop-hop gait. Stacey stopped occasionally to glance back, but saw nothing. Still, it was with great relief that I spotted the pile of stones I'd assembled as a marker for returning to the Kahiko Trail.

We emerged onto the main trail sweating, gasping, and stinking like pigs. I knew this because we'd flushed a wild hog just before finding the trail marker. Stacey asked if she should tend to my twisted ankle—we had a small first aid kit in the backpack—but I waved her off and we continued down the path, speaking not at all until we reached the 4Runner. Stacey grabbed the keys from me. Only when we'd driven out of the forest reserve and were near the main road did I let her pull over. Keoni carried a well-equipped first aid kit in the car that included several wraps, one of which Stacey used to expertly bind my ankle, giving it a pat when she finished.

"Not too bad," she said.

"Nicely done."

"I practiced on my brothers, except for Mark. He never had anything as easy as a sprain; when he was sixteen he broke his leg."

"Ouch."

"All in a good cause. It was the last quarter of the last game of the football season. His team won."

Stacey's brothers, Matthew, Mark, Luke, and John, were all sports enthusiasts, covering the usually array of team sports, plus cricket. Stacey was the surfer.

"I don't think the ankle is too bad; enough ibuprofen and I can surf this afternoon," I said confidently. Even if I had to tape my leg up to my knee.

By mutual agreement, we waited until after we'd made a stop at an ABC Store for cold drinks before discussing our adventure.

"Were we being followed because of your murder investigation?" Stacey said.

"I don't think so."

"You think it was just bad luck that some weirdo decided to follow us on the trail with God knows what in mind?"

"Maybe there was a swimming hole at the end of the path and he thought he could catch us skinny-dipping."

"Like I said, a weirdo."

"Or it could be he wanted to stop us from blundering into his *pakalolo*."

"Marijuana?"

I nodded. "Helicopters can spot the big patches, but if someone has a small plot and hides it under trees ..."

Stacey, eyes on the road, said nothing.

"Think about it," I said. "I'm sure we made plenty of noise, bolting out of the underbrush like a stampede of scared rabbits. Yet he didn't chase us back up the path. He realized we weren't a threat."

Stacey considered this for a few moments.

"Well, I do have one other theory, but I hesitate to mention it," I said.

"What's that?"

"He could have been trying to Honk you."

"Not funny," Stacey replied.

"His card says, 'I was hiking and my compass pointed to you.'"

There was a strangled sound from Stacey. I glanced at her just as she lost it. We were both laughing so hard that she could barely drive the car.

By the time we had parked the 4Runner, our hysteria-induced hilarity had long since abated. We limited our activities for the remainder of the day to surfing and eating, even opting to skip the live music for a quiet evening in my apartment: I with my foot elevated and iced, and Stacey waiting on me. I was taken aback when Stacey asked me to talk about the murder investigation: what I'd done and what I'd discovered. When I'd concluded, Stacey said she'd help me. I was grateful and surprised, and said so.

"My help comes with one condition," Stacey said.

"Name it."

"You absolutely have to control your impulses."

"I don't—"

"You sure enough do, shugah. This morning, you get a great idea and plunge right ahead without thinking of potential consequences.

I'm not blaming you entirely for what happened; I had my reservations about diving off onto a different trail, and I should have spoken right up."

"Face it, I'm a persuasive person."

"Darlin,' the next time you get a great idea to trail a suspect, or hike a suspect trail, ask your little old self, 'Would I do this if I had Rebecca with me?'"

Stacey's comment hit me in the solar plexus. My nearly five-year-old niece was the most precious little girl in the world. I'd never do anything that might harm her. Of course, she was a chip off the old Jones block: I'd given her my old Barbie dolls armed with semi-automatic weapons and she'd developed a penchant for toy guns, even knowing what caliber each of hers were. Barbie could hold her own against a cadre of rogue Kens.

"I'll do my best," I said, much subdued. At the time, I meant it.

"Fair enough. Let's face it Emma, you do need my help. You're making a hash out of this investigation."

"I am not."

Stacey assumed a haughty expression: eyebrows and nose both raised. "Let me see: a drinking party with Wife Number One after which you DWIed your way home; a failure to get Wife Number Two to even speak with you; and a public cat fight with the girl-friend."

"Yeah, but I've learned a few things."

"That you wouldn't cut it as a PI or even a PM, private meddler?"

"Fine, Your Staceyness. Tomorrow after work, you can come with me to interview Greg Walker's lawyer. I plan to ask him for a list of the poor souls embroiled in Walker's egregious litigations; fifty-four additions to my WhoMightaDunnit list."

Stacey shook her head.

"You're not coming?"

"Oh, I'm coming all right, but you're facing way more than fifty-four suspects, shugah; there can be multiple parties to a suit. Have you even the least idea how to manage your way through such a big ol' list?"

"I have one or two ideas," I said. But I knew that Stacey knew that I was bluffing. My real motive in meeting with Walker's lawyer was a vague hope that he would point me toward a viable suspect or two, or he would confess to the murder himself.

Hey, it happens on TV all the time.

EIGHTEEN

"A groundless rumor often covers a lot of
ground."

Anonymous

STACEY DROPPED ME off early that morning and headed out to see the sight. She had adopted the North Shore casual attire of board shorts, *slippahs* and a tank top proclaiming, "I Not Late, I On Aloha Time." However, without a deep tan and a tattoo, she'd still be recognized as a tourist.

Karen arrived and without even a "Good morning" or "How was your weekend," she asked me if I'd seen Edvard.

"Not yet. Why?" I meant "Why?" as in, "How bad is it? How could he possibly be attired that would be stranger than paranoia pants, surveillance-skirting sneakers or his watch-the-watchers watch?"

"I'm worried about him."

Karen? Worried about Edvard? "Something you're not telling me?"

She averted her eyes, which were a little strange today for a reason I had yet to fathom. "Did you hear the news this morning?" she said in a strained voice.

I shook my head. Stacey and I had discussed the virtues of Kona versus Kāʻū coffee, a new entrant from the Big Island, and hadn't turned on the radio, the TV, nor checked the Internet for the latest hysteria-inducing rumor.

"KOAU Radio carried a story about unknown signals interfering with the satellite-based tracking system at Honolulu International Airport. The tracking system is used to precisely locate aircraft and

129

aid in takeoffs and landings. The authorities noticed the interference occurred around the same time each morning and evening and theorized a commuter on the H-1 was using a GPS blocking device. After monitoring the traffic for a week, the FAA identified the suspect vehicle and the driver was arrested last night. No name was given."

Karen didn't need to say more; it required no imagination to believe Edvard could be the culprit. For a man who shielded his cell phone, how big a step was it to install a jamming device on his vehicle? Even I had heard that rental car companies in Hawaiʻi hid GPS trackers to ensure drivers did not take them on unpaved roadways, enter restricted military areas (bullet holes are hell on a paint job), or inadvertently park the car at the bottom of Kaneʻohe Bay (salt water is hell on an entire car).

Karen was rattled: her nail polish was chipped, as if she'd been nibbling on her fingertips, and she had lined only one of her eyelids with kohl, which was smudged so badly she looked like a one-eyed raccoon. Her odd appearance was nearly as unnerving as Edvard's surveillance-fooling, nausea-inducing contact lenses.

"Even if Edvard is using a jamming device, don't you think he'd be smart enough to turn it off when he drove by the airport?" I was trying to comfort myself as much as Karen.

"If he thought only the car rental agency was tracking him then yes. But knowing Edvard's convoluted logic, he might think because he was on a contract for DoD that they'd be tracking his vehicle. In which case his paranoia would override common sense."

"As it so frequently does. We should call him."

We did. There was no answer.

The clock swept past nine and there was still no sign of Edvard. Melia came by his cube dressed as if she were going on a date: sheathe dress, necklace with a small dolphin charm, silver bracelet, and platform ankle-strap shoes, which added several inches to her height and even more head-turning points. Stylish, I thought, but more LA than Hawaiʻi. She canvassed the GDers, even asking Gunnar, Linda, and Karen if they knew Edvard's whereabouts, but no one had a clue. When Melia departed (leaving the cloying scent of *pīkake* and grapefruit) Karen broached the subject of bringing our Edvard-related concerns to Michael.

I questioned how that would help. If Edvard had been arrested, sooner or later Michael would hear the news. In the off chance, decreasing by the minute, that Edvard was not the culprit, we'd expose ourselves and Edvard to Michael's ridicule. He'd lose all confidence in our babysitting skills, ignoring the fact that there was no way to keep tabs on Edvard but to bug, follow, surveil, and in short, conduct just the sort of recon Edvard was assiduously combating.

Karen pointed out that if Edvard had been arrested it would be better if we told Michael rather than have him read it in the news.

"Or receive a tweet," I added. "Under the hashtag #Edvardisindeepkimchi."

We agreed to wait until lunch. If Edvard didn't show up, one of us would talk with Michael: the one whose resume was most up-to-date.

A heavy gray cloud hung over my cube that morning. Karen was similarly affected; her conversations with drop-ins lacked their usual animation and I noticed another of her fingernails had pits in the polish. Peabrain would not approve.

Well past noon, Karen and I were still ensconced in our cubes fighting off hunger pangs. Neither of us wanted to admit it was time for lunch, and time to report Edvard missing.

I was thinking of cold lemonade when a piercing squeal from the next cube gave me a start. I popped up to see Karen throw her arms around Edvard's neck, knocking a fake ear loose as she did so. She pushed it back into place good-naturedly and offered to give it a pinch to keep him even-eared.

Edvard was overwhelmed by Karen's warm reception and pleased to accede to her ear-evening offer. When he saw my grinning countenance and multiple co-workers popping out of their cubes like prairie dogs, his eyebrows headed for his hairline.

I slipped into Karen's cube where she still had Edvard in a bear hug. Or is that a watchdog hug? After I cleared my throat, she released Edvard and gently pushed him into her chair. Amidst the hurried whispers of our worries and concerns, it emerged that Edvard had spent the morning in a dentist's chair having work done on a chipped tooth. Whether it was for "foil dental recognition technology" purposes or "my filling is about to drop out" purposes, he didn't say, but he took umbrage that we believed he had been caught GPS jamming.

"I would never do such a stupid thing," he sniffed. "Besides, I've no need to jam signals. I always travel with a GPS detector and regularly sweep my rental cars."

Of course he did. Why didn't I think of that?

Edvard, noticing Karen's sheepishness over her emotional greeting, kindly offered to sweep her rental for tracking devices.

"Thanks, but no, thanks," she replied.

"What about you, Emma? Want me to check the Toyota in case your boyfriend is tracking your movements from afar?"

Like Karen, I thanked him and declined.

As I returned to my cube, I heard Edward mumbling to Karen about suspecting his dentist might be in the employ of the Chinese government and having swept his new dental work.

I chose to eat and work at my desk over lunch since I had accomplished very little that morning while worrying about Edvard. I paid a call on the vending machine for yogurt, peanuts, and a cold drink and returned to find Edvard lecturing Karen about biosensors that were now the size (and taste?) of Tic Tacs.

"They're impervious to stomach acid and can track information about medication-taking behaviors and how the body is responding," he said.

"I suppose you're going to tell me why that's not a good thing," she responded.

"Because laws have been proposed to make it mandatory to take certain drugs if they've been prescribed, like statins or antipsychotics. The government could use biotechnology to verify you were taking your medicine. If you couldn't stand the side effects of the drug and stopped taking it, the government would know;

'They' could throw you into a sanitarium and force-feed you the drugs."

Before Karen could say anything, Melia came by and invited Edvard to lunch. Oblivious of Melia's date-night attire and clueless as to her real motive, Edvard asked Karen to join them. She politely declined.

After they left, Karen stuck her head in my cube. "I assume you heard his commentary on biosensors."

Mouth full of peanuts, I nodded.

"I must be losing my mind, but his theories are starting to make sense. I mean, it's scary that the government could do that. Think about it; if you're getting your health care through the government, then what's to stop them?"

I swallowed the peanuts, gagged slightly, and sipped my ice tea before responding. "I've read about these biosensors, and it's not the monitoring that bothers me."

"Oh?"

"Think about it; they survive in the body for two or three days before being expelled in the, ah, usual manner."

"That's disgusting."

"Not as disgusting as the government demanding you capture the sensor so it can be recycled."

Karen scrunched up her nose at that, and said she needed another antacid—she'd taken two earlier whilst obsessing over Edvard's absence.

We weren't burdened with any more Edvard conspiracies for the next several hours, partially due to being in and out of our cubes for meetings, and because Melia was camped out in Edvard's cube all afternoon.

Karen and I had just returned from one meeting when she gestured toward Edvard's cube. "Edvard strikes again."

"Excuse me?" I said as we stepped into Karen's cube and sat down.

"He has a knack for attracting women in mid-level positions, typically in their late thirties or early forties. Grapefruiters."

"What's wrong with consuming citrus fruit?"

"That's not what I meant. Studies have shown that women smelling of grapefruit are perceived by men as being, on average, six years younger than their real age."

Only if their thighs didn't resemble grapefruit. Nothing says "old" like cellulite. Not that I had any.

"You're not jealous?" I asked.

"Hah! Not a bit. It's good for business; the more women enraptured with Edvard, the better review for GD from the client."

"Still," I said, "I have to wonder how he can attract competent women when to us, he comes off as a lost soul drowning in the deep sea of paranoia. How can these women not see that?"

"It helps that he's über intelligent, almost handsome, and basically a nice guy. God knows those are in short supply. He's far preferable to a man with several TVs in the living room who spends every waking minute watching multiple sporting events and bellowing at the games. Or a man that leaves beer cans and empty chip bags on every surface and falls asleep with the TV blaring and the remote in his hand."

The voice of experience?

"When you put it that way, Edvard seems like a real catch," I said.

I pushed back my chair and stood up. "I guess it's my turn to pop a head in before Edvard tells Melia that the government is wasting money on this project with GD because aliens will invade Earth sometime this year and bless us with their super-advanced technology."

Karen jumped to her feet. "Don't know that Edvard believes in aliens, but you can go back to work; I don't mind interrupting their tête-à-tête." She quickly walked toward Edvard's cube.

As long as Karen was the babysitter, Edvard would be safe from the clutches of Melia and every other citrusy seductress.

NINETEEN

"A little nonsense now and then, is relished by
the wisest men."

Anonymous

"I STILL DON'T understand who you are and why I should be talking to you."

Stacey and I had been ushered into the office of Alan Nakamura, Greg Walker's lawyer, on the nineteenth floor of a high rise on Bishop Street. Judging by Nakamura's luxurious offices, the litigation business was lucrative. Nakamura's assistant had stayed just long enough to ensure no one wanted anything to drink before making an obsequious exit. I began my spiel about investigating Greg Walker's death on behalf of Kealoha Kanekoa, when Nakamura's question slashed through my explanation.

"As I said, we're working for Mr. Kanekoa and would like to ask you a few questions about the suits you were handling for Mr. Walker's business dealings."

"Are you private investigators?"

"We are conducting an investigation on behalf of Mr. Kanekoa," I equivocated.

"Are you licensed investigators?"

"We're experienced in investigative work, particularly murders," I said.

To use a hackneyed but undeniably accurate analogy, he was like a dog with a bone. A sketchy bone whose *bona fides* he was attempting to ascertain.

"Are you licensed as private investigators in the State of Hawaiʻi?"

"No."

"Do you know that without a license, you are not permitted to advertise or furnish investigating services?"

"We haven't advertised, nor are we being paid to investigate. Though we'd be happy to take your donation to the Kealoha Kanekoa Legal Defense Fund," I said, hoping levity might loosen his legalistic logjam.

"You left the impression with my assistant that you had an official standing in this case. I can see that you are merely impertinent busybodies wasting my time." He used the intercom to summon his serf.

"I prefer the term 'empowered amateurs.'" Actually, I hated the term "empowered," but it was one of those trendy management terms one found oneself using often to impress people, like "one" instead of "I." Therefore, I, er, "one" used "empowered" because it was "impactful." Even if "impactful" was another trendy term one hated.

"Out," he said, throwing his arm toward the door. That wasn't trendy, but it was direct.

The assistant held the door open, her deep frown registering disapproval.

I couldn't think of anything to say. Nakamura was rightsizing his office in an impactful way.

"Out," he said again more firmly. "Or would you like me to call security?"

"We're going," I said as I moved my chair backward and stood up. "Why are you reluctant to answer a few questions? What are you afraid of, Mr. Nakamura?" I'd watched a number of journalistic expose TV shows, and "What are you afraid of?" was always the question where the hidden camera zoomed in on the subject of the inquisition.

He picked up his phone and punched a button. We didn't wait to see if he was ordering up a half-caf skinny soy chai latte with sprinkles or calling for reinforcements. We exited the premises under our own empowerment. In other words, we vamoosed at warp speed.

There were other people in the elevator as we slithered in before hitting the close door button frenetically. Two of them appeared to be interns who opined for twelve floors on like, Allie and Justin's, like, breakup. After eight floors of "OMGs" and fifteen uses of "like" as an adverb instead of a transitive verb, I decided I was like, on Justin's side, totally. Stacey and I refrained from speaking until we'd left the building and were a good twenty-five yards beyond the front door.

"Sorry," I said to Stacey once we turned the corner. I expected her to be either upset I'd wasted her time, or sympathetic to my plight. I didn't expect her to start laughing.

"What?"

"Oh, God," she said. "It was like a grade B movie. 'Just what are you afraid of, Mr. Nakamura?'" she mimicked. "I was waiting for the Dramatic Music to cue. Violins. Cymbal crash after a suitable pause. Close-up of angst-ridden Nakamura. Fade to black. Commercial break for a laxative advertisement."

I couldn't help it; I giggled, too.

"No wonder you're not making any progress on this investigation," Stacey said after her laughter had subsided. "You're playing police detective."

"What do you mean?"

"Find a nice place for dinner and I'll explain."

STACY AND I wound our way through the downtown jungle, feet pounding on the hot concrete and enveloped in exhaust fumes and traffic noise. Thank goodness Honolulu's downtown occupied a small area, but it was still more purgatory than paradise.

Stacey must have been thinking along similar lines as she announced she wanted to go "some place tranquil."

We agreed that meant Waikīkī was out, unless we wanted to eat bobbing on our surfboards, far away from tourist crowds. I'd known surfers to do that when a swell was running; they'd stay out in the water for a full eight hours and pay a food truck owner to carry *kaukau* out to the lineup on a jet ski. I'd tried it once, but keeping a sandwich dry in a six-foot swell was beyond my skill set, and who wants a BLT and saltwater on whole grain?

Thirty-two minutes (and 3.26 miles) later, we entered my apartment with pizza, a prepared salad, and a bottle of white wine. Stacey was in favor of flopping on the floor and digging right in, but I had my standards, or rather, I had my Grandmother Swenson's standards.

"Dishes, cloth napkins, and stemmed wineglasses? Seriously, Emma, who are you trying to impress?"

"Paper plates and napkins just ends up in landfill—and in Hawai'i, land is at a premium—while cloth can be laundered. The stemware keeps your hands from heating the glass and the wine. And Stace, please use the coasters; I don't want to leave rings on the table."

"It's laminate." Stacey delivered an eye roll worthy of a surly seventeen-year-old girl.

Once we'd settled on the couch with our meals, Stacey launched into the Nakamura fiasco.

"Tell me, shugah, how did you go about investigating Laguna's death, when you didn't know her friends or work colleagues?" Stacey stabbed at her salad, piercing a black olive.

"You know darn well how I did it. You were part of it." I grabbed my wine to wash down the too-hot bite of pizza I'd consumed. Shoot, I'd buwned the woof of my mouf.

"Did you ever once go up to people, introduce yourself, and tell them you were trying to solve a murder?" Stacey speared another olive.

"Of course not." An insistent throb from my mouth. More wine didn't work. Cheese pizza: an instrument of torture. The CIA should consider it as an alternative to waterboarding.

"Why are you taking that approach here?"

I'd just noticed that Stacey had given herself all the olives. I didn't see any in my portion of the salad. All I got were the radishes.

Was that fair? I speared an extra-large slice of avocado from the salad bowl. I'd need the vitamins to rebuild the skin in my mouth.

"Well?"

"I have kinda been hired by Uncle Kimo; he wants regular reports and when I have questions, or need more information on people, he's there to provide it."

"Sugah, you are not a PI. This frontal assault may work for the police, but you have no authority to compel people to answer your questions. Besides, that's not what worked for you in solving Laguna's murder."

Darn. She was right. My entire approach was flawed. "May I please have one of your olives?"

"Y'all need a cover story." Stacey speared a small olive on her fork and shook it over my plate.

"How about a grieving girlfriend? And thank you for the olive."

"Your acting abilities aren't that good."

"I posed successfully as a member of Lime-O!"

"True, but all you had to do was parade around with a placard in the name of peace, wearing a shade which flatters almost nobody, hon. A bereaved girlfriend requires a little more emotion and a better wardrobe, unless you are Kermit the Frog's ex. Considering what you've told me about Joline, your vocabulary and grasp of grammar would give you away in two minutes, even if you were attired in a tight little black dress, sans underwear. Not to mention the incredulity of anyone grieving a jerk like Walker."

"Peabrain gave a tearful endorsement of Greggers."

"You believed her?"

"Point taken. Maybe I could be a spurned lover, instead."

"That makes you a potential killer, not someone investigating how he died."

"Colonel Mustard in the library with a candlestick? Though, since a bookend has more heft, I don't know why anybody would use a wussy old candlestick. I kind of like the Wicked Queen in the kitchen with a cleaver. Which, after all, is better than Greg deserved."

"Emma, focus. Who is next on your list to interview?"

"Raymond Tam, Walker's business partner in the taro lab."

Between bites, I told Stacey about Walker's investment in Loʻi Kalo Labs. It smelled fishy to me, like a mass die off of anchovies in Redondo Beach. Walker was a land developer, not an angel investor. Why would he involve himself in a controversial lab?

Stacey agreed Tam was a good next step, and invented a cover story for the interview. I convinced her to take the lead role, pointing out that if she was going to criticize my methods, she, to use the overused business cliché, had to be "part of the solution, not part of the problem."

"Gladly," she replied. "Plus I promise to practice inclusive empowerment and incubate game-changing ideas that will level the playing field."

Game, set, and buzzword match to Stacey.

TWENTY

"All the world's a stage, and all the men and
women merely players ..."
William Shakespeare

BECAUSE I EXPECTED the next two days would be hectic at work, I made an appointment with Dr. Raymond Tam for Thursday at his laboratory. While I was slaving away for the good of my country (cue "America the Beautiful"), Stacey was not lost for things to do (cue "Happy"). On Tuesday, she surfed her brains out. The next day she dropped me at work early and took the 4Runner for her excursions.

I'd barely seated myself when Karen popped into my cube, dropped onto my spare chair and slumped down so her head was below the top of the chair. I knew it was bad news: her manicure was a mess.

Her hidden camera had arrived earlier in the week and she had it at the ready when Gunnar came by around 6:30 the prior evening. He'd hit on her with "nothing so overt that anybody nearby would stand up and scream 'knock it off, you pervert,'" yet enough that she felt weirded-out. Pen in hand, Karen clicked on the camera and did her best to hide the flashing recording light, point the lens at Gunnar, and act naturally.

"About as easy to do as a nonchalant striptease in church," Karen said in one of her rare witticisms. "The video bounces all over the place, like it was taken by a covert operative frog."

"Can you edit out the worst parts?" I asked.

Karen handed me a memory stick. "See for yourself."

A few minutes into the video, I had to disagree with Karen. The frog wasn't a covert operative but palsied and using a mind-altering drug.

"I don't think we can use any of this," I said.

Edward chose that moment to stick his head in to say good morning and exchange pleasantries.

I half-listened, frustrated that I didn't have a clue as to what to do for Karen. At least, that's my excuse for what happened next; I asked Edvard what was new on the hacking front. I know, it's like bringing a bucket of tennis balls to a litter of retrievers. I was in that kind of mood and Edvard didn't disappoint.

"Luxury toilets," he replied.

"Excuse me?" I said.

"Luxury toilets made by Japanese firms. I'm sure you've seen them in the hotels around here. My rental apartment has one: automatic opening and closing of lid, flushing, bidet spray, music, and fragrances. You can control everything wirelessly through an app on your phone. However, since there's no security a hacker could download the app and activate any of the functions."

"Is this a national security concern?" Karen asked.

"I like to keep current on hacking and spying opportunities," Edvard countered. "This is just another example of how the move to wireless everything is leaving us vulnerable."

Sudden inspiration struck. An improbable idea, but …

"Edvard, what do you know about ways to covertly videotape?"

"Quite a bit, actually. Did you know—"

"Would you consider helping a friend, like me, in a case where someone was doing something they shouldn't, and I needed evidence of what this person was doing so I could threaten to expose him or her. Not for money. Just to get this person to stop."

In rapid succession Karen's face registered comprehension, horror, and thoughtfulness.

Edvard, taken aback at being interrupted, blinked rapidly. Registering what I had said, he assumed an air of thoughtfulness and peered over the other cubes to ascertain whether he would be over-heard. When he spoke, he lowered his voice to a whisper. "Has Gunnar been hitting on you?"

I was astonished. Had Edvard bugged my cube?

"How did you know?" Karen blurted.

"Educated guess. He thinks he's a Sir John. He flirts with every female and tries to sleep with them."

"He hasn't flirted with *me*." I said, temporarily affronted that Gunnar didn't find me worth pursuing.

Edvard's confusion was unmistakable.

"It's me he's after," Karen said. "Making noises that if I don't play ball he'll give me a bad performance review."

"It is I," I said, automatically correcting her grammar.

Karen explained the Gunnar situation to Edvard, including her unsuccessful dance with the recording pen. "I don't need an award-winning film, just enough to make him stop. Restore the balance of power, one might say."

Edvard flashed Karen a big smile. "It would be my great plea-sure to help."

The sound of voices signaled the arrival of Gunnar and Linda, effectively ending our discussion. In hurried whispers, Edvard suggested that he and Karen rendezvous after work to review op-tions. I begged off from further involvement, as it was clear I was no longer needed. But, I did have one question for Edvard before he left.

"Who or what is a 'Sir John?'"

"The famous Spanish lover. Is he not Sir John in English?"

"Don Juan," Karen said. She flashed Edvard a smile and he beamed back.

STACEY PICKED ME up after work replete with stories from her World War II Wednesday; she'd visited the USS *Arizona* Memo-rial, the Pacific Aviation Museum on Ford Island, and the Punch-bowl, the National Memorial Cemetery of the Pacific. The last put her in a reflective mood.

"Thousands of markers, each one telling a story," she said. "Like the man in his fifties who died in Viet Nam, after serving in both World War II and Korea."

Without waiting for my response, she continued. "One grave had a serviceman and his daughter. She was eight when she died, poor man. And there were graves with a son buried next to his parents, and both the father and son served in the military."

"Uh-huh."

"And graves of men with Japanese last names who served in the 442nd Battalion. I remember you telling me about them." The 442nd, made up of Americans of Japanese ancestry, fought in Europe during WWII and was one of the most highly decorated units in the war.

"Right."

"I mean, it was just so ... if you'll forgive me for using a cliché, awesome."

"Uh-huh."

"Of course, you've seen it all before and are probably blasé about the whole thing."

"Sorry, Stace. I'm just concentrating on the traffic."

After a few minutes I realized Stacey had fallen silent. I felt badly about cutting her off.

"Keoni took me to Punchbowl one year on Memorial Day. The Boy Scouts, God bless them, decorate each grave with a *lei* and an American flag. A second, special flag is planted for Medal of Honor recipients."

"I bet that's a moving sight."

I nodded. "If the consulting assignment is extended and I'm here through the end of May, I'd like to see it again."

"If you're here at the end of May, I'll come visit again."

"Can you get the time off?"

"I'll take the time." Stacey launched into a diatribe about work and her search for a new position. She was spoiling for a confrontation with her boss if he wouldn't give her time off.

"Don't get yourself fired, yet. I can't promise I'll still be here because I don't know how the project will play out."

"If your assignment is over maybe Uncle Kimo will pay your way out here. It's the least he can do after using you."

I would have pressed Stacey on her comment, but at that moment, the white Honda Accord behind me decided to swing across two lanes of traffic to make a right turn. A screeching of brakes, horn blasts, and a sickening crunch followed. Stacey turned around to assess the damage as I gripped the wheel more tightly.

"A white car and a red pickup. The drivers are out of their vehicles and yelling at one another," she said. "Where's that ever-present *aloha* spirit?"

"It doesn't apply to driving," I said. "Or murders of twice-divorced, litigious real estate developers who cheat on their girlfriends."

TWENTY-ONE

"Self control is the chief element in self-
respect, and self-respect is the chief element
in courage."
Thucydides

I WAS RELIEVED the following evening to find the traffic lighter and less frantic as Stacey and I drove to Loʻi Kalo Labs. Stacey had spent most of the morning surfing, but had used the afternoon to gather intelligence.

"After an Internet search on taro, I did a quick recce of the lab," she said.

"'Recce?' That sounds like an Italian form of bowling."

"You're thinking of bocce. 'Recce' is recon, reconnaissance."

"I think you spent too much time yesterday with the ghosts of World War II."

"So what if I did?" she replied. "I learned a thing or two, like the importance of spying on your enemy before you attack."

"Remember that we agreed on a cover story of you as a journalist, not a CIA operative."

"Fine, call it prepping for the interview. In either case, I unearthed a few interesting tidbits. You'll try to manipulate me into telling you what they are, but I won't say because I want your unbiased reaction to Dr. Tam and his lab. If you'd like to offer me a bribe, however, I'll listen, just to hear how far you are willing to go to get me to talk."

Stacey had piqued my interest, and she knew it. For the moment, I remained quiet; I wasn't going to give her the satisfaction of seeing me beg.

Lo'ı Kalo Labs was a single-story industrial building surrounded by taro fields on the windward side of the island. We approached along a freshly paved road through a new housing development, still under construction, and past taro fields to reach the lab. Telephone-controlled gates of a chain-link fence led to a nearly empty parking lot ringed with monstera, humongous leaves with eye-like holes, evoking Jurassic Park. Happily though, no velociraptors were clawing apart vehicles in search of fresh prey.

As if Edvard were hanging over my shoulder, I spotted a surveillance camera outside the front door and one inside the small lobby where we entered. The sumo wrestler-sized gate-operator-cum-receptionist announced us on the phone as "two *wahine*" (girls), and Tam appeared *wikiwiki* (quickly).

Stacey eloquently delivered our cover story and Tam escorted us to his office, apologizing for the "lack of a welcoming presence, but we're concerned about security here because of recent *pilikia* (trouble)."

I admit to being poor in estimating the age of people with Asian features and no, it isn't because they all look alike. It's more that I know many people of Asian extraction who seem ageless, such as Noelani's Auntie Momi. The first time I saw her she was attired in a long shapeless *mu'umu'u*, her snow-white hair piled on her head in a graceful chignon, and dancing a hula to "Hi'ilawe." Her graceful movements, expressive hands and swaying hips told the story of the love affair under the mists of a waterfall. I pegged Auntie Momi to be in her mid-fifties. Noelani corrected me; Auntie Momi was in fact her great-aunt, and on the far side of seventy-five.

Tam could have been anywhere from thirty to sixty years old. He radiated nervous energy; his steps were short and rapid and his hands gestured constantly like a hyperactive fluttering bird.

He leaned forward when seated as if ready to jump up at a moment's notice. I found myself sitting on the edge of my leather chair, ready to leap up with him, infected by his energy. Stacey, on the other hand, leaned back in her seat and folded her arms, her turquoise-polished index finger casually tapping to music only she could hear.

"It's sweet of y'all takin' the time to meet with us," Stacey said in as thick a Texas drawl as I'd heard her affect. "Particularly as we're just bustin' in on y'all's busy day." She flashed a brilliant smile at this last statement and I could see, even in Tam's dark eyes, his pupils dilate. I was long since used to Stacey's effect on the average male: even when she wasn't deliberately stoking the boiler, she had men trailing in her wake, like cabooses chasing her charming choo-choo.

"You said you were a reporter from … Texas?" Tam said.

Stacey affirmed that she wrote for *Texas Businessmen*. "From time to time, we do features outside of Texas, just to give our readers a fresh perspective on the world. As I was coming here to see my good friend Emma," she nodded at me, "my boss thought I could also do an article on a business in Hawai'i that's unlike anything we see in Texas. You, Mr. Tam, have a very unique business. It's just fascinatin' to me and ah'm sure it will tickle our readers."

I cringed at the "very unique" phrase as my mother had drilled into me that unique meant "one of a kind." There was no such thing as "very one-of-a-kind," darlin'.

"I'd be more than happy to give you an overview of what we do here," Tam said, "but please call me Raymond."

I might as well have been a plastic plant. During his entire spiel, Tam eyes were fixated on Stacey and he did his best to impress her. Tam mentioned his Ph.D. in genetics from Stanford and current employment as a professor at the University of Hawai'i in addition to his side business of the lab where he performed genetic research on taro.

"A few hundred years ago, taro yields averaged 48,000 pounds per acre. Today, diseases and non-native pests have crippled the taro and yields are down to 11,000 pounds per acre. I'm working on altering the basic structure of a Tahitian cultivar by selectively inserting disease-resistant genes from rice, wheat, and grape crops. If successful, we could similarly modify those genes in Hawaiian taro."

"Well ain't that interestin'?" Stacey said. "However, I thought there was a law against genetically modifying Hawaiian varieties of taro."

"There is, but once I can prove how we can effectively strengthen the plant, or save it, I think there will be a push to repeal the law. Even if that doesn't happen, we'll have a stronger Tahitian taro to grow in the islands."

Stacey inquired how long Tam had been working on the taro issue. He responded that he began his research six years ago. However, local opposition to GMO products had put pressure on those doing research in that area, such as Monsanto and the University of Hawai'i where he was working. Funding had dried up. To continue his research, Tam had started his own lab and he acquired land to grow Hawaiian taro for market, the proceeds of which funded his research.

"The yields of the Hawaiian taro, Lehua Maoli, are shrinking, but taro demand is growing thanks to resort restaurants specializing in Hawaiian or Hawaiian fusion cuisine. *Hale* Alex—the number one restaurant in Honolulu—buys a lot of my taro. You drove past my fields on the way in."

"Really? Why I always thought y'all grew taro like rice, in big ol' ponds," Stacy said.

Tam laughed. "Common misconception. Most taro is grown that way, but for upland taro all you need is good soil and plenty of rain."

"So Raymond, if you don't mind telling me, is taro lucrative? Should I tell the Texan business community to sell their oil fields and invest in your business?" Stacey uncrossed and re-crossed her legs, letting her short skirt ride up a bit. Work it, girl. "Or are you keepin' this li'l ol' taro patch to yourself?"

I detected a distinct lift to Tam's eyebrows. I'd bet on his pulse doing the cha-cha, too.

"Taro's a hard business and I already have a partner, had a partner …"

"Yes?" she said, her head cocked to one side. Only the yes came out with three syllables: ye, ee, and es.

"He, my partner, died a couple weeks ago in a car bombing."

"Y'all don't mean that explosion at the golf club?" Now Stacey was all wide-eyed and innocent.

Tam nodded. Stacey gave a little gasp. "How horrible! Why Raymond, whatever are you going to do, now that you've lost your partner?"

By this time, Tam was out of his chair and patting Stacey's shoulder.

"How's your research coming?" I thought it best to get the interview on track before Tam offered Stacey his handkerchief, a brandy, and his undying love.

Tam started, as if he'd never heard a plastic plant speak. "Fine, fine. It's just taking more time than I'd like."

"Will you have the time? I mean, I've heard about the protestors trying to shut you down."

Tam waved his arms. "Not to worry. They'll be gone soon."

"What makes you think that?"

This time, Tam didn't even deign to answer me; he was too busy tending to Stacey, who asked for reassurance that Raymond wasn't "grieving deeply for his dear, good friend who'd died." He confirmed he was not. Stacey discreetly probed about his problems with the protesters, amidst Tam's questions about her visit: how long was she here, where was she staying, what type of food did she like, had she enjoyed the fine music the islands had to offer, and would she like him to show her "the real Hawai'i." By the time we left, Stacey had given him a telephone number and a peck on the cheek.

"Where to now?" she asked once we were back in the car.

I pulled out of the lot. "I'm too embarrassed to take you anywhere else when you're channeling Scarlett O'Hara: I kept waiting for you to say 'Fiddle-dee-dee' and wave a fan in front of your face."

"I was acting, shug."

"It's a good thing you don't act for a living, shug. You dropped more terminal 'g's than the Ole Miss Kappa Kappa Gammas do in a year."

"It worked, didn't it? He's obviously scared of the, what did he call them, 'Neolithic' protestors? In addition, he's barely scraping by, money-wise."

"I sensed that, too."

"I'm sure of it. I told you I did a little advance work. Turns out the margins on taro are, in a word, pitiful. There's a glut and buyers are easily able to buy what they need cheaply. Also, I find it hard to believe his research is fine when there is no one working here. Unless invisibility is a side effect of eating GMOed taro."

"Employees often start early and leave early in Hawai'i. It's not unusual to have an empty parking lot after five."

"How about at one o'clock in the afternoon? I drove by here then and found no one home, not a single car in the lot. Just in case it was a company-wide lunch, I drove into Kailua for a bite and returned at 2:30, or thereabouts. Still no cars. Drove around the fields, too. Didn't see a soul."

I pulled onto the Likelike Highway and headed for the Pali. "Okay, I admit it, your recon was a good idea," I said.

"I do know how to wrap up an operation and make an exit."

"Right, the phony cell number."

"Oh, it wasn't a phony number, it just wasn't mine. I give that number to guys I never want to see again. I like to let them down easily, you know, by providing access to other single women."

"Dare I ask?"

"Sacred Heart Convent in Houston."

TWENTY-TWO

"He aloha 'ia no a'o Waikīkī, eā, ka nehe o ke kai
hāwanawana, kaulana kou inoa i nā malihini,
eā, ka'apuni kou nani puni ka honua." (Beloved
is Waikīkī, the rustling of the whispering sea,
your name is famous to visitors, all your beauty
known around the world.)
"Waikīkī Hula," Traditional

STACEY AND I were sipping coffee and picking at the remains of our breakfast: eggs and bacon for me, pancakes and pork links (finger-shaped, eew) for her. We'd barely been able to pull ourselves out of bed that morning to meet Uncle Kimo at the Moana Surfrider for brunch, having done sunup to sundown surfing the day before. Or, as we preferred to describe it: tiki torch to tiki torch. When we paddled out at Pops early in the morning, they were dowsing the tiki torches in front of the Royal Hawaiian, and when we paddled in from our last session, they were lighting them again.

There is no better place for breakfast than the terrace at the Banyan Court. The hungry sparrows—or were they wrens? I can't tell the difference—visiting the umbrella-covered tables and hopping around underfoot were a minor nuisance in light of the beachside location, views of Diamond Head, and impeccable service. If the waves weren't calling to me, I could spend all day there, sipping coffee and listening to Hawaiian music in the dappled shade of the hundred-year-old Banyan tree that crowned the courtyard.

I'd given Uncle a summary of what I'd learned from Marla, Jo-line, and Danny Estrada. Stacey did the honors for Raymond Tam, without mentioning her hammy southern belle act.

"We haven't discovered anything that clears Kealoha of suspicion," I concluded.

"On the other hand, it seems shortsighted of the police," Stacey added, "to focus on Kealoha considering that Walker was less popular than Rasputin with ex-wives and business partners. Why aren't the police investigating them?"

A sparrow lit on the back of an unoccupied chair, cocked its head, and hopped down on the table. It skittered up to my plate before I shooed it away with a decisive "*A'ole.*"

Stacey surreptitiously dropped a piece of pancake on the ground, whereupon Mr. Cheep and two of his noisy friends fell upon it like Assyrians on the fold.

Uncle Kimo had listened patiently as his gaze wandered to the workers in subdued aloha shirts wiping off the leaves of the plants that ringed the Banyan tree while mourning doves cooed their supervisory approval. At Stacey's accusation, he stirred. "The police are evaluating other potential suspects," he said, "but only Kealoha has a motive, can be tied to the bomb material, and was in proximity to the explosion. Unfortunately for Kealoha …"

The hesitation told me bad news, like an ill-tempered bull at Pamplona, was around the corner.

"…he has an arrest record."

"Carrying a concealed bomb?" I inquired. One might as well assume the worst.

"Not quite that bad. Aggravated assault and resisting arrest, incurred during protest activities when he was younger, before he married Pikake and calmed down."

"Lovely." I wondered how long Uncle had been holding back that little gem of information. My tone of voice must have said as much.

"I didn't know about it either, until the police told me."

"The police are apprising you of their findings?"

Uncle smiled. "The police, no. Detective Al Karratti, yes."

"A cousin, brother-in-law, or other blood kin?" I asked.

Surprisingly, he was not. Kimo and Karratti had played football together at Saint Louis, an all-boys high school. Saint Louis won the state championship Uncle's senior (Karratti's junior) year. Karratti wouldn't tell Uncle everything, but he knew Uncle was working with "an investigator from the mainland" to help Kealoha. Since the police didn't have enough to convict Kealoha—discovering explosives in Kealoha's house or the trigger device would have helped—Karratti had said he was open to other possibilities, as long as Kimo's mystery investigator didn't *hana lepo* (make a mess) of the case.

"Do you think your friend would give us HPD's list of suspects?"

Uncle laughed. "I've been careful what I ask Al, so he doesn't have to say no. Requesting the list would cross the line."

"Too bad. It would be nice to be able to focus in on just a few people. I don't know how I'm going to investigate all of Walker's business dealings in hopes of discovering the killer amongst the suers and sue-ies? Wait, that can't be right."

"Plaintiffs and defendants: plaintiffs sue, defendants are sued," Uncle Kimo said.

"Whatever, that's still fifty-four suspects," I said.

"More. A number of the suits involve multiple plaintiffs."

"Toldyaso," Stacey muttered under her breath.

"I don't have that much time," I said.

"Perhaps," Uncle responded, "instead of asking who would want to kill Greg Walker, you should focus on why he was killed *now*."

"You mean, for example, someone with whom he had a recent run-in."

Uncle nodded. "Consider who benefits from the timing of his death."

"Wouldn't that be everyone he sued? Now that he'd dead, aren't they off the hook?" Stacey asked.

"Not at all," Uncle replied. "Suits don't disappear just because of death. The executor of the estate will make the determination of whether or not to proceed. If the suit has merit, it will probably go forward."

"Would all the people he sued know that?"

"Possibly not. Again though, why was he killed now and not three months ago, or three months from now? What triggered his murder?"

"A recent action taken by Walker, or plans he had made that threatened someone," Stacey said.

"Exactly. You should examine Walker's business dealings in the last week or two of his life. A conversation with his lawyer, Alan Nakamura, would be in order."

Stacey and I looked at one another and giggled.

"What?" Uncle said.

"Emma and I did try to interview him. He wanted to know if we were licensed PIs. When we admitted we weren't, he threw us out," Stacey said.

"That's not entirely accurate," I said. "He picked up the phone to call security and we *hele*-ed out before the heavies arrived."

"That sounds like Nakamura. I'll give him a call and let him know you are working with me. I'm sure he'll be happy to do what he can, without revealing anything confidential, of course."

"You're sure he'll help, huh? Let me guess," I said. "A cousin?"

Uncle shook his head.

"Played football with him?"

Another head shake.

"Surf together? See the same chiropodist? Spent the night in jail together?"

"No, no and no."

"I give up."

"He married my *wife's* cousin."

"THERE'S A GOOD one," Stacey said, as she snapped another photo. A stretch white limo had arrived and disgorged a bride, her small head peeking from a mountain of white lace, and a smiling groom in gray tux and tails.

"Every half hour," I said.

Stacey and I were sitting on the veranda of the Moana Surfrider Hotel, killing off the last hour of her visit by sipping iced nutty Hawaiian lattes, munching on macaroons, and watching the parade of tourists. White railings and gracefully turned posts enclosed the old-fashioned front porch where eighteen wooden rocking chairs, each one occupied, perched like sentinels overlooking the Moana portico and Kalākaua Avenue.

Barnum and Bailey had nothing on the carnival that regularly patrolled the main street of Waikīkī. Stacey was particularly taken with the Japanese bridal parties arriving for weddings at the Moana. In the high season, which we were approaching, the hotel hosted forty weddings a day without batting a fake eyelash.

Stacey snapped shots as the latest wedding party approached the entryway and glided into the hotel.

"Black socks and sandals approaching," I said, alerting her to a young couple (honeymooners?) emerging from the hotel into the bright sunshine.

"Mmm. Japanese grunge. I have enough of those." Stacey said.

Many of the young Japanese males visiting Waikīkī sported the preppie-meets-grunge style: rat-pack hat, plaid shorts, non-matching plaid shirt, sandals, and dark socks. The women had their own style: diaphanous dress, leggings, at least one Hello Kitty accessory, wide-brimmed hat, and sleeves so long that merely the tips of fingers were exposed to the sun. I guess it was okay to have suntanned nails.

On the sidewalk a scramble was taking places as parents pushing a doublewide stroller met a couple holding hands carrying surfboards under their arms. Instead of parting, the surfboard couple veered to the side, forcing a family of four into the street to avoid the boards.

Stacey shut the lens of her digital, dropped the camera in her purse, and picked up her coffee. "Done for now, but I reserve the right to pull it out should a photo-op present itself," she said. "That is, if I have any room left. I'm near maxed out on my memory card."

"I hope you had a good visit. I appreciate your company and help with the investigation."

"I don't know that I did much and I'm still concerned about you being involved in another murder."

"Worried about my safety?"

"That's part of it; being in paradise is no protection against evil. Just ask Eve."

A bare-chested man in a Speedo and flip-flops walked by sporting copious amounts of chest, back, and leg hair. Also a copious belly roll.

"Eew," Stacey and I said in unison.

"Where's a wax bar when you need one?" Stacey said.

We watched the apparition stroll out of sight before Stacey continued her harangue.

"I'm ticked off with Uncle Kimo and Keoni for taking advantage of you," Stacey said. "Here you are in Hawai'i for a few short months and between work and this investigation they've inveigled you into, there is precious little time left for you to surf, hike, snorkel, and engage in other activities."

"Activities like watching hairy fat men in Speedos parade up and down Kalākaua Avenue?"

"If that's what turns you on. Although I think the weirdo factor is higher in San Francisco, particularly along Folsom Street."

"Touché." I paused for a moment. "I'm sorry if you feel this investigation has cheated you out of play time this week."

"Oh shugah, it's not about me. I had opportunities to do things during the day while you were working. I'm worried about your psyche. You're not making any progress on this murder. What if you don't solve the murder and return to San Francisco knowing that your only accomplishment was missing out on great surfing? You'll be angry, and blame Keoni."

Stacey was right. Even though I would be partially to blame for pursuing the investigation, I'd dream up reasons why it was all Keoni's fault.

We said no more on the subject, but when I dropped Stacey at the airport, part of me wished I were going, too. Never before had I felt the need to escape Hawai'i.

THAT EVENING I paid bills. God Bless Magda Basilone, the best landlady *evahs*. When I couldn't get home every week, she sorted through my mail, dumped the obvious junk, and batched up the rest.

Too bad Magda couldn't wade through my email, too. I'd been reading a number of Big Data articles on sites where I'd been required to register. The annoying email was now in full flood: invitations to attend a seminar to hear the "Rock Stars of Big Data," take a course on "Demystifying Big Data," and meet like-minded professionals in "Big Data Dating." Okay, made the last one up, but who wouldn't succumb to a pickup line of "Wanna check out my algorithm?"

I was sick of the constant tracking of one's movements on the Internet to support targeted ads, the invasion of privacy, and the correlation of one's wine bar preferences with cleaning habits. (Big Data proves Merlot drinkers use toilet cleaner pellets.) I needed a way to shield my activity from … darn, I was channeling Edvard, again. Never mind.

Lodged amongst my remaining email was yet another missive from Jennifer with a reminder that the "BIG SHOW" was fast approaching. She had attached a .PDF file of her latest wedding news including how she planned to coordinate our manicures with our bouquets and how Madison, the labradoodle ring-bearer, had learned to march down the aisle without marking his territory. Shoot, I didn't even know she was a he.

Jennifer reminded us to each practice the "Thriller" routine with the video—done that—and record a video of our practice session for her and Madison (the choreographer) to critique in order to smooth out rough spots before the wedding. Ain't gonna happen. I could handle Bridezilla but no way was I going to submit to Cruella the Choreographer.

What happened to the Jennifer I once knew, the girl who had not yet succumbed to bride mania? For the sake of the old Jennifer, I resisted replying with a scathing email or a link to the elegant choreography of Hermes Pan, as danced by Fred Astaire and Ginger Rogers, or Fred Astaire and a hat rack, either of which would be preferable to Madison's twitching, stomping, and drooling gaggle of ghouls. Was there any Big Data analysis linking marital longevity with precision dance routines?

Keoni called in the midst of my email purge and I brought him up to date on Stacey's and my activities including our report to Uncle Kimo.

"Perhaps, *ku'u pua nani*, you have done enough."

"Huh?"

"Maybe it was wrong of me to ask you to help, but I had hoped you would discover information to help Kealoha. You have tried, but it is not your responsibility to find Walker's killer."

Well that was out of left field. Had Uncle Kimo called Keoni and told him I was of no use whatsoever? No, that didn't make sense. Uncle had given me advice about how to proceed. This was Keoni's assessment of what I just told him. I confess my glossy pride felt smudged.

"I've just dented the surface of this case," I said. "I have a whole work plan laid out." Not true, but it sounded good.

"But is that how you want to spend your free time in *Hawai'i nei*? You should be surfing and playing in the sunshine."

It dawned on me I'd heard that spiel just a few hours earlier. "Have you been talking to Stacey?"

"Why are you asking that?"

"She gave me the same advice: drop the case and spend more time surfing."

"Maybe Stacey and I both want what is best for you."

I noticed Keoni did not deny that he had spoken with Stacey.

"I promised Uncle Kimo that I would speak with Alan Naka-mura, Walker's lawyer. If nothing comes of that, if he doesn't give me any good leads, then I'll think about backing out."

"Good. Let me know if you want to drop the case and I will speak with Uncle Kimo; I will tell him I've asked you to cease and desist."

"Cease and desist? Aren't we getting all lawyerly?" I could hardly wait until he started in with the Latin, like *sic utere tuo ut alienum non laedas*, which, despite how it sounds, has nothing to do with a uterus or aliens.

For the next forty minutes we talked of other things. Or should I say, Keoni talked: about his classes, his professors, and interesting (to him) law cases. I was pleased that Keoni was excited about his new calling, but I didn't want to live the experience with him. His delight in legal minutiae reminded me of being next to a new mom at the last wedding I'd attended. During the excruciatingly slow dinner service I heard way too much about the horrors of a long labor and subsequent Caesarean delivery. I desperately attempted to change the topic, but to no avail; I was treated to a soliloquy on the joy of breast-feeding and challenges of excretion control (don't ask). I skipped the dessert and coffee and hid out in the ladies' room until the dancing started.

Like that self-absorbed mom, Keoni was tone deaf to my attempts to steer the conversation elsewhere, forcing me to resort to my old standby. I pleaded an urgent need to use the bathroom and fled the phone. In Hawaiian, the phrase for the bathroom was "*ka lumi ho'opau pilikia*," the room where trouble stops. Indeed.

TWENTY-THREE

"Men are nearly always willing to believe
what they wish."

Julius Caesar

THE PERCENTAGE OF consulting projects without client changes is infinitesimally small. This scope creep allows a consulting company to raise the price of the contract and push back the deadline (which it wasn't going to meet, anyway). Once in a long while, the consulting company will absorb the extra work, for which it expects to be rewarded at a later date with a contract for another project (on which it can make obscene rather than merely indecent profits). Michael had to decide which tactic to employ on the DFAS contract.

Asphire, an IT consulting company, had been hired by DFAS the prior summer to perform data cleansing. Not a high colonic for one's database, I hasten to add, but an improvement in the quality of DFAS data, such as correction of inaccurate data, elimination of multiple spellings, and supplying missing data.

Edvard, Linda, Gunnar, and I had been testing GD's work, but inconsistencies in the DFAS data were invalidating our test results. As an example, the Marshall Islands were in the database as Republic of Marshall Islands, The Republic of Marshall Islands, and Kwajalein Atoll, not to mention the multiple misspellings of Marshall, Kwajalein, and Atoll and the seven different ways to abbreviate "republic." On a positive note, since the Marshall Islands were under threat from polar ice melt and a rising ocean, maybe we could wait a few years and the problem would disappear, literally.

Gunnar aptly summarized the situation: "The data's crap; Asphire screwed up royally."

"If the NSA has used Asphire to clean their data, we could all be on the terrorist watch list," Edvard added.

Michael looked worried. "Does anyone from DFAS know about this?"

"They know our analytics test is having problems, but not that the data is the cause," Gunnar replied.

"If they don't know then don't tell them; I will talk with David about how to handle this."

I didn't think any more about it until the next morning when Edvard dropped by to chat. Karen and I had become entirely too accommodating of Edvard's paranoia, to the point that his conspiracy monologue had become a near-daily occurrence: our morning caffeinated conspiracy confab. Goodness knows there was plenty in the news each day to feed his fever. Just that morning the local news-radio station carried a story about an Internet search engine promising to encrypt data to protect users from the prying eyes of government. Edvard had given this particular search engine the moniker "mackerel" because it would sell users' data to anyone who would pay. (Karen had clued me in that the French words for mackerel and pimp were the same.)

Therefore, I was prepared that morning for an Edward diatribe on "mackerel," but he surprised me by not even mentioning it. Instead, he opened the conversation with a declaration of interest in joining David Blanchard's government practice.

"You're kidding me," I blurted out. No way could Edvard be considering working for the government, the source of his over-the-top paranoia.

Edvard's eyes blinked in astonishment.

"I mean," I said, "why do you want to work for Blanchard?"

"Growing business, more opportunities for promotion," he responded. "I'd like to be a project manager and the government practice seems the fastest way to get there."

I didn't burst Edvard's bubble by mentioning that his eccentricities were an impediment to being given project management responsibility.

Karen was non-committal, almost disinterested in Edvard's pronouncement and abruptly changed the subject. "Edvard, what do you think will happen with this Asphire mess?"

Edvard waved his hand vaguely. "It'll be swept under the carpet. We're not going to even mention it to the client."

I sensed a wild Edvard theory was forthcoming and I decided to have some fun.

"You are so right," I said.

Edward was tongue-tied momentarily, having expected my usual pushback to his proclamations. I could see the wheels turning in his head as he sought a new approach. "You know about the deal, then?"

"Sure. It's common knowledge. Know all about it." I nodded at Karen and gave her a meaningful look, hoping she'd play along and we might stop Edvard in his tracks.

Edward's disappointment was writ large upon his face. My behavior was petty, but I was enjoying its effect.

"I give up, what deal?" Karen said.

Clearly, my meaningful look needed meaningful work.

Edward brightened. "The deal between consulting companies. They cover for each other. To the world they are in competition, but in reality, it's a big fraternity. Senior consultants and partners move back and forth between companies, sharing pricing information and colluding on big projects. That's why you never hear of one ratting out another. Michael will talk to David and he'll want us to cover for Asphire. I'd bet on it."

"You've nailed it, Edvard," I said, continuing my act of sycophancy.

Karen nodded. "Other than pricing collusion, I agree."

Indeed. Had she finally understood my meaningful look or was Karen, God forbid, becoming Edvard's acolyte? I studied her demeanor, but discerned nothing.

Satisfied he'd made his mark for the day, Edvard retired to his cubicle.

THAT EVENING I was ushered once again into the office of Alan Nakamura. This time he met me with a handshake and a huge smile. By tacit agreement, neither one of us mentioned our earlier encounter, and pretended as if we were meeting for the first time. To be safe, I'd worn flat shoes with rubber soles, in case I had to sprint for the elevator again if he called security.

"Call me Alan" pointed out the sites from his office and we exchanged a few pleasantries before he turned the conversation to the litigious Greg Walker.

"Kimo asked that I give you what information I can about Walker's legal actions."

Ah. He said Walker, not Greg; doesn't sound like they were BFFs.

"As you know," Alan continued, "I am limited to sharing information that is in the public record."

"You can't tell me anything new?" I put on my best "Santa bypassed my stocking" face, hoping for sympathy.

"New facts, no. But I've organized the information in a manner that might be useful." Alan handed me a spreadsheet listing all the outstanding suits. The first four pages were filings by Walker and the last page listed the suits against him, sorted by monetary size.

"Now, since I am litigating, I can't offer opinions on the outcome of the litigation, other than I think we'll win them all. What kind of attorney would I be if I didn't believe that?" He smiled broadly and handed me a second spreadsheet. "These are the results of litigation settled, both in and out of the courts, over the past several years. Those highlighted in green were significant wins, those in red were losses and no highlight means it was a wash."

Red was the predominant color. Clearly, he was leading the witness, so I played along. "With this track record, why was Walker suing every little thing that moved? If past is prologue, he shouldn't have expected to win many." I was careful not to imply anything about Nakamura's ability, or inability, to win a case for his client.

"I can't answer that. But, I can give you an informed opinion on why real estate developers in general are litigious."

According to Nakamura, developers might fire up a lawsuit in the expectation of a loss on a project, or out of pure greed. Their targets could include the general contractor, previous land owner, local government, bank, or little old lady who walked by the site with her incontinent West Highland Terrier; a picture that portrayed developers barely above bail bondsmen and local politicians on the slimewad scale.

"So Walker filed suits with little or no merit just to extract money from those who didn't want to go to court or pay legal fees. That sounds like blackmail."

"I don't want to comment specifically on Walker's suits," Nakamura said. "But for developers in general, the suit isn't always about the money; sometimes it's a way to buy time."

"Can you tell me on a one to ten scale of ecstasy over Walker's death, which of his legal foes are at twelve?"

Alan eyed me strangely before responding. "I'll deny this if you repeat it."

I nodded.

"The Ewa Groves Home Owners Association has been locked in a longstanding disagreement with Walker about the size of the amenities center. The HOA thought they were guaranteed a Junior Olympic-sized swimming pool, tennis courts, a tot lot, and a large area for entertaining. Walker built homes on some of the proposed common area and the pool he constructed was quite small. The home owners and Walker have been locked in a three-year battle in the courts to come to terms. There have been anonymous threats from some of the homeowners."

I must have shown my eagerness because Alan added, "We haven't been able to determine which of the over two hundred homeowners sent the menacing letters."

Precisely 199 more than I felt like interviewing. *Auwē.*

"Who else?"

"HuliHuli Construction. Two years ago HuliHuli completed a project for Walker on Kauaʻi. Walker claimed he lost money on the project because of HuliHuli cost overruns. HuliHuli agreed to absorb the costs in return for being given the Nani Kai project on a cost plus guaranteed profit basis. Just last month HuliHuli walked off the Nani Kai project and filed suit, alleging Walker was significantly behind in his payments. HuliHuli claims that they have lost significant amounts of money on the two projects."

"Darn. Kealoha Kanekoa works for them."

"So do many others; it's a large construction company. Because they weren't paid, HuliHuli didn't pay some of their subcontractors, so there are a number of suits filed on both projects."

"And anyone at HuliHuli working the HART project could steal explosives. Do you have any ideas who in particular at HuliHuli might want to murder Walker?"

Alan shook his head. "Wouldn't tell you if I did."

"Not even for your old friend Kimo?"

"Especially not for Kimo."

Whoa. That was a shock.

"Listen, Kimo is like a brother to me; an older brother who manipulates others to get his own way. When Kimo called about your visit, he said you were not a PI, but had good investigative skills. I told him it was dangerous for you to be entangled in this investigation and I did not want to be involved. Yet, Kimo exerted his charm and here we are. I love the man, but not the way he uses people."

He put up his hand before I could say anything.

"I advise you to succeed where I so often fail and tell Kimo you will not do his bidding."

All I could say was that I'd think about it, and Alan seemed satisfied with that.

"Alan, one last question. Do you know anything about Walker's investment in Loʻi Kalo Labs?"

He nodded. "The Kalolani Project."

"The what?"

"The Kalolani Project. The owner of the lab and the surrounding land was in financial trouble. Walker heard about it and offered to infuse some money into the business. He didn't care about the lab, of course. Walker figured it was only a matter of time before the owner went under and then he would have the inside track on picking up the land cheaply so he could develop single family housing.'"

"Wouldn't he have to get it rezoned?"

"Yes, and normally that would be a problem, even though Walker was better than most at working the system. However, this particular parcel is already surrounded by residential areas. Walker might not get the density he wanted, but he was confident of being able to put up housing on the land. He'd recently had a survey done and commissioned a site plan."

"Did Tam know about this?"

"He knew about the survey. He was furious and pulled up all the survey stakes."

TWENTY-FOUR

"Fate saves the living when they drive away
death by themselves!"
Beowulf

"YOUR GOING TO GET HURT IF YOU DON'T STOP," the note read. Black ink, block letters, plain paper, just as before. Why didn't the threatening letter writer include a return address so I could thank him for his grammatically impaired concern? I scanned the area to see if perchance my pen pal was watching for my reaction. The street seethed with activity: spandex-sheathed women jogging along the sidewalk, ponytails swinging side to side; men in aloha shirts and black pants—the universal Hawaiian work uniform—striding purposefully into the day; an Asian woman pushing a stroller carrying a toddler and an infant, shrieking in stereo; and cars darting from lane to lane in vain attempts to bypass stopped city buses impeded by tourists asking whether the bus would take them to Ala Moana, or Pearl Harbor, or Maui. Nobody with a handlebar moustache, a trench coat, black pants-beret-turtleneck-and-Ray-Bans attire or other professionally evil mien appeared to be checking me out.

Apart from me, the sole immovable person was a man in faded blue jeans outside an ABC Store sipping coffee and staring at me. I stared back at him and took two steps in his direction when a white panel truck stopped in front of the store, the man got in and the truck peeled away from the curb.

Not the killer, it would seem. Just as well. What would I have said to him? "Excuse me, sir. Did you leave this threat on my windshield

171

and have you deconstructed anyone recently via a small, yet tastefully appropriate incendiary device using locally sourced ingredients?"

I examined the note again. My pen pal displayed an appalling ignorance of the written word, unless I owned a "going" and didn't know about it. If the language reflected the writer, then Joline was an obvious suspect; six months of training in Critical Cuticle Care didn't include how to write an effective threat. On the other hand, had the message read, "Cease your investigative activities or risk bodily harm," I would immediately have thought of Raymond Tam or Alan Nakamura. But then, both men presumably were too smart to reveal themselves quite so easily.

On the way to work amidst the mostly stop and some go traffic I called Uncle Kimo and reported on my conversation with Alan Nakamura.

"He's an A-number one guy." Uncle said. "Somebody you can always trust."

I was non-committal. I didn't feel like telling Uncle that Nakamura had called him a bully, nor that I couldn't warm to a person who flooded the court system with lawsuits on behalf of an unscrupulous client. Okay, slime-wad client. No wonder the most popular Shakespearean phrase was "The first thing we do, let's kill all the lawyers." I bet Will had been sued.

I also didn't mention the menacing notes. My agreement was to share what I had discovered in my investigation. Strictly speaking, I hadn't discovered anything about the person threatening me, except they'd not had my eighth grade English composition teacher, Mrs. O'Dell, who was O'Hell on poor grammar and spelling.

I asked Uncle to arrange for me to meet Ortiz and Abbott, the two men mentioned in Pikake's note at the *lūʻau*. Uncle's background report noted they both worked at HuliHuli. After Alan's revelations, Ortiz and Abbott had moved up on my Sinister Suspect Scorecard.

"You think HuliHuli had an employee kill Walker because of non-payment?" Uncle said when I explained my reasoning.

Put that way, it did sound stupid. "Not exactly. I'm not sure what to think, but Ortiz and Abbott have as much reason to kill Walker as Kealoha."

"Fine. I'll tell Kealoha you want to interview them and he can set it up."

"No, no. Don't do that. I'd like to speak with them without them knowing I'm investigating Walker's murder. Maybe Kealoha can take me to a Kūlohelohe meeting and introduce me as distant cousin from San Francisco with professional protest expertise as a member of Lime-O."

"Isn't Lime-O an anti-war group?"

"Yes, but they're branching into other area of social concern, like the environment and genetically modified foods." Having spent several months pretending to be a Lime-O member in order to track down a killer, I was well versed in their strategy.

Uncle wanted to know if I still believed Walker's wives and girlfriends were suspects. "I would question not whether they have motives, but what would cause them to kill Walker now, and with a bomb; hardly a typical woman's weapon," he said.

"Since Marla and Carmen didn't see much of Walker, poisoning him would be difficult," I responded. "And bomb making is so easy even Joline could do it. Well, maybe not Joline, but anyone with an IQ north of ninety."

"But you've not interviewed Carmen. Have you ruled her out?"

I assured him my plan included speaking with Carmen in the next few days. It was only a small lie; one which I rectified after I hung up by giving Danny Estrada a call to ask if he would let me know when Carmen next appeared at the golf club.

Candidly, I wasn't concerned about Carmen. Marla had fingered her, which meant by the Rules of TV Murder Mysteries, she was innocent; the first suspect always is. And by the "Rules," the killer is either the first or second person interviewed by the detective, so either Marla or Joline was the killer. Or was it Kealoha or Marla? No, it had to be Marla or Joline. Each exceedingly garrulous, it took little effort to imagine either one confessing to the murder in gory detail while holding the detective at gun point. Oh, wait. That would be me! Note to self: no confrontations with suspects.

DANNY CALLED ON Thursday; Carmen had a 9:40 am tee time with her gal pals to play nine holes. Danny predicted that the earliest she'd be done was 12:15 pm, so I took an early lunch break and arrived a few minutes after noon. When Danny pointed out Carmen's car I parked nearby and waited. No more than twenty minutes later Carmen and Danny approached in a golf cart. He efficiently unloaded her clubs, placed them in her trunk, and departed. Carmen began changing her shoes in front of the open trunk. Time to tee up my interrogation.

"Get away from me or I'll call security," Carmen snarled when she recognized me. The least she could have done was preface her threat with an *"aloha"* or *"howzit."*

"I thought you'd like to know that your ex-husband's business dealings were the likely cause of his death."

"I've no interest in what you *think* you know. Now go away." She placed one golf shoe in the trunk and began unknotting the second.

"You could help me find Greg's killer by sharing what you know about his business partners."

"The police have already identified that Kanekoa *kanaka* as the killer."

"What if the police are wrong? Surely you want the real killer to be found?"

Carmen threw her other golf shoe in the trunk and slammed it. "Out of my way. Now. Or I'll scream."

"Don't your children deserve to know the truth?" Okay, it was hackneyed, but it was all I could think of at the time. Besides, doesn't playing the 'for the sake of the children' card always work?

Carmen breathed deeply as if preparing for an ear-splitting screech, then whirled around with her fists clenched. Those long talons could do some damage. Red nails, too, so my blood wouldn't show. I wonder how she swung a golf club without chipping her polish.

She took a step in my direction. Sideways, as if preparing a roundhouse kick. Best not to find out. "I'm leaving, I'm leaving," I threw my hands in the air and slowly backed up.

Carmen stomped to her car—as much as you can stomp in the spiked heels she'd slipped into—started it up, threw the car in reverse, and shot out of the space with nary a backward glance. Or maybe she had checked her mirrors, because I had to jump out of her way to avoid becoming fresh road kill. With a lurch and a roar Carmen zoomed away, leaving me engulfed in exhaust fumes.

A hui hou to you, too.

"WE'RE GOING TO eat the cost to do this?" I said.

Michael had just told us that GD was not going to mention the Asphire mess to DFAS. We had to find a way—any way—to get our software analytics package to work properly, even with the data issues.

Michael glared at me and for good measure, added a scowl. He may have expected me to wither in the face of such reprobation, but in my propensity to speak without thinking I'd faced worse. I hadn't wilted since my ten-year-old self told my father that Latin was a stupid language for stupid people to which my father had given a typically Ovidian reply: *rident stolidi verba latina* (only fools laugh at the Latin language). Michael's glare didn't approach my father's near-Medusan expression and I found it relatively easy to stare him down.

"If you must know," he said in staccato syllables, "David Blanchard is working with Asphire on a joint bid for a large government contract in Ottawa. It's a multi-year program and the potential profits dwarf anything we can make on this project. We need Asphire's expertise to land the Canadian contract."

Since Edvard had predicted this, I discreetly turned my head slightly to check out his reaction. His expression gave absolutely nothing away. Feigned innocence in his case was doubtless an acquired skill for the day when "They" came after him.

A few minutes later, our staff meeting was over and Gunnar left the room with Michael. Karen followed with Edvard dogging her heels. I dumped my root-beer bottle in the blue recyclable container (the gray can was for white paper, the black for trash, and the mesh basket for newspapers) and deep in thought, followed the others. Michael's revelation was disappointing, but not shocking. It hadn't taken me long after coming to work for GD to learn that the company and its clients at times engaged in questionable activities: not illegal, but not squeaky clean either. A prior boss had pushed me to slant a report in favor of outsourcing a client's business to GD. His arrest for murder left me free to prepare an unbiased report. Friends had told me worse stories. About unethical companies, that is, not about working for cold-blooded killers.

Karen and Edvard were chatting in her cube when I stopped by.

"We were just talking about Canada," Karen said.

"Be great if we and Asphire landed that contract," Edvard said. "I've heard that Ottawa is a nice town with a bit of European flavor."

"Bit of European flavor" could mean anything from a comment on Ottawa's architecture to the ability to get dark beer on tap.

"Have you ever been there?" Karen directed the question to me.

I shook my head. "No, and I've no interest in the frozen tundra." I said. "Remember, I grew up in Minnesota. In Canada, summer is only two days long and there's no surfing. No good surfing, anyway." For one month of the year, crazy Canadians would don wetsuits and surf the near-freezing Ottawa River on standing waves formed by the huge runoff of melting snow and ice. That factoid alone was enough to make me happy our attempted Canadian land grab in the War of 1812 had failed.

Edvard tried to persuade me not to be hasty. After all, wouldn't it be terrific if he and Karen and I all joined the government practice together?

"For the record, I'm not interested in being part of a practice that might send me to Islamabad or Abuja. If I can't spell it correctly on a first attempt, I am so not going there."

And I wasn't; I truly was not.

TWENTY-FIVE

"Hawai'i pono'ī, nānā i kou mō'ī , ka lani ali'i, ke
ali'i." (Hawaii`s own true sons, be loyal to your
chief, your country's liege and lord, the chief.)
"Hawai'i Pono'ī," King David Kalākaua

I WON'T ADMIT it to others, but I'm aware of my impulsiveness, and that it is not a blessing. At best, it is an accidental virtue.

Once, I accused a coworker of killing our boss. At the time, I was alone with him and unarmed, except for a steaming hot mocha. Let's just say the way I used it lent new meaning to the phrase, "wake up and smell the coffee." Once on a dare I skied a double diamond mogul-covered run named "Widowmaker." Truth in advertising, as I found out.

Close friends and family, aware of my proclivity to act first and think later, wonder how I made it to twenty-six with no major broken bones, except my right thumb, which was Virgil's fault. He slammed the door on it, and I'm still planning to get him back for that someday when he doesn't expect it.

Saturday dawned bright and clear: another dang beautiful day in paradise. The surf report was more Iowa than idyllic: flat and boring. I had hoped—really, really, really hoped—to surf a few hours before my flight that afternoon to the Big Island to meet Keoni, who was flying straight to Hawai'i from San Francisco. With surf-less time on my hands, I elected to sniff around into Walker's murder. Since I had been unable to interview Carmen, despite my best efforts, I'd proceed straight to checking out her

179

ex-boyfriend, Tony Perello. Perello might know about Carmen's relationship with Greg, like whether she hated him enough to blow him up into a thousand charred pieces. Eew.

Uncle had provided an address for Perello in Waipahu. My GPS led me through an industrial area to a downtrodden three-story apartment building, one of several dozen crammed together. Broken-down pickup trucks festooned with Da Hui stickers and "shaka" signs, rampant trash, graffiti-adorned walls, and chain link fences crowned with barbed wire added to the overwhelming feeling of depression and desperation.

Three teenaged males leaning against a fence smoking *pakalolo* (weed) eyed me suspiciously as I walked toward Perello's building. Coming here alone might have been a mistake; the *aloha* spirit did not extend to certain places in Hawaiʻi where outsiders were resented. I didn't think I'd be attacked in the middle of the day, but my mental antennae were up and searching for trouble. Not for the last time, I wished I hadn't left my *lei o mano* in San Francisco. Nothing says, "I'm a badass, don't mess with me" to Hawaiians like an authentic Hawaiian weapon, especially when used with a culturally appropriate *haʻa* (war chant). In lieu of the *lei o mano*, I had my pepper spray key chain handy.

I threw my shoulders back and added a bit of swagger to my steps as I mounted the outside staircase to the second floor and strode along the open passageway. Several plastic chairs and small tables perched outside doors as residents annexed the space as a *lānai*, and I stepped over and around a number of toys left out by their young and trusting owners. Stopping outside Perello's paint-chipped door, I became conscious of the faint smell of ammonia; at least one resident was making an attempt at cleanliness.

I knocked and the door opened almost immediately to reveal Adonis: a deeply tanned, dreamy, dark curly haired, dark-eyed man, thirty to forty years old, barefoot and clad solely in very form-fitting board shorts. I closed my open mouth before I drooled on his floor. It was easy to understand how Carmen, of the expensive clothes and car, might be attracted to a male who was clearly not of her economic strata. Pecs and sex, for example. Yes, indeedy, that might do quite nicely.

Adonis spoke: "What do you want?"

Nice baritone.

"Mr. Perello?"

"What if I am?"

"I'm Krista Williams from the *Honolulu Star-Advertiser* and we're doing a follow-up story on the man who was killed by a car bomb a few weeks ago, Greg Walker." Using the cover story of a reporter as we'd done with Raymond Tam might indicate a lack of originality, but I preferred to think of it as "repurposing a successful stratagem." Extra points for me since I had used the name of a real reporter and had dummied up a fake business card earlier that morning.

"I'm writing an *exposé* on how Mr. Walker used and abused people in his personal and business lives. Do you have a few minutes for an interview?" I stepped forward confidently and, *kupaianaha* (surprise), Perello stepped back and allowed me to enter.

"Who gave you my name?" Perello said.

I barely registered his question as my eyes fixated on the humongous tiger shark lying in a plastic wadding pool in the center of the room. I had no idea kid's wading pools were so large nor how Perello had schlepped the shark up the stairs. Fortunately, the *Galeocerdo cuvier*—Latin for "if you see one coming, paddle like hell"—wasn't alive and kicking, paddling or backstroking. The astringent odor of ammonia, now overpowering, emanated from the pool.

"How big is it?" I asked.

Perello grunted. "Barely a five-footer. Was just about to finish cleaning it. Now, who gave you my name and why are you here?"

Doing my best to ignore the shark as well as the large carving knife on the floor, spear gun on the sofa, and the half dozen shark jaws piled in the corner, I launched into my spiel.

"Greg Walker was an important player in the local real estate field. The *Star-Advertiser* is preparing a series of articles on the gross failure of the local police to thoroughly investigate his murder. We're aware that Greg Walker created many enemies through his real estate developments and in his personal life. I have been told by an anonymous source that Walker tried to control his ex-wife Carmen's social life including threatening to withhold child support unless you and Carmen stop seeing one another. Is it true that you planned to marry Carmen and Walker's action destroyed her one true chance of happiness?"

I knew as soon as it came out of my mouth that it was a ridiculous statement straight out of Grade "B" Detective School. Carmen enjoyed nothing better than spending money on herself. Perello might be a fine—exceptionally fine, sigh—boy toy, but she'd never marry a moneyless man.

Ares replaced Adonis as Perello growled and demanded to know who in the world told me such equine excrement. (He used shorter words.)

"I can't reveal my sources."

At that, he declared my information was big bovine bowel movements (he used really short words and fewer of them) and that I should am-scray. Here I thought nobody over the age of nine used pig Latin.

Having clearly hit a dead end, I had but one option. "Do you think Carmen is capable of murder?" I said as I backed out the door.

To my consternation, Perello lunged at me. I turned and am-scrayed really ast-fay down the passageway. Perello followed me down the stairs and out to my car; stopping at the foot of the stairs when he saw I'd reached my car. I jumped in the 4Runner and took off as if a Great White Shark were slicing toward me.

I WISH I COULD SAY that the showdown with Perello was the low point of my weekend, that Keoni and I had a perfectly scintillating time on the Big Island, so much so that I didn't think a millisecond about murder or lose a wink over work. I really do wish I could say that.

My big weekend on the Big Island didn't start well, through no fault of mine. Keoni, arriving shortly before I did, was waiting for me in Kailua-Kona with his parents. Not one for exuberant displays of affection in public, Keoni and I exchanged an all-too-brief hug and kiss. Keoni's *makuahine* (mother) Kalena greeted me with a *lei tuberose* from flowers she had cultivated herself and Keoni's father, Makua, gave me a big hug. So far, so flowery good.

Makua drove us to their modest, plantation-style home a mere three blocks from the ocean. The plantings around the home were as beautiful as I remembered. Kalena was a demon gardener, not that gardening success was necessarily all that difficult in the fertile soil of Hawai'i.

As expected, Keoni and I were given separate rooms. At opposite ends of the hall. After unpacking we joined his parents for happy hour. I for one was thankful to see the *pūpūs* did not include *nigiri* or any item resembling fingers. The mini-Portuguese sausages were somewhat suspect, but I love them so I just closed my eyes when taking a bite.

In my parents' home, the cocktail hour was the time to discuss contentious issues, perhaps because alcohol, judiciously, not indiscriminately applied, could loosen inhibitions about taboo topics. One could go too far though, like the time my younger sister Ariadne announced she was dating an atheist and planned to bring him home for Christmas and my father wondered why, if he were an atheist, he wanted to join anybody for a Christian holiday? By the time we had all expressed our increasingly heated opinions several times over, the creamed chicken in the oven was closer to sun-dried roadrunner.

Keoni's family had a slightly different approach; they waited until dinner to dig in, literally and emotionally.

It started innocently enough, with Makua asking Keoni how his studies were going. Keoni responded with a description of his first-year law classes and expounded on how the classes might apply to native Hawaiian rights. The conversation thereupon degenerated as fast as the ice melted in our mango teas.

"I'm tired of these native Hawaiian movements for sovereignty," Makua said. "Half of them just whine about what was taken from our ancestors over a century ago as if that event is responsible for their current troubles. They blame *haoles* for everything. My great-grandmother was a *haole* of missionary stock, yet she wrote down many Hawaiian *mele* that are still sung today. She helped preserve our Hawaiian culture."

"Ah yes, the missionaries, who prohibited our gods, our language, our *mele*, our *hula*." Kalena interjected.

I kept my head down and focused on the salad: Waimanalo greens, toasted macadamia nuts, and grilled papaya. Was that Big Island goat cheese? '*Ono!*

"Your grandmother may have undone much wrong, but much more was taken from us, and is still being taken," Kalena said. "Why can't portions of our islands be reserved for *nā kānaka maoli*—we who are true Hawaiians?"

"Are we going to start doing DNA tests to determine who is authentically Hawaiian?" Makua said. "Because, you know, I have that background, too."

I was uncomfortable; I never heard Kalena use the term "true Hawaiian." She had always treated me with respect, but was this the respect of *aloha* and nothing more? Did she prefer Keoni fall in love with a "true Hawaiian?"

"The *haoles* took our sovereignty and robbed Queen Lili'u of her throne. Why shouldn't we Hawaiians have recognition under law as the people we are?"

"Please pass the Hawaiian bread," I said to Keoni. Which, technically, wasn't Hawaiian at all but Portuguese *pão doce*, sweet bread.

"Who are true Hawaiians: the 150,000 who reported themselves as ethnic Hawaiian on the census, half of whom no longer live in the islands? What about the much larger number who said they were Hawaiian and another ethnic group? What about the *haoles* who were born, raised and still live here?"

"We should be able to strike that balance, so that those who are suitably ethnically Hawaiian—"

Makua interrupted. "This obsession you and your brother Kimo have over a Hawaiian nation will destroy that which makes us all truly Hawaiian, the *aloha* spirit."

"A tourist industry creation."

"What about the one God, *ke Akua*, who teaches us to love thy neighbor, regardless of his ethnic background? Do you agree with the separatists who want us to return to worshipping the old gods of Hawai'i?"

"You know I don't."

"Then why are you channeling the god Kū?"

The back and forth continued, but Keoni seemed barely aware of it. He helped himself to seconds on the *kālua* pork while occasionally fueling the flames. "Dad, don't forget to remind Mom that Princess Ka'iulani was only half Hawaiian, and yet her heart was completely broken over the loss of her kingdom."

I realized then that his parents' dispute was of long standing. The arguments were lyrics to a family anthem, to which they all knew the melody.

Makua nodded at Keoni's point and added that the Hawaiian kings believed that if you were born or served in Hawai'i, you were Hawaiian.

"That was before our kingdom was taken from us," Kalena responded.

"Does that mean we should secede from the United States?"

"What do you think?" Kalena said, suddenly turning to me.

I finished chewing a delicious bite of salad.

"I think the mango slaw is *nō ka 'oi*. Are the mangos from your garden? Oh, and if you are going to secede, please take New Jersey with you."

At that, Makua laughed and took Kalena's hand.

TWENTY-SIX

*"Silence is one of the great arts of
conversation."*
Marcus Tullius Cicero

I FLEW BACK to Oʻahu Monday evening. There had been no more discussion of Hawaiian rights, but I tread carefully around Keoni's parents for the rest of the visit, even after Kalena apologized Sunday morning.

"My passion gets the best of me," she said. "Even Makua has given up trying to calm me down when the subject comes up and I erupt like Kīlauea."

We'd attended church followed by a humongous brunch. Afterwards, Keoni fell asleep on the couch, not able to muster up the energy to surf. I shouldn't have been surprised; since he'd been in San Francisco, we'd seen much less of each other than I expected or wanted, and our outings were low-energy affairs, rarely involving surfing, biking, hiking or long walks around the city. The most energetic thing Keoni did was hunt for the remote.

Keoni had been entirely and eternally exhausted since he started law school. I tried to cut him a little slack, knowing that he hadn't been a serious student at UH and was now having to study very hard. But, I missed the Keoni I used to know, whose surf stoke surged under any and all circumstances including shark sightings and small/funky/blown out conditions. We'd once surfed through an electrical storm (and yes, it was one of the dumbest things I ever did). Sigh.

Monday wasn't a top-ten day, either. Keoni asked me what was new on the investigative front. I told him about my chat with Nakamura and, without thinking, my meeting with Perello.

"Stacey was right," Keoni said.

"About?"

"She called and read me the riot act; by the way, do you know the legal and historical context for that term?"

"As a matter of fact, I do. Under English common law, a group of twelve or more could be forced to disburse. I wish that applied to bridal parties forced to do a choreographed wedding dance."

Keoni shook his head. "How can you be flippant about a very real danger? Stacey shared a few details from your previous investigation that you conveniently if not cowardly failed to mention."

Ruh-roh. "What did she say? Her birthday is coming up and I want to know whether to get her a stuffed pig. On account of her squealing on me."

"She was honest. You weren't. You told me that Laguna's killer swung at you before you swung back with the *lei o mano*."

I knew what was coming next.

"You didn't say that you invited him into your apartment—"

"'Invite' as in he forced his way in."

"And that he tried to strangle you with his bare hands."

The feel of the smooth *koa* wood of the ancient Hawaiian weapon had calmed me when I was attacked and had grasped it instinctively. I had felt a surge of triumph when the shark's teeth connected with the attacker's shoulder and ripped a jagged wound through flesh and muscle.

"Stacey said I had the brains of a sand flea and the compassion of a rattlesnake to get you involved in Kealoha's problems."

"That sounds like Stacey."

"After she stopped lecturing me, I explained that your tales were 'G' rated, leaving out sex and violence."

"There was no sex," I said. "Except those occasions where you were present, and since you have intimate knowledge of those times, I didn't think you needed a recap."

Keoni was in no mood to banter. He gave me a full five seconds of what I call his Kū-eye—Kūkaʻilimoku is the Hawaiian god of war—before speaking. "I'm calling Uncle Kimo tomorrow and telling him you will no longer be involved."

That did it. I let Keoni know in words of one syllable—except the Hawaiian ones—that no one, not even he, could tell me what to do. After a few long, tense seconds whereupon I tried to flex and pump my five-foot-seven and more-slim-than-stocky frame to intimidate his six-foot-one and Kamehameha-warrior physique, Keoni backed off and we negotiated a compromise. I would attempt to contain my impulsiveness ("attempt" in my mind meaning any sustained effort for, oh, ten seconds or more) and I promised to tell Keoni everything I discovered. I didn't specify when I'd tell him and he didn't ask. He, in turn, would refrain from trying to bully me into dropping the case.

I also suggested that for my birthday Keoni could make me another *lei o mano*, the kind that was the Hawaiian warrior form of brass knuckles. "Smaller, more portable, fits in a purse, and I can slip it around my hand in dicey situations. Not that I plan to be in any of those situations."

Keoni readily agreed. Nothing says "true love" like a handmade weapon. My mother would be pleased, too, as she felt a woman could never have too many weapons. At least, I think she felt that way considering she supplied me with a self-defense gizmo nearly every holiday and birthday.

I wondered briefly if Stacey or Keoni had told my mother of my misadventures. No, friends wouldn't do that. Besides, I would have received an instantaneously anxious phone call if Mother had had any inkling of my brushes with death. At least Stacey, and by extension Keoni, were unaware that I'd had a similarly close call apprehending the killer of my boss, Padmanabh. My brother was the only one in whom I had confided. Stacey and Keoni had no reason to talk with Virgil; however, if they told my mother and then she canvassed my siblings, Virgil might feel compelled to break his silence about the first attack. My mind boggled at all the ways I could be exposed. I now understood why killers got rid of all witnesses: so much easier to lie/omit/deceive with impunity. Sigh.

Large-scale lying was entirely too complicated. Maybe I needed a spreadsheet of lies I had told and to whom, beginning when I was five and blamed my brother for throwing a snowball through the window of our home in Minnesota. Mother found out when she was reliving our childhood over Thanksgiving dinner one year. I temporarily forgot that I'd blamed Virgil for that particular malfeasance for years and owned up to it after a too-large glass of Pinot Grigio. Big mistake: I got the smallest piece of pumpkin pie for dessert and no whipped cream or candied pecans on top.

By the time Keoni put me on the plane Monday evening, we'd both chilled out. Keoni claimed he was happy that I'd witnessed his parents' disagreement. "The native Hawaiian rights issue is one of several areas where my parents hold profoundly differing views. Yet, they love and cherish each other."

His point was clear: he didn't believe the issue would stand between us. I wasn't as sanguine, but I forced a smile and gave him a kiss. "See you next weekend at Jennifer's wedding."

He nodded and his beaming face lit up my world.

TUESDAY MORNING KAREN arrived at DFAS with two grande coconut lattes, a vente triple shot latte, and a box of malasadas. Sugar and caffeine, breakfast of champions. Malasadas, fried sweet dough with a filling, comes from the Portuguese for "you seriously do not want to know how many calories this has."

"The vente is for Edvard," she explained, handing me one of the coconut lattes. Ah, still hot, as were the malasadas.

"Imf era rsmn fr allda mmood?"

"Excuse me?" Karen said.

"Is there a reason for all the food?" I said, after swallowing a very large bite of malasada, licking my lips of the filling and rubbing the sugar off my cheeks. I was a mess, but a mess initiating a blissful carbohydrate coma.

She smiled and nodded. "Edvard is a genius. I'll tell you more over lunch. Why don't we go back to that place in 'Aiea and we can talk in private?"

I assumed the celebration was for getting the goods on Gunnar, and I was proven correct at lunch. Edvard not so modestly explained his success over island plates and live music in the form of Kekoa's Auntie Anani's falsetto singing.

As soon as our meals arrived, Edvard launched into an overly detailed explanation of the Deep Web or Undernet. No, it's not an uncomfortable woman's undergarment. Comprised of web sites that cannot be accessed through traditional search engines, the Undernet requires a special browser constructed to preserve the anonymity of the searcher. Like a blender, these anonymizers whir your nosy inquiries through servers around the world before knocking on a digital door for information. The return information is encrypted numerous times and then gift-wrapped such that only you can unwrap it.

I'd done completely innocent research into bomb-making in the open web—I was surprised Edvard's "They" hadn't come after me yet—but a bona fide evil-doer could research bomb making, untraceable poisons, methods of hacking a neighbor's webcam and more through an anonymizer with a reasonable certainty that Nobody Else Would Know.

Edvard had taken just such a route to discover a few tricks for catching Gunnar in the act of "acting inappropriately," an HR catch-all term for everything from failing to be inclusive to offing a client.

Edvard paused in his geek-speak as the waitress approached for our dessert orders. While Karen was deliberating whether to have coffee and/or dessert, I noticed Manoa, my friend from the surf lineup, arrive and take a seat near the window. He saw me and we exchanged waves. The waitress noticed and smiled. "You friend of Manoa?"

I nodded and explained we'd met surfing and it was he who recommended Kekoa's.

"He eat here most days. Big customer, ya?" she said. *"'Ōpū nui* (big stomach)."*

Karen cleared her throat, loudly, and asked for the *liliko'i* crème brûlée and a cup of decaf with room for cream.

The waitress departed and Edward returned to his soliloquy. He had learned how to configure Karen's computer to run the webcam without the LED flashing to indicate its operation. Result: a spycam! Note to self: don't undress in front of your laptop, as you will neither know when it is filming you nor will you get an airbrush option.

Edvard also modified Karen's phone to act as a silent microphone. Second note to self: don't take cell phone in bathroom or bedroom during, ah, er, certain activities. Additionally, Edvard had procured several inexpensive items with video capture capability, designed and sold by Eastern European entities. Who knew a Beanie Baby or a Smiley Button could be recording your every move? Strategic placement of said items gave Karen 360-degree video coverage of her cube and several audio recordings.

Edvard waxed eloquent about how the recordings left no doubt that Gunnar was harassing Karen and that Karen could take the tape to HR tomorrow and get Gunnar fired, if she wanted to.

The waitress delivered our desserts and coffees and departed. Before Edvard could start up again, I took the opportunity to puncture his balloon.

"Far be it from me, Edvard, to criticize your methods, but I was told in no uncertain terms by a private investigator that bugging is illegal in most states. I would expect Hawai'i is one of those. I know we're planning to use these recordings just to, ah, persuade Gunnar to change his behavior, but we won't be able to use the recordings with HR; I think they'd be concerned about the legal consequences of using illegally obtained information to discipline employees."

Edvard shook his head. "Don't worry. I checked and it's legal in Hawai'i to record a conversation as long as one participant in the conversation is aware of the recording and the recording occurs in a place where one has no reasonable expectation of privacy."

Karen chimed in. "No one expects privacy in a cubicle."

"Secretly recording can be illegal if the recording, or the information in it, is used in violation of the law, such as blackmailing. We don't intend to use it for blackmailing, do we?" Edvard flashed Karen a conspiratorial smile.

Karen grinned in return. "Not at all. We plan to give Gunnar a copy in case he'd like to share it with friends, coworkers or bosses." She giggled. "I can hardly wait to see the expression on his face."

Karen had set the bait by working late Monday night and, like a fish to a winsome worm, Gunnar made his approach. Artfully, Karen's protests had been made with her back to the cameras, thus hiding her coquettish smiles. "I felt like a heel," she confessed, "subtly encouraging him, but it's not like he needed or got encouragement before. Ever."

Edvard's eyes never left Karen as he praised her performance and assured her that all was fair in war. I wondered if he also meant fair in love; I'd seen that same longing gaze from dogs, eyeing a favorite treat just out of reach. Or surfers checking an incoming six-foot swell.

The mutual admiration society was in full swing; Karen was effusive in her praise of Edvard although she tossed me a crumb of credit for the idea of asking "brilliant Edvard" to help.

At least Karen's problem was solved. Almost. Karen admitted she needed to think through the confrontation with Gunnar. She unequivocally turned down Edvard's offer to accompany her for protection, although she seemed happy to have him take her arm on the way to the car.

Was this a sea change in their relationship, or just an interlude until Edvard began upping the ante on surveillance foiling, like cross-dressing to fool surveillance cameras? Michael wouldn't be happy with that but I'd be okay with it as long as Edvard didn't wear the same outfit to work as I did—and look cuter in it.

TWENTY-SEVEN

"I wouldn't take a bullet for you, because if I
have time to jump in front of the bullet, you
have time to move."

Anonymous

I GAVE UP my evening surf session to meet Joline at Duke's. I chose an outdoor table with a view of the ocean and watched a doting father tandem surf with his little girl as I sipped a virgin strawberry daiquiri. She was all of four, and dressed in a pink bikini with a purple inflatable vest, complete with a purple shark fin on the back. Every time her dad caught a wave, he hoisted his daughter on his shoulders and the lineup whooped and cheered at the duo. Watching them surf put me in a great mood, which was abruptly shattered when Joline blew in, barged by the musicians setting up to play, and dropped into a chair across from me.

I'd received several frantic voice messages from her earlier in the week, demanding that we meet. After the wreckage of our last meeting, I was surprised she wanted to talk, and I said as much after the attentive waitress had taken her drink order. .

Joline shrugged. "I told you that I want Greggers's killer caught. If that means taking a few insults from you, I can handle it. I've had to deal with nasty people in the nail salon, too. Some ladies just don't get that square nails are so last year and won't listen to we experts."

I winced at her misuse of "we" for the proper "us," but then I had always valued grammar over grooming. I also resisted the temptation to ball up my fists, concealing my aqua-colored squared-off nails. No doubt Joline had checked out my manicure and categorized me among the heinous-handed.

"I admit that I was less than tactful at our last meeting," I said, smiling through gritted teeth. "I apologize and so appreciate your call. Like you, I want the real killer found."

Joline didn't seem interested in my apology, searching the crowd anxiously as I spoke. What or whom did she fear?

When Joline next spoke, her voice was barely above a whisper. "The Yakuza are after me."

The band, Maunalua, chose that moment to launch into their rendition of "Koke'e," one of my favorite songs. I listened to a few bars before reluctantly focusing again on Joline.

"You'd better tell me the whole story," I said.

Four days earlier, Joline had been visited by two men whom she claimed were Yakuza, the Japanese Mafia. Greg owed them money and they had come to collect. She let the men search the apartment—what choice did she have?—but they found nothing of value. They took Greg's bank statements and deliberately left a huge mess. She was warned that when she came into money from Greg's estate, they'd be back to claim their share. That's the short version, anyway. It took her more than a few minutes to get the whole story out, amidst her fretting about the future for her and her beloved daughter Chloe.

"What makes your sure they were Yakuza?"

She explained they were Japanese, had similar and intricate tattoos, and denied they were Yakuza.

Not much to go on. "Why would Greg owe the Yakuza money?"

"Well, Greggy like to gamble from time to time and he, uh, didn't always win. But one of the men said they wanted their investment back with interest."

"What investment?"

Joline shook her head. "I don't know."

I shrugged, not knowing where else I could take the conversation.

"I want you to go to the police for me," Joline said.

"Excuse me?"

"I want you to tell the police that the Yakuza killed my Greggers."

"Why don't you tell them?"

"The men told me that until I deliver the money I will be watched. One of them said that if I go to the police, Chloe would lose her mommy." Joline's eyes filled with tears.

Seriously. Did the Yakuza use the word "mommy?"

"So the Yakuza may be watching us now. By your logic, if I go to the police, I could be killed."

"I'll pay you. Greggy told me he'd taken out a three million dollar life insurance policy for me, in case anything happened. I promise you can have five hundred."

I got it; okay to put my life in danger, but not her life. Since I had squared-off nails, I was expendable. Worse, my life was only worth a paltry $500, before taxes. Joline had clearly been inhaling too much polish remover if she thought I'd go for that deal.

I resisted the urge to walk out on her. "Nice for you that Greg took out a large insurance policy."

Joline's narrowed eyes told me she wasn't as dumb as I'd hoped. "Greggers was worth more to me alive. I loved him and we were going to get married."

After Joline's willingness to toss me to the Yakuza, I felt no compunction about returning the insult.

"So you say. But you just told me he owed the Yakuza. It sounds like Greggy had money problems. Good thing you got the money from the insurance before he went bankrupt … or ran off with that gorgeous and talented waitress from the golf club."

Joline stiffened. Before she opened her mouth again, I threw down the rest of my drink like a shot of tequila, dropped a twenty-dollar bill on the table, and stalked out. Or tried to stalk. The large gulp of the frozen daiquiri gave me a cold headache such that I shut my eyes and grabbed the bridge of my nose in agony, stumbling into a hotel employee carrying a fruit basket. Grace is not my middle name.

Fifteen minutes later, I was in my apartment, headache-free and changing into surf gear. The waves were calling and I wanted to not think about death for awhile.

Per my agreement with Keoni, I called him that evening to tell him about Joline and the Yakuza. Predictably, he was less than thrilled at this latest development. "*E ku'u pua*, this is why you should listen to me. This investigation should be *pau*."

"You've often told me that you like my perseverance in the face of challenges."

"This is pig-headedness."

"Hey, I'm trying to abide by our agreement and tell you what happened, but if you're going to dump on me …"

Keoni apologized for his remarks and I for my temper. He claimed to know little or nothing about the Yakuza except rumors. "The ubiquitous *Kepanī* (Japanese) boogeyman," he said. He also reminded me that Joline's safety wasn't my problem.

That evening I read up on the Yakuza. According to the Internet (I know, it's not an authoritative source) the extent of Yakuza-purported underworld activities was staggering: extortion, gambling, money laundering, drugs, pornography, slavery, gun running, and fake cellulite cures. Okay, I made that last one up.

They did indeed invest in legitimate businesses such as real estate and Hawai'i was one of their favorite playgrounds not just for the weather, but because they could blend in easily. Tattooed Asian men don't stand out here like they might in, say, Laramie, Wyoming.

On the surface, then, Joline's story was plausible. The Yakuza might be another in a long list of disappointed investors in Greg Walker projects and the Yakuza were not known for using the court system to resolve their business problems. Reputed Yakuza methods of execution invoked knives, guns, and grenades. Devoid of mention were IEDs. Could it be that Greg Walker's death heralded the expansion of Yakuza standard business methods?

If Joline's story were to be believed—and I was skeptical—I was facing a new set of suspects whom I didn't much fancy interviewing.

Excuse me; is that a Yakuza tattoo on your arm? Do you know anything about the death of Greg Walker? Are you in favor of human sushi?

If Joline's story were untrue, was she planting a red herring to divert attention from her guilt? And why are herrings red; couldn't they be blue, green or a nice, go-with-everything taupe?

Shoot, I was wandering off topic again. Let's see, Joline, angry about Greg's dalliances and failure to marry her, or even wanting money, kills Greg with a bomb. Possible, but not likely. Despite easy-to-assemble bomb instructions, there was always the danger that one might chip one's polish when packing the bomb, or break a nail screwing down the wires. Nope. Couldn't see Joline taking that risk.

I wasn't ready to believe Joline's story without more evidence, so I called Noelani to inquire whether her mother had ever mentioned the Yakuza in connection with any Hawaiian real estate deals.

"She's mentioned the Yakuza a time or two, but I don't pay attention when she's venting about work," Noelani said. "I'll ask her, though."

UNCLE CALLED TO let me know that Kūlohelohe had scheduled a meeting in the Auloa Community Center on Thursday—he didn't know the agenda—and with the additional tidbit garnered from Karratti that neither Ortiz nor Abbott had alibis for Walker's murder.

When I arrived I made a beeline for the coffee pot, poured myself a small cup, and was searching the crowd for Kealoha when I saw Raymond Tam. What was he doing here? For all of 1.35 seconds I maintained the hope that he wouldn't recognize me. After all, he'd never taken his eyes off Stacey when I met him. Nevertheless, it might be safer to slip out to the ladies' room until the meeting started, and hide in the back of the room during the proceedings. I made it halfway to the door before I was spotted as the sore thumb—or sore scalp—that I was. Blonds were many in Minnesota but obscure on Oʻahu.

Tam stormed over. "What are *you* doing here? Where's your so-called reporter friend?"

Oops. I guess he'd called the convent. I hoped the nuns at least blessed him before hanging up. "Can't talk now; on my way to the ladies' room." I managed a weak smile as I sidled out the door.

When I returned, the meeting was underway with Kealoha moderating the raucous discussion. Kūlohelohe was asking for a moratorium on the work of Lo'i Kalo Labs while Kūlohelohe reviewed the lab procedures to prevent the contamination of Hawaiian taro.

I slumped into a chair at the back to observe the crowd.

Raymond Tam insisted that contamination was a non-issue and he'd consent to share certain lab procedures only if Kūlohelohe turned over those who had spray painted the lab buildings and cut the fences. Several members of Kūlohelohe ignored their own group's proposal and argued for a permanent moratorium on genetic engineering of any *kalo*.

After forty minutes of rancorous debate, Tam walked out, giving me the *stinkeye* (dirty look) as he left. Unless his sneer was meant for someone else and I got caught in the crossfire.

Like a convention of sea gulls arguing over a seal carcass (eew), squawking continued for another twenty minutes as attendees argued among themselves. At last, Kealoha called a halt to the proceedings and suggested withdrawal to a nearby bar. Bars are a much better place for bloodletting than a community center.

I was in the mood for a mango margarita but this didn't appear to be a margarita kind of place, more like a *pia* (beer) and more *pia* place. Kealoha bought me a Longboard without asking, apparently remembering that I had one in hand at the *lū'au*. We chatted a few minutes about the meeting before he took me over to the table where Kevin Ortiz and Sam Abbott were sitting, and introduced me as a cousin and member of Lime-O and Babes Against Biotech. (Actually, I was all for biotech if it could prevent zits and large pores.)

Both men were muscular and nearly as wide as they were tall. Kevin, bedecked with numerous tattoos (even on his neck), was the more garrulous of the two. He'd been vocal at the meeting, expressing the opinion that nothing short of a complete shutdown of the lab would be acceptable.

In contrast, Sam had been content to observe others and occasionally voice his opinion stated as fact. No "maybe", "perhaps," or "I think." Such was the forcefulness of his delivery than no one contradicted him.

The topic of discussion at the bar was not Loʻi Kalo but a recent mountain ball game, a local version of softball, played earlier that evening against a rival construction company. I attempted to steer the conversation to the evils of GMO, but Kevin in particular was more interested in venting his spleen about the eyesight and corruptibility of the umpires. After awhile, I fell silent. If I couldn't delve into their opinions of Greg Walker, at least I could use the time to assess their personalities and batting averages.

I swear they spent more time recounting the game than it had taken to play it. Kevin, complaining about the ump's call at second base, nearly lost it when Sam contradicted him, declaring that Kevin was the only one who didn't realize he was "out by a country mile." Kevin launched into a stream of profanities that ceased when Sam pointed out that a lady was present. By ten I'd seen and heard enough. I excused myself and Kealoha got up to escort me to my car.

"I hope after meeting Sam, Kevin, and the others tonight you see that they could not be murderers," he said as we stepped out the door into the warm evening.

Since I lacked a divining rod when it comes to identifying killers, I opted for a few non-committal words. I think I used the "salt of the earth" cliché.

Kealoha nodded, as if I'd cleared them of all suspicion.

"Too bad your meeting with Tam did not go well," I said.

"I did not expect an agreement, but we must try to find areas of compromise or we will forever be butting heads and nothing will be accomplished. So, we keep talking with Mr. Tam, praying for opportunities for *ho'oponopono*, making things right."

I unlocked the Toyota, but paused before getting in. "I guess Uncle Kimo didn't tell you, but I met with Raymond Tam. He said something curious, that the protests against the lab would soon stop. Do you have any idea what he meant by that?"

Kealoha shook his head.

"Could he have meant that you'd be arrested and the movement would end?"

In the dim light of the parking lot, I thought I could see frown lines crease his forehead. "Perhaps, but I am not the center of Kūlohelohe. There are many who are passionate about the cause."

As I pulled out of the lot and headed for Waikīkī, Kealoha's last words echoed. There had been passion in abundance at the meeting: raised voices and clenched fists. But not from Kevin Ortiz. He voiced his opinion frequently, but without fervor. Not until he spoke of mountain ball did Kevin display strong emotions. What did it mean, if anything, and was it relevant to Walker's murder?

TWENTY-EIGHT

"Great things are won by great dangers."
Herodotus

SURFING THE NEXT morning provided much-needed relief; I was definitely On It, catching several good waves and carrying on a flirtation with a baby *honu* floating in the lineup. I was dropped in on twice, both beginners, and I let them slide in the interests of *aloha*. I'd uttered only one bad word when I'd hit coral on a bailout.

My inner calm and peacefulness lasted all of ten minutes after returning to shore. I'd finished a quick rinse-off and was strolling through Kapi'olani Park to get to my car when I heard a loud buzz. Glancing overhead, I spotted a drone hovering ten feet off my right shoulder. Instinct took over and I dove for the shelter of a nearby *hau* tree. When raised my head to search for the drone, it was gone. A child's laughter and a few cries of "Mommy, look!" penetrated my consciousness. It was nothing more than a small radio-controlled plane: just a boy with a toy, not a surveillance drone. I resolved to spend less time listening to Edvard.

ON THE WAY to work in surprisingly light traffic, I found myself singing one of my favorite Hawaiian songs, "Ku'u Home O Kahalu'u." "But I fear I am not as you left me, *me kealoha ku'u home 'o Kahalu'u*." Wailing on the last "u" I remembered I'd promised to bring in goodies for the morning staff meeting. I swerved suddenly to avoid the ramp to the H-1 and heard the expected horn serenade behind me, followed by an echoing chorus of horns.

203

I glanced behind me to see that a black SUV with tinted windows had executed a similar maneuver, eliciting a corresponding response from the driving public.

I thought no more about it until I pulled out of Leonard's parking lot with a box of pastries—well, a box less one since I'd had to sample the coconut strudel—checked my rearview mirror and saw a black SUV with tinted windows behind me. Where did he come from? The SUV followed me to the entrance ramp onto H-1. Was I being paranoid: first mistaking a toy for a drone, now imagining evil men in every black SUV?

My analytical self went to work calculating the odds of seeing a black SUV in my rearview mirror. I estimated the percentage of black SUVs in the inbound lanes of H-1, factored in the number of vehicles I could see when I checked my mirror, checked the number of times a black SUV was in my mirror on the route to DFAS, made a few wild assumptions, and came up with 63.5 percent. That is, I was 63.5 percent certain I was being tailed and 100 percent certain the tail was the killer, because the tail is always the killer—or a G-man—in the movies. But who was it?

Of course, 63.5 percent was far from a sure thing and my calculations were a guess. (Taking the number to a decimal point was not a sign of accuracy, just my obsession with precision.) Worse, if I truly believed I was being shadowed, I'd have to tell Keoni; this was way more serious than notes on the windshield. We'd be together in San Francisco this weekend for Jennifer's wedding and, after the less than stellar weekend with his parents, I didn't want a blowup of any kind. I put the thought out of my head and refused to check my rearview mirror during the remainder of my morning commute. Until and unless my tail ran me off the road or attempted to dispatch me, there was nothing to report to Keoni. *A'ole mea.*

In the staff meeting I was enjoying one of the crème horns—hey, I'd surfed off the calories from the strudel—when Mike brought up the issue of the Asphire data shambles and announced that Edvard had devised a "brilliant and elegant solution" to the problem and was "a genius."

Edvard smiled broadly as Mike sang his praises, stopping just short of calling for the heavenly choirs to sing hallelujah. The intricacies of Edvard's solution weren't explained, not that I'd understand since data cleansing was not my area of expertise. Truth be told, I'd probably just recommend a good detergent: one with bleach. Mike was thrilled that Edvard's solution would take less than two weeks to implement and that we had a good chance of staying on schedule provided we worked even longer days and a few weekends.

Trailing Edvard to the kitchenette after the meeting, I noticed he slightly dragged one leg in imitation of Lon Chaney, Jr. in *The Mummy's Curse*. He was too young for bursitis and I hadn't heard anything from him about rheumatoid arthritis, incipient tennis knee, or a torn ACL. I held my tongue as Edvard poured himself a cup of coffee and I purchased a calorie-free cola from the machine. Following him as we returned to our cubes, I saw Edvard hitch up his pants and change his gait as if performing the Monty Python Minister of Silly Walks sketch.

Nosiness trumped my resolution to ignore Edvard. "Jockey shorts a size too small, static electricity buildup in your khakis, or did rubber-eating roaches snarf the sole of your left shoe?"

"What?"

"You've gone through four styles of walking in five minutes and even for you that is weird."

"Oh, that. I'm just practicing—"

"Surveillance avoidance," I filled in. "What else?"

Mentioning the "s" word was a clarion call for yet another Edvard lecture on the advances in surveillance technology; in this case, how "They" determined identity based on gait. However, bad legs, failing knees, or even carrying a backpack could alter one's gait enough to fool the current technology.

"As a biometric system, it's vulnerable. All I'm doing is ensuring that my gait is inconsistent enough that I can't be identified," he said proudly. "Especially since Michael won't let me wear my fake ears anymore."

"I suggest you not change gaits every two minutes; that's a dead giveaway that's it's you. Also, the little tap dance you tried attracts too much attention; no one is taping you here, either for surveillance purposes or to audition for a revival of *A Chorus Line*."

"You can't be too careful. Smart phones can be used to track gaits. Androids and iPhones contain accelerometers. In case my cell phone is hacked, this is one way to fool it."

Techno-curiosity got the better of me. "Won't your lead-lined smart phone case prevent any hacking?"

"Can't be sure, that's why I need to find alternatives. Maybe if I encase the phone in gelatinous material it will throw the accelerometer off. Or maybe I should just jailbreak my own iPhone and turn off the accelerometer."

Despite what Stacey says, I'm not one to stir up trouble, but I couldn't pass on the opportunity Edvard had given me.

"While you're musing over your options regarding the accelerometer, I have a suggestion about your ears."

"Yes?"

"If women are allowed to wear fake eyelashes, color their hair, and dare I say enhance their breasts to alter their appearance, why can't you wear prosthetic ears for the same purpose? You might want to have a chat with Michael about our policies regarding gender discrimination."

The rest of the day I worked like a dog: a sheepdog, rounding up stray software code, not the serial nap-taking canine my parents had. It didn't help that I had to sit in on two of Edvard's meetings to stay informed on critical issues (in other words, baby-sit him with the client). Karen had done more than her fair share recently in keeping Edvard on topic. I had one close call when a client made a joke about connecting everything to the Internet, including his toaster. Edvard warned the client that Chinese-manufactured appliances, like refrigerators, toothbrushes, TVs, and smoke detectors were being sold below cost to the U.S. market because the Chinese planned to use them in a massive cyber attack on U.S. infrastructure.

At that point, I staged my own hack attack; I doubled over, coughing and gagging. When the not-too-helpful back pounding began to hurt, I recovered, apologized, remarked on Edvard's sense of humor, and brought up a work-related issue.

I LEFT WORK at the last minute possible to still make my plane to San Francisco and arrive in time for the wedding day activities. (Although, I was missing the rehearsal dinner and the "final-final" dance practice—oh darn.)

On the way to the airport, I called Uncle Kimo with a brief summary of the activities of the previous night and my observations on Kevin Ortiz. Uncle agreed it might be nothing but said he'd pass my comments on to Kealoha.

Between the phone conversation and my excessive speed (I was running late), I only checked twice for a trailing black SUV and was relieved to see no sign of one. I looked forward to leaving the investigation behind even if it meant putting up with Bridezilla Goes Zombie.

TWENTY-NINE

"E kukū ana i ke kai, i ke kai hāwanawana,
'ōlelo o Kawaihae, hae ana e ka naulu."
(At mid-tide on the sea, the whispering sea,
speaking of Kawaihae, stirred by the sudden
shower.)
"A Kona Hema 'O Ka Lani," Traditional

THE RED-EYE deposited me in San Francisco in plenty of time for the bridesmaid's eight o'clock mani-pedi. It's crucial that the bridesmaids all have identical nail polish. I personally knew a couple of marriages that had foundered on that point, to say nothing of the hurdle to marital happiness caused by having a boutonniere that didn't match the groomsmen's cummerbunds. The horror.

The mani-pedi was heavenly and I fell asleep while my toes were drying. I was awakened, rather grumpily, for the mandatory makeup application. The makeup artist who clucked-clucked over the state of my pores didn't improve my mood. "Clogged!" she informed me, but cut the conversation short after my snotty rejoinder: "Matches my bowels!"

I returned home to my apartment by eleven with black talons (white tipped, no less, in what was the fashionably undead version of a French manicure), and more makeup than I generally apply in a month. My face was flawless in a "mortician to the stars" type of way: very pale, with dark brows, and even darker, smudged eyeliner. I had taken notes and would be ahead of the game for Halloween.

I indulged in a two-hour nap, my head bolstered by pillows so I wouldn't roll over and smudge the makeup. I woke to feel only slightly dead; I suppose that made it easier to get into character. The restorative powers of sugar and caffeine—double latte with shot of caramel, a few sprinkles, and two cinnamon cookies—imbued me with sufficient energy to complete my preparations.

I curled my hair (grateful I hadn't been asked to go Goth and add a white streak), dabbed a touch of perfume at my throat and temples, shimmied into seriously uncomfortable underwear so no straps or lines would show (even ghouls have their fashion standards), and then donned an odious dress that even the bridesmaids of Frankenstein wouldn't wear. I added pierced earrings in the form of silver skulls, a gift from the bride to her attendants, and slipped on a pair of open-toed black shoes. Thank Heaven, or is it Hades, that ghouls wear flats, not stilettos.

When I opened my apartment door to Keoni, he didn't move. The edges of his mouth were twitching as he tried and failed to subdue a smirk. "It's, ah, well, different," he finally said.

"So is a thong made of chili peppers, but I don't relish wearing one of those, either."

If the color, amethyst purple, wasn't bad enough, the dress featured a too-tight princess-cut bodice with an overlay of black lace and long sleeves ending in a large quantity of black lace up to the elbow. The overall effect was enough to make me question whether Jennifer was deliberately trying to make every other woman in her immediate vicinity resemble a refugee from a polygamous religious cult. Not that there's anything wrong with that.

"I'll gladly trade outfits," I said.

Keoni was attired in a charcoal gray suit, white shirt, and tie. I'd never seen him in a suit before, unless one counted those of the "swim" and "wet" variety.

"What do you think?" he said, doing a slow turn. Big Hawaiian guys do not pirouette.

The suit fit well across his back, showing off his broad shoulders to good advantage. His dark hair was slicked back, he smelled of exceedingly nice aftershave, and he was darkly handsome.

"Very nice." I gave him a slightly lingering kiss, but only slightly, since I didn't want my makeup to get mussed just yet.

I gathered up my purse, keys, and not-totally horrible pale pink lip-gloss: I'd drawn the line at the black lipstick preferred by Jennifer's makeup artist, or should I say, *artiste*. Doubtless the extra e added a couple of zeros to her fee.

"There's a surprise waiting below," Keoni said as we started down the stairs.

"Is that 'surprise' as in a hungry werewolf or 'surprise' as in a fifth of gin to brace me for the coming ordeal?"

"There you are," a familiar voice said. My landlady Magda and her miniature red dachshund Chesty were waiting at the bottom of the staircase. Chesty barked at me and made a fake charge toward the stairs. As Keoni and I continued down, he gave another bark before retreating behind Magda's legs from which he whined and shivered. I couldn't say I blamed him: I wouldn't let anyone dressed like me in a respectable home, either.

"I saw Keoni coming in and he told me he was escorting you to a wedding," Magda said. "I want to get a picture of you two."

"I don't feel all that photogenic," I responded.

"Women do very strange things to make their weddings perfect and memorable. Invariably they require their friends, families, and future husbands or future ex-husbands to take part in the insanity. She must be a good friend of yours for you to wear …" Magda's voice trailed off and she snorted, suppressing a giggle.

"We went to high school together," I said. "She's a close friend, for now."

She nodded her head knowingly and we both laughed.

"Let me get a couple pictures. I promise I won't put them on the Internet, and years from now, if she remains a good friend, you can laugh at the pictures together."

"And if she doesn't?"

"You and Keoni can laugh at her," she said.

Keoni and I dutifully posed at the bottom of the stairs. As Magda snapped a couple of shots, Chesty grew bold enough to cautiously approach. I think he finally recognized my scent because his whole body started wagging as he gave off excited yips and I was forced to give him ear scratches before departing.

"Have a good time." Magda said as we left. "Remember, you only have to wear it once."

We had a three-block walk to the car and received exactly zero curious looks. In San Franfreakshow, a zombie princess with a handsome prince in her clutches was no big deal.

I remember very little of the ceremony, doubtless because I was concentrating on breathing in a tight bodice and avoiding making eye contact with strangers lest we both burst out laughing at my sartorial silliness. I remember a reading from 1 Corinthians 11, though I considered whether "love bears all things, believes all things, hopes all things, and endures all things" included awful bridesmaid dresses.

The "Thriller" number went as one would expect when most of the participants had skipped rehearsals. Jennifer had chosen to take the undead theme through to the food, which I discovered when a black-gloved waiter placed two breadsticks on my bread-and-butter plate that resembled long, tapering fingers, complete with hair (rosemary) and red fingernails (sun-dried tomato). Eew. The "eyeball" floating in my glass of champagne and the finger sandwiches festooned with plastic roaches didn't bother me nearly as much. I halfway thought about reminding Jennifer that "undead" was considered a non-inclusive term by the zombie community, who preferred "living-challenged" as a descriptor.

With my usual aplomb I skipped the bouquet toss by hiding in the ladies' room. All in all, a good enough time to raise the dead.

BACK ON THE plane to Honolulu, I was happy that Keoni and I had not argued and grateful to have a week without visitors. Not that I'd been besieged, yet, but one problem with living in paradise is that But Everyone wants to visit. No less than five friends at the wedding inquired as to a good time to visit me in Hawai'i, one of whom I hadn't heard from in nearly two years and whose idea of friendship was limited to bragging updates on Twitter and Facebook. I don't begrudge friends taking advantage of a free place to sleep, a car, and a tour guide (me), but I was there on GD's dime, or more correctly the U.S. Government's dime, and I had to work fifty-five hours a week. Surfing and sleuthing were already making that difficult. I told the self-inviting guests that I was bombarded with work and I'd get back to them when work settled down. Meaning, "when I moved to the next assignment in a less-desirable location like Cleveland, Ohio."

Leave it to Kaitlyn, who'd been missing in action for the past year, to push back, insisting she and her boyfriend Josh would be no trouble, they'd stay out of my way, etc. I smiled sweetly and responded that I would love to spend quality time with her and that it would be a shame if I were not able to entertain her properly. I suggested we get together later in the summer, when I was back in the area and what weekend would she suggest. Her promise to name a date soon rang as false as her artificially enhanced cup size. Meow.

I had plenty on my to-do list in preparation for Mother's arrival on Saturday, starting with washing Keoni's jeep and clearing out the granola wrappers, empty water bottles, broken bars of surf wax, and a lot of sand. I'd need to lay in food and pick up the apartment. Although the lease came with a cleaning service, the pile of dirty laundry, slightly damp rash guards and board shorts, flip-flops, and the last week's worth of newspapers on the floor were out of scope.

Oh, and a trip to Goodwill was happily in order. I'm sure some poor soul on O'ahu needed a black lace and amethyst dress. Perhaps a hula dancer who needed to dance to "Monster Mash."

THIRTY

"A conspiracy is nothing but a secret
agreement of a number of men for the
pursuance of policies which they dare not
admit in public."
Mark Twain

LEAVING WORK MONDAY evening I was again tailed by a black
SUV. I had hoped the SUV incident the prior week had been due
to a fog of paranoia impacting my synaptic processing. In other
words, a figment of my over-active imagination. I knew, however,
the threatening notes were real and I had not returned to Honolulu unprepared. My purse now carried my Shrieker, an electronic
noisemaker Mother had given me.

On a previous trip to Hawai'i I had shown the Shrieker to Noelani and set it off by accident. The loud, penetrating howl sent
beachgoers heading for high ground, fearing the tsunami sirens
had gone off. Even though I've handled it carefully since then,
there have been several other embarrassing, ear-splitting, raise-the-
dead incidents. I used to pack it on blind dates in case I needed to
end them early and loudly. Now, I carry it during dicey investigative endeavors.

As I neared Waikīkī, I attempted several maneuvers to trick my
tail into approaching closer: sudden slowdowns, pulling into driveways unexpectedly, and veering onto the shoulder before backing
up. Okay, I didn't back up, although I've seen it done. I hoped
to draw the SUV close enough to read the license plate number.

Surely Uncle Kimo's friend, Detective Karratti, would run the plate for me. I succeeded in eliciting honking horns, vulgar gestures, and obscenities galore, but the SUV remained well behind me. Since I'd promised Keoni I'd curb my tendencies toward precipitate action, I did not stop in the middle of a street, get out of my vehicle and charge the SUV with my pepper spray. Doesn't mean I didn't think about it.

The next morning the SUV was back. I was certain my threatening notes pen pal was behind the wheel. He, or she, was stepping up the intimidation. What would the next step be? Ramming my car?

I was grateful to arrive at work, where U.S. Marines manned the gate. Even if my stalker penetrated their cordon of defense, a scream for help inside DFAS would bring a squad of men and women well-versed in hand-to-hand combat.

My mother did not raise me to be a doormat. If I couldn't confront the SUV driver, at least I could give him a headache. That evening I again engaged in evasive driving: running a red light, turning right out of a left lane, and numerous sudden lane changes made all the worse by the squishy responsiveness of the 4Runner, which swayed alarmingly when I made a sharp turns. It wasn't easy to lose a tail, particularly in heavy traffic, but finally I did. To make it harder for him to find me in the morning, I parked ten blocks away from the apartment in an out-of-the-way spot, and then hoofed it home. There was no SUV outside my apartment building, so it appeared that he didn't know exactly where I lived.

When I emerged that evening to walk along Waikīkī, I kept my hand in my front pocket where I'd stashed my pepper spray key chain. (I'd never again put it in a tight back pocket, having been unable to dislodge it once when I needed it desperately.)

I spent a lot of time peering over my shoulder although the surge of humanity made it difficult to deduce if I had a tail. I dodged into a slinky lingerie store, figuring that if my tail were male, he'd stand out. I was wrong. All the customers were men. At least one was buying for himself; a 6'3" dark and hairy man draped in a feather boa was preening in front of a mirror.

After emerging from the store, I took to making sudden changes in direction, hoping I could spot or lose any pursuer. During one of these maneuvers, I ran into an elderly man with a silver-handled cane who nearly pitched into a stroller holding twin toddlers. The rapid reaction of a heretofore immobile Silver Man kept the old man from falling. The street performer received the grateful thanks of the elderly man and the mother of the twins, along with the applause of his audience. I got dirty looks and fist gesticulations as I slunk away.

I was being silly. It wasn't like my follower could easily attack me in a crowd, poking a poison-tipped umbrella into the back of my leg. The sole umbrella carriers in Waikīkī were Japanese girls, protecting their skin from the sun, which had long since set.

I slid into a vacant chair at an empty umbrella table at the Royal Hawaiian and let a white wine and Kapala singing "Makee 'Ailana" take me away from all harm.

THE NEXT MORNING I surfed Populars, where my safety was assured with Manoa and friend policing the lineup. For a time, I forgot that I had a stalker.

I did a quick rinse off and shimmied into my work clothes back at my apartment. I was rushed for time, so I took the King Street ramp to the H-1, where my tail picked me up. Note to self: vary route to work.

At least the SUV didn't engage in any threatening moves, like approaching closely then backing off, tailgating, or rolling down the window and pointing an Uzi at me. It was just there and annoyingly out of reach, like a mosquito bite between your shoulder blades. Nevertheless, I planned on being careful. Just that morning, Manoa had recommended a great restaurant "*out Waipahu way with da best sashimi evahs.*" I made noises about trying it even though I'd no intention of going anywhere where I might run into Perello, with or without his spear gun.

I didn't have a playlist for "De-stressing from Surveillance," though Edvard probably did, but I listened to Erik Lee sing

"Hōkūleʻa Hula," and thought about the long voyages of the Polynesians crossing the Pacific Ocean, and the resurgence of wayfinding in the 1970's that enabled such voyages.

"Auwē, Hōkūleʻa te vahine o ke kai."

My cell phone rang just as I pulled into the base.

"You put me in big trouble with Momma and Rissa." Noelani's voice came through loud and clear.

"What? No *'E, Emma!'* or *'Howzit?'"*

"Momma wanted to know why I was interested in the Yakuza. I told her Rissa finally was moving on from Tomas and had a new boyfriend. He said he was in real estate, but one of her friends thought he had Yakuza tattoos."

"Why did you tell her that?"

"First thing that popped into my head," Noelani said. "Momma didn't even wait to finish the conversation. She called Rissa to find out about the new boyfriend and to warn her about the Yakuza. Rissa didn't know what she was talking about and said so. Momma figured out I was lying to her and, well, it wasn't pretty."

Noelani's mother had stormed over to the condo (to which she had a key) and confronted Noelani, who was pressed to confess all. Her mother gave her an earful about butting into unsolved murders and not hanging out with those who do.

"Mom cooled down after and hour or so, and I don't think you're on her bad list any longer," Noelani said, "but if you run into her, don't expect a hug. Or any of her award-winning *haupia*, either."

Despite the blowup, Noelani had learned that the Yakuza had invested in a number of projects in and around Honolulu. Not that the Yakuza had registered their activities with the local authorities, but "everyone" in the real estate community knew the Yakuza had played a role in selected luxury developments. Noelani rattled off a short list. One of the projects was on the list of Walker's suits. Another, Koʻolau Towers, was not on the list but sounded familiar. It took a moment before I recalled Marla mentioning it as one of her successful investments.

Noelani brushed off my groveling thanks and hung up. I expect she was a miffed about being reamed by her mother, the latest in a series of strained relationships attributable to this case. Would that my tail would get oh-so-teed-off with me and depart in a huff of exhaust fumes, never to darken my rearview mirror again.

WORKING IN THE early morning quiet of humming fluorescent lights, I gradually became aware of murmurs from Edvard's cube; he and Karen were conversing in low tones. Even holding my breath, closing my eyes, and leaning back in my chair until I almost fell out of it, I couldn't discern the topic of their conversation. Their hushed voices implied a private *tête-à-tête* rather than a conspiracy rant. Weren't they getting chummy now? Particularly Karen, who'd been so *nice* to Edvard lately. Was it just his help with Gunnar, or was there more?

When Karen went to the kitchen for a coffee refill, I tagged along behind her. Not that I was nosy or anything. I was just trying to be a supportive colleague, which of course meant that I'd need a complete debriefing on her interpersonal relations with co-workers. Her excitement was palpable; she was practically walking on air. I wondered how to bring up Edvard when Karen mentioned that she had "great news."

"You're engaged?" I said loudly.

Karen stopped in mid stride and turned toward me. "What on earth are you talking about?" she hissed.

"Sorry, brain cramp. I meant, what great news?"

"I have a meeting with Gunnar at lunch, about his behavior. Why did you think I was engaged?" she said, her voice still tight with anger.

"Nothing," I lied. "A couple friends have announced engagements lately. I guess I have matrimony on my mind."

Karen appeared to accept my weak explanation although not without a little more slamming of the refrigerator door and sloshing of the coffee pot than was strictly called for. She reminded me that Dave Blanchard would be at DFAS next week to schmooze with the client. His visit was an opportunity for her to speak with him about joining the government practice. First, however, she wanted to be rid of the speed bump called Gunnar. She'd arranged to meet him for lunch at Kekoa's and asked me to find another place to eat today. Since I'd brought in leftover pizza, I had no problem complying with her request.

I was restless all afternoon. Not from the pizza, although the too fatty sausage did a number on my intestinal tract. I was dying to know what happened with Gunnar. Upon her return, Karen immediately dove into consecutive meetings, leaving no chance for a discreet talk. Or a rant-filled one, either.

The DFAS stampede for the exits occurred on schedule at 4:30 p.m., but the activity level around our cubes remained high as fellow GD consultants popped in and out with questions. Around six, I poked my head into Karen's cube and said I was going to the kitchenette for a cold drink and snack and would she like to join me.

"I'll be there in a few minutes." Her tone was less than enthusiastic.

The kitchenette was deserted, except for the geckos and they seemed more interested in swirling up the walls than eavesdropping.

I grabbed a cold drink from the vending machine and took a seat at a small table in the corner. While waiting, I read the bulletins on the wall: reminders of the upcoming Combined Federal Campaign, a reprint of an old WWII "loose lips sink ships" poster, and a Marine Corps recruiting poster. Seriously? I thought everyone at the command was already a convert.

Karen shuffled into the kitchen, and before she even reached for a paper cup, I blurted it out. "How did Operation 'get Gunnar in your gun sights' go?"

"Can you keep your voice down?" She sounded tired.

"Sorry."

Karen poured a cup of coffee from a pot that had probably been half empty for the past two hours. Yuck. She said nothing as she jammed the pot back under the drip machine and slowly and deliberately doctored her coffee. Was she trying to up the suspense?

She stirred her coffee three times clockwise and five times counter clockwise before tapping the spoon on the rim, rinsing it off, and putting it back on the drain board. With agonizing slowness, I might add.

"It's not easy to answer," she said as she sat down at the table and slumped in her chair.

That didn't sound good and Karen seemed dejected. Before I could press for details, Rafe walked in.

"I thought you'd left," I said.

My tone was accusatory and Rafe reacted accordingly. "I, uh, sorry, I mean, I was in a long meeting this afternoon and was trying to catch up on email. I'm just getting a cold drink."

He popped a bill into the vending machine which immediately spit it back out. Rafe smoothed the bill and then tried again. No luck. He slid his wallet out and checked inside. "I, uh, only have twenties." He looked at me in silent appeal.

Karen, who hadn't turned around at Rafe's entrance, was still studying the wall behind my back. I got up and reached into my pants pockets, discovering enough quarters to spot Rafe a drink and shoe him on his way.

He tried to give me his crumpled five-dollar bill, but I waved him off. "It's on me; my apology for snapping at you. I was just asking Karen for help on a personal issue."

Rafe seemed satisfied with that and scuttled out.

I returned to the table and sat quietly as Karen told her story.

She thought she had him at first; Karen had taken a laptop and earbuds to the restaurant and let him view the video as she "savored the coconut shrimp appetizer." It was the last part of the meal she enjoyed. Gunnar was unrepentant. They'd gone back and forth about the tape, but the bottom line was that Gunnar didn't think the it proved anything; he could claim that she had come on to him earlier and he was just responding to that. Furthermore, he didn't believe she had the guts to go to Michael or HR with it and jeopardize her chances of joining the government practice.

Karen feared that even if the existence of the tape kept Gunnar from harassing and blocking her move to Blanchard's group, he would find a way in the future to undermine her, perhaps to the point where she'd be fired. If she then showed the tape, her superiors would wonder why she didn't come forward sooner and think she was blackmailing Gunnar. Which, technically, she was.

I was at a loss. I felt as if I'd let Karen down. Maybe I should have spent more time helping her than chasing an elusive car bomber. I might not know whom to kneecap to keep Kealoha out of the clink, but maybe I could help her get Gunnar for good.

THIRTY-ONE

"Sweater, n.: garment worn by child when its
mother is feeling chilly."

Ambrose Bierce

SERENDIPITY IS A wonderful thing. Like Joseph McVickers play-ing with wallpaper cleaner and realizing it could be turned into a toy, thus launching Play-Doh. Or Manoa being at Kekoa's when "Emma's *hoaloha* (friend)" was talking with a *kanaka*, noticing how upset she was, mentioning it to me the next morning in the lineup and listening to my explanation of Karen's problem with Gunnar. Manoa came up with a plan to, as my brother Virgil would say, "kick a#$ and take names."

Before Mother's arrival that afternoon, I decided to follow suit. I didn't confront anyone directly, not wanting to risk bodily harm or further criticism of my manicure. Instead, I wrote letters. Threaten-ing letters that said: "I have proof of your guilt, which I will give to the police. This is your last chance to turn yourself in and plead for a lighter sentence." The notes might lack a few well-chosen sinister adjectives, but at least they were correctly spelled and punctuated. If I were arrested, it wouldn't be by the grammar police.

Of course I didn't sign my name. Had I more time I would have cut and pasted letters from magazines for each note; somehow that seems scarier than getting a left-justified Times New Roman double-spaced letter. I thought about it but ultimately decided that adding "sincerely yours" detracted from my wanna-be-menacing tone.

I prepared letters for Marla, Carmen, Joline, and Raymond Tam. Kevin Ortiz and Sam Abbott I dithered about, finally deciding to send a note to each. Alan Nakamura got a pass, only because he was Uncle Kimo's *hoaloha* (dear friend) and therefore, almost *'ohana*. Deep down, despite the fact that Keoni wanted to join the profession, I believe that lawyers are always guilty—of something.

I mailed the letters from Hawai'i Kai, not wanting a Waikīkī postmark that could point to me. Of course, I used gloves in addressing the letters and water, not saliva, to moisten each stamp and seal the envelopes. Just for fun, the return address was the Honolulu police station in Kaimukī.

I knew the whole "politely threatening letter" thing was hokey, but I wouldn't be able to do any investigative work during Mother's visit. Maybe, just maybe, the notes would precipitate a response, like the killer showing up at the police station to offer a full confession. Hey, it could happen.

On the drive to the airport, I began to second-guess my actions: not the sending of the notes, but my grammatical exactitude and choice of professional font. Should I have misspelled a few words and misplaced a few commas in an attempt to emulate an uneducated thug? (Not that all thugs were uneducated; the IRS employs college graduates to shake down children who don't pay taxes on their lemonade stand profits.)

I'd also not imposed a deadline. Did that imply a lack of seriousness? I wasn't well versed on how to dish out threats. Maybe I should have done an Internet search on "getting the most from your menacing missives" or downloaded *Seven Habits of Highly Effective Evildoers*.

To think of other things, I popped in my Kapala CD. The combination of jazz and Hawaiian music filled the 4Runner as I bounced along to "Chigasaki," a cheerful Hawaiian song about a Japanese surf town.

It was nearly five when I met Mother at the airport with a plumeria *lei* and a hug. The *lei* stands at the Honolulu International Airport sold more expensive and more stunning *leis* than plain old plumeria, but on her previous visits Mother had made it clear that she loved the scent of plumeria more than ginger or even *pīkake*, and although she admired the beauty of an orchid *lei*, she didn't know why anyone would wear odorless flowers. I stopped at Maile's *Lei* Stand and selected a *lei* of alternating white and pink plumeria blossoms. I took a good sniff before placing it over Mom's shoulders and kissing her, in *ho'olei*, the correct *lei*-bedecking fashion.

"How was the flight?" I asked dutifully after I hustled her and her luggage into the 4Runner.

"Interesting. I wasn't able to select a seat on this flight and was assigned a middle seat. An eight-year-old unaccompanied girl occupied the window seat."

"Joy. Maybe the airline thought a woman traveling alone would be less annoyed than other travelers."

"Possibly. She was quite delightful, as it happens. She chattered on for most of the trip; I think the poor girl was bored. She didn't have any books or anything to read. When you kids were that age you'd have four or five books in your backpack for even a short trip."

"Still do. I love having hundreds of e-books at my fingertips, but sometimes, I prefer the flesh and blood, or paper and ink, of a real book. Did she talk for five hours?"

"No, she watched cartoons on her tablet when she wasn't nattering. She didn't seem to have any toys along, either. Not even a Barbie doll equipped with a flamethrower."

We laughed together. As a kid, I'd convinced my parents to purchase G.I. Joes in order to appropriate their weapons for my Barbies' pitched battles with my brother Virgil's action figures. Because Barbie was bigger and better armed, I'm convinced she always won.

Mother fell silent for a few moments, absorbed in the scenery clicking by as we continued down the Nimitz Highway toward Waikīkī.

"Are you hungry?" I asked as we neared Waikīkī.

"Not immediately. Why, what did you have in mind?"

"Mānoa DNA is playing at Lulu's tonight: I gave you their latest CD last Christmas. I thought we could see them and grab dinner at the same time."

"'Ah, music. A magic beyond all we do here!'"

"Shakespeare?"

"J.K. Rowling. *Harry Potter*."

I parked a few blocks from the apartment. I didn't think I'd been tailed coming back from the airport, but I couldn't be certain, so I continued my new custom of parking in odd places to make it harder for the tail to locate my vehicle.

Mother questioned my choice of parking space, spotting several open spots in the four-block walk to drop off her luggage. I explained that open spaces this close were highly unusual. She seemed to believe me, but I was going to have to come up with better excuses for the next six nights.

As music venues go, Lulu's was downscale, loud, and intimate. Stacey had loved it, but I wasn't sure about Mother's tolerance for loud music. I asked for seats well in the back, but I need not have worried. Mother was enchanted by Mānoa DNA's mix of traditional Hawaiian and 1970s' music with a few songs in Japanese for an international flavor. Our conversation was compressed between songs, and even when the band was on break, the street noise penetrating the open-air restaurant made casual chatter difficult. I occasionally watched the surf tape loop on the flat screens ringing the restaurant and bar; the usual head-banging music on mute, thank heavens.

After dinner we retired to the Mai Tai Bar at the Royal Hawaiian, an old hotel set on the water, well back from Kalākaua Avenue in an oasis of what feels like old Hawai'i. Known as the Pink Palace of the Pacific, the Royal Hawaiian is pinker and more famous than the similarly clad, prominently placed Tripler Army Hospital which can be seen from downtown Honolulu. It goes without saying that most people prefer staying at the Royal Hawaiian to Tripler, and it's not just the view, the food, or the drinks.

Kapala was playing "Nani Hanalei" as we walked in. We sat down at a table close to the musicians, and ordered a couple of Mai

Tais as soon as a waiter swooped by with two waters and nibbles. Kanoe, the regular hula dancer, gave me a hug and asked if I had any special requests, knowing I'd ask for "Raising Hāloa," the song they'd written about farming *kalo* (taro).

Mother and I sipped our drinks and bathed in the music before engaging in gentle conversation. Mother had seen my brother and sister-in-law before she'd left and Ashley, expecting her second child in a few months, was "even bigger than the first time." I hoped Mother hadn't shared that assessment with Ashley. Dad had recently "assumed the mantle of a Greek hoplite" as he prepared to do battle over a proposal—put forth by a recent transplant from the East Coast—to designate their neighborhood as an historic area. There was no news on the Ariadne front. "She's probably hiding something unpleasant," was Mother's assessment. I had to agree; my younger sister had a wild streak and my parents were just as happy *not* to know about all her activities.

"What would you like to do tomorrow?" I asked after Mother had completed her family update.

"I don't want to interfere with any plans you may have," she responded. "Is there anything on your agenda: getting together with friends, work commitments, investigative obligations?"

"Excuse me?"

Mother smiled mischievously. "You heard what I said and there is no use denying it. Keoni told me everything."

"The stoolpigeon. Maybe he and Stacey should just start a Facebook page: Emma's Investigations. And what do you mean by 'everything?'" I wracked my brain, trying to think of the Hawaiian word for "blabbermouth." "*Kulikuli*" was "noisy," which wasn't quite right. "*Niele*" was "nosy." Close, but no *kīkā*. Wait, *'iole* would do: rat.

"Keoni came to see me after he returned from spring break and told me it was his fault that you were involved in another murder investigation. He hadn't known the full story of your previous adventures when he asked you to get involved. Until he heard the truth from Stacey, he was unaware, as he put it, that you lost all sense of self-preservation in your crusades to protect the innocent."

Keoni was going to get an earful. "And what possessed him to soothe his conscience at the expense of worrying my mother?"

"Now dear, be fair. Keoni is concerned about you. I'm glad he told me the truth so I can keep an eye on you while I'm here."

"You can keep an eye on me? Because Keoni thinks it is okay to put my mother in danger? What gives him the right? And oh, by the way, I've done a good job taking care of myself so far." My voice had risen in volume and, had we been any place less public, I might have shifted into shouting mode.

"Emma, please. Keep your voice down. Keoni did not ask me to keep an eye on you. I think he wanted me to convince you to drop the investigation. And I'm more than a bit confused by your thinking that I might be in danger when you've told Keoni that you're perfectly safe."

She had me there.

"Furthermore, I had a feeling you weren't telling me everything about your investigation into Padmanabh's death, so I had a heart to heart with Virgil. He told me about your assailant pulling a gun."

"Dang."

I expected to be reamed out on the spot, but instead Mother suggested we retire to my apartment. She'd packed a full arsenal of protection devices she wanted to show me.

It might have been my imagination, but I could swear my stuffed bunny Fred had new creases between his ears at the sight of all the self-defense gizmos Mother pulled out of her suitcase. As far as I could tell, she didn't have anything that fired bullets, but she had just about everything else. Except a catapult: too hard to get in your purse and anyway, how often does one need to engage in siege warfare?

"You can clip this to your purse, your key chain, even a belt loop." Mother handed me a two-inch handbag fob with a short chain. I wondered if it came with a gold as well as silver chain, since I favored gold jewelry and everyone knows that coordinating weapons with wardrobe is *de rigueur*.

"Not my style." I peered at the cherry-blossom enamel design. Seriously? A weapon with a floral design?

"It's a personal alarm," Mother responded. "One hundred thirty decibels of a woman screaming. People tend to ignore anything that sounds like a car alarm, but will respond to a screaming woman. If you are in trouble, just pull the chain."

"Does it come with ear plugs for me?"

"Be careful you don't accidentally catch the fob on a hook, in a seat cushion, or the like. It could be embarrassing."

Been there, done that with the Shrieker.

"Which color would you like?" she said, holding up two key chains in the shape of cats.

"What are they?"

Mother put two of her fingers in the holes for the eyes and made a fist. "Hopefully, an assailant won't get close enough that you have to resort to blows." The sharply pointed ears of the cat poked up from the back of her fingers like brass knuckles.

"I see. In that case, I'll take the lime green."

Mother tossed me the key chain and picked up a silver perfume container. "Pepper spray. I carry one of these, just in case. It fires five bursts that reach up to six feet. I just have to remember not to mix it up with my real perfume. I put a piece of tape on the pepper spray. Sans tape is my Jessica McClintock perfume, I think. Anyway, I know you have the pepper spray key chain, but I thought you could use more spray," she said, picking up a pen, which she tossed in my direction. "Just pull off the top and press the sprayer. Couldn't be easier. Oh, and the other end is a functional pen. You can do very nice calligraphy with it, in fact."

Indeed. You could use the pepper spray, then immediately write an apology note. Grandmother Swenson would approve.

Without waiting for comment, she continued. "Here's a toy I'd love to try out." She pulled a cell phone out of a pink leather holder. "It's a stun gun. One hundred thousand volts." She made a thrusting move as if stunning an imaginary assailant. "I can think of a few people I'd like to use it on," she muttered to herself. "More specifically, a few body parts on those people."

She handed the device to me. "Be careful with it."

"That goes without saying," I said dryly, holding the phone a little away from my body, lest I accidentally hit the wrong button, which would lend new meaning to the concept of a wrong number. More like a dead wrong number.

"I didn't mean it that way. Stun guns and TASERs are illegal in Hawai'i. With the exception of pepper spray, just about every other defense product is illegal or severely restricted; I don't know how the state government expects a woman to defend herself."

"Run fast, I suppose. Tough to do in *slippahs*, though." I should know since I tried that with Padmanabh's killer.

"Best keep the stun gun out of sight. Oh, and be sure to charge it regularly. The battery dies if it sits idle for too long."

I half-wondered where to find a portable charger for a pocket stun gun. Probably the same place you'd find press-on nails with poison-dispensing tips. Of course the nails would be fashionably rounded and not so-not-stylish square-tipped.

"Maybe you should carry it, Mom, just while you're here."

Mother agreed quickly. So quickly, in fact, I think she was hoping to get a chance to use it.

Mother continued to rummage around in her bag with the same air of anticipation I'd seen from my siblings exploring their Christmas stockings. If Santa Claus were an arms dealer, that is.

"I'm a bit surprised you made it through security with this haul."

"It was all in checked luggage, disguised as something else. Besides, I think TSA is focusing on finding agricultural products, and I didn't bring even an apple. Ah, here it is." She pulled out a plastic bag containing what appeared to be Christmas ornaments.

"What's with the snowflakes?"

"Ninja stars, eight points." She removed one of the flat, white shapes and held it up.

"Do you know how to use them?" I said.

"You throw them at people." She frowned at me as if I were dense.

"I know that, but isn't there a certain technique?"

"Probably, but it seems to me that you could throw it like a Frisbee, snapping the wrist to induce a spin." Suddenly she turned, flicked her wrist and the star flew at my bathroom door, where it bit into the wood, just missing the door handle. A gecko on the wall near the door jam scuttled to safety, disappearing behind a picture frame.

"Low and left." Mother eyed the star in the door, its points still quivering. "I need to practice my throw."

"Maybe outdoors," I said, thinking GD wouldn't want to pay for "unspecified damages" to my rental apartment. Unless, of course, one of our customers conveniently menaced me in my apartment, in which case I'd just charge the repair bill to DFAS.

My mother's actions unsettled me. Although I'd always thought highly of my family—I didn't trash my parents like many of my contemporaries did in high school and college—I hadn't given them, and in particular my mother, much credit for being more than just parents. I recognized they were professors, experts in areas in which I had barely a smattering of knowledge. They had tried to inculcate me in the finer points of literature and dead languages, but that was in keeping with the teaching part of parenthood. I couldn't imagine them as people with real lives, interests, quirks and passions. Now I saw my mother, whom I regarded as safe and predictable, playing with illegal and potentially lethal weapons. This was a woman I did not know, but it did explain where I got my urge to arm my Barbie dolls with M16s, laser guns, and camouflage stilettos; nothing says you can't be both stylish and lethal.

Mercifully, the ninja stars marked the last of her weapons. Mother seemed willing to talk about more mundane topics after that, like how my murder investigation was coming along, had I "ID'd the mad bomber," and where the closest place was to get a "fat pill" to go with her morning coffee (Leonard's for a malasada, *any kine*).

I gave her a summary of my activities and conclusions, such as they were.

Mother looked thoughtful. "You wrote letters to each of the suspects telling them you knew they were guilty?"

"Right, but I didn't sign my name."

"Still …" Mother fingered the ninja star, stroking the edge as if feeling the sharpness. "You may have thrown blood in the water. We should charge up the stun gun tonight. I want to carry it starting tomorrow, just in case the sharks start to snack."

THIRTY-TWO

"Maka'ala ke kanaka kahea manu." (A man
who calls birds should always be alert.)
Hawaiian Proverb

MOTHER AND I enjoyed Leonard's malasadas for breakfast. Mother licked her sugar-covered fingers after scarfing down a custard-filled one. "Mmm. I love empty calories. How about we have these for dessert tonight?" We purchased a few extra and were on our way.

First stop was the *USS Arizona* Memorial. Mother had seen it before, but it's always impressive, particularly the columbarium on the memorial, where men who had survived the attack and lived out a full span of years had their ashes laid to rest with their shipmates.

The afternoon featured shopping, specifically the Kapi'olani Park monthly Waikīkī Artfest, a good place to pick up one-of-a-kind gifts and an opportunity to once again park a few blocks from the apartment with the excuse "it will be less of a walk to the Artfest." Not that we'd been noticeably tailed by a black SUV. However, there were an inordinate number of white cars in Hawai'i, doubtless due to the rental fleets, and I couldn't be sure I wasn't being tailed by one; every time I checked there were four or five in my rearview mirror. Why couldn't tails all agree on a standard car, like a hot pink Mini Cooper? I cast several glances back as we walked toward the park, relieved to see no stalker in evidence. Once at the Artfest, Mother cut loose. She was in her element, popping in and out of almost every booth. I kept my eyes open for any artifact

233

made of native wood, particularly a *lei o mano*. I espied a few like the ones Keoni had made for me; they were upwards of $300 each. Not that one could put a price on an object hand-crafted with love that had proven its mettle in battle.

When I stopped to watch the hula dancers perform a beautiful *hula kahiko*, I lost sight of Mother for a few minutes. I found her in a small booth pulling out her credit card to pay for two framed Art Deco Matson Cruise Line menus.

"Where are you going to put them? Your walls are full." I'd been searching for Matson prints for ages. Tentacles of envy reached out, lending a distinct whine to my voice.

"I'll find a place." Mother's confident response when challenged to fit another piece of furniture or artwork into the house. "If I can't, I'll just have to find a deserving recipient." Her smile assured me that the pictures were destined for my birthday or Christmas stash.

"Those will make a nice gift." The voice came from over my shoulder. I turned to find Marla Matsumoto, clad in flowing multicolor-paisley-print pants, a tight pink top, and pounds of jewelry.

After an awkward hello, I introduced Marla to my mother.

"Emma told me you have wonderful Hiroshige woodblock prints in your home," Mother said, her charm on full blast. Marla brightened. Before I knew it, they were discussing Asian art and walking off together. I followed in their wake wondering if this was a chance encounter, or if Marla had been following us? If so, why had she approached? To confirm the identity of my mother so she could threaten her to get to me? I stayed close to the pair, and slipped my hand into the cat knuckles in my purse, ready to do battle. Several times Marla or Mother would pause at a booth to examine the jewelry or crafts and I was able to overhear snatches of conversation, which assured me they were not trading information on murders, bombs, or messy divorces.

With Marla setting the pace, we wound our way through the crowd. I heard Mother ask Marla about a place to get a cold drink and she led us to the Queens Café, a small snack stand just off the beach. All the tables were occupied so Mother did her best vulture imitation, leaning over a couple that had finished eating and were talking. It embarrasses me when she does this, but it invariably works; we were able to snag a table with already-warmed seats—not that we needed them in eighty-degree weather—and order refreshments.

The afternoon sun glared off the ocean and although we were seated in the shade, we kept our sunglasses on. Consequently, I was unable to read Marla's eyes when she turned to me and launched her missile.

"Why is Coconuts not in jail yet?"

Was she teasing, or serious?

"Did you know that Greg was almost broke?" she added.

Okay, not teasing. "How do you know that?"

"My nephew is, or was, his accountant. Did you know that Coconuts had a multi-million dollar insurance policy on Greg?"

"Joline said that she was the beneficiary of Greg's policy. In fact, she offered to pay me $500 if I'd do her a small favor." If one called ratting out the most powerful gang in Japan a "small" favor.

"What favor?" Marla frowned.

"It doesn't matter; I'm not doing it."

"Well, anyway, that's not the policy I'm talking about. Carmen took out a life insurance policy on Greg and she paid the premiums. With Greg dead, she'll collect millions."

"Did she have a bona fide financial interest?" Mother asked, leaning forward in her chair.

Marla nodded. "Child support from Greg."

Seeing my confusion, Mother explained. "One can't take out an insurance policy on just anyone. You must have a financial interest that would be harmed by his or her death."

How did Mother know these things?

"With Greg broke, he became more valuable to her dead than alive," Marla said.

"You couldn't have told me this earlier? Like, say, when we first met?"

"I didn't know it then, but I've been doing some investigating."

"And while you were snooping, did you turn up anyone who saw her at the scene of the crime? Because by my count, there are over fifty people with motives for killing Greg." Just call me Ms. Snittypants.

"No. I thought you might have done that. Just how many weeks, or years, do you need to prove Coconuts' guilt?"

If she was going to be snitty back … "Has it occurred to you that Coco, er, Carmen could have hired a trained killer, like a member of the Yakuza? But then, they're not for hire unless one is Japanese, or part-Japanese, and has business interests with them, like maybe real estate investments. You would know all about that, wouldn't you? Talked to any of your Yakuza investors lately?"

The gauntlet flung down, I awaited Marla's reaction.

She laughed. "Is that what you think? Weeks investigating a murder and you blame it on a shadowy organization? A boogieman that I ordered up, no less?"

Put like that, it did sound weak.

Marla was enjoying herself way too much. "Do tell, why would I order a hit on Greg?"

"I heard that when you divorced, he promised to pay the college tuition for your kids and that he reneged on it and you were angry."

"To think that the San Francisco police rely on you to solve their toughest cases and a book is being written on your exploits."

Mother gave me a speculative look, which I ignored for the moment.

Marla continued. "Greg made a lot of promises he didn't keep, like wedding vows. Even having his commitment in writing meant nothing, as many an unpaid contractor or upset homeowner could tell you. I wouldn't be surprised if right now Greg is trying to get out of a pact he made with the devil, and if the devil is smart, he'll let him go and good riddance."

She paused to take a sip of her drink and shoo an inquisitive sparrow that perched on the edge of the table, cheeping loudly for a handout.

"I had nothing to gain by his death, except the removal of an annoying boil from my backside, and I would not do anything to hurt my children who, despite Greg's behavior, loved their father and feel his loss."

I didn't have an answer for her, but Mother did.

"I'm sorry your feelings are hurt, but Emma is doing her best to find Greg's killer. I'm sure you realize that in her position, everyone is a suspect. If you want to help your children, you might think about using your connections to search for any and *all* information that might be useful, rather than conducting a vendetta against Carmen. As Emma pointed out, there are other suspects with motives."

Carmen appeared surprised. "You're a PI, too?"

"Absolutely not. But I know a bitter ex-wife when I see one."

"Well, excuse me," Marla said. Although it came out more like, "Weeelllll, excuuuuuuuse, me." Marla stalked off, without saying goodbye, no less.

"Accusing people of murder to their face? Is that your normal investigative style, from the V.I. Warshawski School of charm?" Mother said.

I shrugged. "Sometimes it works."

"And what's this about being a consultant to the police and being written up in a book?"

"I'm guessing that Keoni, in trying to impress Uncle Kimo, may have exaggerated my value to the police. The book thing probably started with him, too. A woman I worked with last fall wanted to use my adventures as a basis for her next bare chests and heaving bosoms romance novel. Uncle Kimo fed the rumor mill and the tale has mutated. Perhaps in another week or two the rumor will include the made-for-TV movie based on my exploits. No, a direct-to-video movie. Better yet, a blockbuster movie in 3-D. Emma Stone is playing my part."

Mother shook her head. "Anything else I should know that you haven't told me? Like why you are parking blocks away from your apartment?"

Busted, again, I reluctantly told Mother about my encounters with the black SUV. She took the news stoically, although during the recitation of my evasion attempts her eyebrows went up so far it appeared as if she'd overdosed on Botox. She cautioned me yet again to carry the self-defense gizmos and not drive or walk lonely streets at night. Since my apartment was in the midst of Waikīkī, lonely was hard to come by. As for the self-defense gizmos, I assured her that the Shrieker, pepper spray, and cat knuckles were in my purse.

"Take the ninja stars."

"I'm not sure I can throw them with any accuracy. Anyway, I'd need a shoulder bag the size of Molokaʻi to carry all that."

Mother suggested I practice by throwing the ninja stars against the bathroom door. I mentioned the issue of damages to the apartment coming out of my pocket and she countered with my safety being more important than the cost of a door. My mother won the argument (so what else is new?) and that evening I worked on my technique. By the end of the session, I was feeling confident that I could hit an assailant, provided he was exactly twelve feet away, stationary, brightly lit and had a brass knob on one side.

Mother promised to drop off a check with building management and a note that a woodpecker had entered the apartment and damaged a door.

I didn't tell her that there are no woodpeckers in Hawaiʻi and blaming a rogue gecko was more plausible. One with a very small chain saw.

THIRTY-THREE

"Stalking is when two people go for a long
romantic walk together but only one of them
knows about it."

Anonymous

I HADN'T PARKED far enough from the apartment; I found another
note on my windshield Monday morning: "STOP SNOPING
NOW. THIS IS YOUR LAST WARNING." Like the others, it
was written in ink—red this time. Now that I was a veteran threat
recipient, I must say I found the use of block letters unimaginative.
At least my bully could have used an appropriate font, like Angry Arial, Hate-Filled Helvetica or Paranoid Palatino. Torn edges,
crumpled paper, and blood spatters would have pulled the entire
threat thread together, too.

"What is it, Emma? A parking ticket?"

"Another note from my tail. Wants me to stop 'snoping.' The
only 'snope' I know about is the urban legend web site. Honestly,
the last time I used it was nine months ago when I was trying to
determine …"

Mother gave me one of those "Tell me everything right now!"
looks. Her deep blue eyes bored in, unblinking: level nine on the
fury scale and way more scary than my father's best efforts. Virgil
and Ariadne had been in trouble regularly and they'd become in-
ured to Mother's stare downs. I had not.

"They're from the person tailing me," I said, assuming a false bra-
vado. "His, or her, grammar and spelling leave a lot to be desired."

Although she'd met the news of my ubiquitous tail with aplomb, this clearly had her unnerved. She wanted to know if I at least had the common sense to tell Kimo and Keoni about the notes.

My diffident shrug sent her into orbit. According to her I was "cavalier" and "gave no thought to those who loved me."

I'd not heard every lecture Mother had bestowed upon my siblings, but her reaction to the note was over the top. Was it my fault that I was being stalked by a grammar-challenged, third-rate menace? I may have investigated a little murder now and then, which was bound to entail risk, but unlike my siblings, I didn't throw myself into life-threatening situations. Well, not knowingly. Two years ago Ariadne hiked to Everest base camp, when we all thought she was vacationing in Orlando. Virgil had tried hang-gliding and even contemplated getting his own rig.

"No one on this case has actually pointed a gun at me, or tried to strangle me." Perhaps not the best rejoinder, but all I could come up with at the time.

"Someone who leaves a note could just as easily leave a bomb."

"But probably not both." I argued that Walker had left his car windows down and his sunroof open, in flagrant support of the Terrorists with Disabilities Act: all the killer had to do was drop a package in the back seat. If someone broke into the 4Runner, which I always kept locked and with the windows up, I'd notice.

Mother suggested I quit the investigation. "Right now," she said, in a tone of voice previously employed for exhortations to write thank-you notes, sit up straight, and clean up your room This Instant And I Really Mean It.

I protested that I wanted to stay involved. Yes, the investigation was eating up my free time and taking away from surfing. Yes, there was an element of danger. Yes, it was probably my pride talking, but with all my self-defense gizmos and a little caution on my part reinforced by Mother's hovering, I should be okay.

This time I stared her down and won the point.

"I can't stop you, but you must tell Kimo and Keoni about the threats, and anything else you haven't mentioned."

I agreed, and to further placate her, I checked under the car and the hood for any devices with blinking red lights and sagging wires. Not that I recalled the online bomb making instructions saying anything about blinking lights, but all the bombs on TV shows had them.

No one tailed us to work and I waved as Mother drove off on her way to the Polynesian Cultural Center.

Following up on my agreement, I called Uncle Kimo first thing. Not surprisingly, he was peeved that I hadn't told him about the threats or the tail.

"*E Emma*, I thought we agreed you were not going to try to find the killer and you would inform me of everything you discovered."

I caught myself before explaining the difference between what I found out versus what happened to me, which didn't constitute discovery as much as unpleasant experience. As if I were going to win that argument against a lawyer. I simply apologized and said he was right.

Uncle said he'd have a good talk with his nephew about full disclosure of facts, seemingly unaware the I'd not told Keoni anything, either. As long as Uncle planned to speak with Keoni, I figured I didn't have to. Keoni would be angry when he heard the news second-hand. I'd talk with him later, when he'd cooled off—in 2020, maybe.

The GD staff had an impromptu feel-good session with David Blanchard and when he expressed appreciation for our hard work and how our success on this contract would make it easier for him to market and build the business, Karen slumped in her chair.

I'd barely reached my cube after the meeting when Edvard stopped by. That is, he stopped by Karen's cube and peered over the top at me in an "aren't-you-going-to-join-us" look that I couldn't resist.

"I'm reconsidering whether to join the government practice," he said without preamble. "Michael says David wants me to write a blog, but I'm not doing it."

During the feel-good session David had stressed the importance of social media accounts in driving new and repeat business and he encouraged us to connect through LinkedIn, Twitter and Facebook if we had not already done so. I was already on all three, but barely used them for personal purposes, and was adrift as to the business benefits. I couldn't imagine tweeting, "Wow, found totally cool chart of accounts at customer x!!! Who knew you could expense your mistresses' lingerie? LOL!" to anybody I wanted to impress as a potential business client. To say nothing of pictures I'd seen of women on LinkedIn that looked like selfies taken at a strip club after way too much alcohol. Not the professional image you wanted to project—unless you were in the world's oldest profession.

"No offense, Edvard," Karen said, "But why does David want *you* to write a blog?"

Edvard shrugged. "My technical wizardry in database analytics; David thinks that if I shared tips and tricks, I'll build a following and a name for myself. I told Michael that I didn't want a name, and I don't do social media."

"Everybody does social media. Even my surf buddy Harrison's dog has his own Facebook page," I said. The dog had more friends than I did.

Edvard was unconvinced. "Social media is prime hunting grounds for 'Them.'"

"Which 'Them' are we talking about? The corporate 'Them' or the government 'Them?'" Karen said.

Edvard took a big sip of his coffee and sighed. He shifted in his chair and gave another sigh. I thought I caught an ear adjustment; did he have on fake ears, again? Had Edvard challenged Michael about the gender discrimination issue?

"The government, your employers, corporations, all of them," he said. "'They' analyze your clicks and sell your information to advertisers and marketers. A startup based in the DC area uses facial recognition technology in uploaded photos to link with your social media accounts. A tourist could be taking a selfie on the beach, catch you in the background, and this software identifies you. Suddenly, your social media sites are showing that you are on Oʻahu."

"I know all that," Karen said. "Why should I care?"

"It's the stalker's friend. I take a picture of you on the street—you are kind of cute, Karen—I use the facial recognition software to find your social media accounts, get access to all that information about you like where you live, where you went to school, and that check-in you just did at a favorite restaurant. Now I know where to find you. Wherever, whenever I want."

"But you're not, are you?"

"Not what?"

"Well, you know. We ran into each other on Saturday at Kapiʻolani Park. That was a coincidence, right?"

Edward averted his eyes. Were his ears turning red? "Not exactly," he said.

Karen leaned back in her chair, as if to distance herself from Edvard. "What do you mean, 'not exactly?'"

"I, uh, have seen your social media sites, and you talk a lot about soccer, and I noticed you had a skinned knee a couple weeks ago, and I figured you were playing soccer, so I checked out where women's teams play and I've been watching you for the past two Saturdays. It was an accident that you made me. I'd just taken off my hat and wig because they were hot and scratchy when you walked by my car. You're a good soccer player. Missed a great opportunity on Saturday, though. If you'd made your run to the goal a bit earlier and used your left foot instead of contorting your body to use your right, you'd have scored."

Karen just stared at Edward.

"Of course, it's easy to say that in retrospect. I've played a little soccer myself and I know it's difficult sometimes to judge when to make that run."

"Now's the time, Edvard," she said. "Now's the time to make that run; run back to your cube."

THIRTY-FOUR

"I must speak of a certain leader named
Artemisia, whose participation in the attack
upon Greece, notwithstanding that she was a
woman, moves my special wonder."

Herodotus

I STASHED THE car four blocks from my apartment and Mother and I strolled over to the Sheraton Waikīkī for drinks and Hawaiian music. I played tourist and ordered a Hula Girl: gin, triple sec and lemon. We all need more vitamin C in our diets. Besides, it came with a cute umbrella toothpick. Mother, sipping a white wine, was telling me about her day when she broke off in mid-sentence. I followed her gaze toward a scruffy-looking man purposefully approaching our table. In his twenties or thirties with a two-day-old beard, sunburned arms and nose, plaid shorts, and a cheap Hawaiian shirt—plastic, not coconut-shell buttons—every inch screamed tourist. He ignored Mom, came straight over to me, and slammed a note on the table.

"Read it," he commanded, and turned to leave.

Years before at a family picnic, my six-year-old sister was plunging out of a tree when Mom hurdled a picnic table, dodged two active toddlers and made a flying catch of Ariadne in 1.2 seconds. Never underestimate the protective instincts of a devoted mother.

The man was on the floor holding his nose with Mom standing over him before I knew what happened. Good to know she hadn't lost her touch when she thought her chicks were threatened.

245

Had she known the note promised an evening of fun if I dumped "the old lady," she might have hit him harder. And lower.

Twenty-two minutes later with the help of the hotel restaurant manager, an onsite nurse, and a prepaid drink coupon for Ryan, Mom's victim, we were on our way. As a parting shot, Ryan said with a leer that he was a forgiving type and his room had "the best view in Hawai'i." I replied that he should try honking, and left him to figure out what it meant. (Mom requested an explanation of what geese imitations had to do with sleazebags, which I provided.)

"What I don't understand," I said when we stopped to pick up a pizza, "is why you hit him in the nose with the pepper shaker. Last minute substitute for pepper spray? What happened to your self-defense gizmos? I thought you and the U.S. Coast Guard are both *semper paratus*, always prepared!"

Mom was embarrassed. "Too much stuff in my bag; I couldn't find any of them quickly. From now on, I'm keeping everything in the outside pocket of my purse."

KAREN WAS WALKING on air the next morning. I found out why when she slipped into my cube just before lunch.

"I've set up face time with David on Wednesday morning to discuss moving to his practice area."

"Good for you."

"Gunnar is a changed man. He was waiting for me in my cube this morning to apologize for his actions. He admitted he'd been totally out of line but that it wouldn't happen again. Ever. He wanted to start over in our relationship and asked that in the future, if he was insensitive in any way, I was to let him know. Can you believe it? It's like he had an encounter with a burning bush."

"*Maika'i nō!*" I couldn't resist a knowing smile: a very large, expansive, Cheshire cat-like smile.

"I should have guessed. What did you do; get pictures of Gunnar with a prostitute?"

I wiped my grin with the back of my hand. "Let's just say that I used my connections."

"You *have* to tell me."

So I did. In whispers I gave Karen a quick overview of surfing etiquette, like dropping in, and how Manoa and his friend Solosolo acted as enforcers in the lineup. Big sweethearts but weighing between 500 and 600 pounds collectively and each over six feet and heavily tattooed, they could intimidate anybody.

"If they tell you to be more polite to other surfers, you are going to be more polite or you aren't going to surf anymore. See?"

"What does this have to do with—?"

"Hear me out." I explained how Manoa introduced me to Kekoa's restaurant, had seen me there with Karen, and had seen Karen's ill-fated lunch with Gunnar and mentioned it to me on Saturday morning in the lineup. Manoa and Solosolo decided to have a chat with Gunnar. Edvard contributed to the effort by sticking a GPS tracker on Gunnar's car. Manoa and Solosolo cornered Gunnar in a parking lot outside a Foodland Monday night where Gunnar was shopping for dinner.

"They told Gunnar that if he didn't stop bugging *sistah* Kalena, as they call you, that they would see to it that his genes didn't get passed along, *evah*. And they convinced Gunnar that they were part of the Yakuza and could reach him anywhere. I'm sure Gunnar checked up on the Yakuza and discovered their Mafioso-like reputation."

"I owe you, big time."

"One last thing," I said. "The price for not saying anything now, and letting my friends take care of it, is that we need to be vigilant to ensure Gunnar doesn't do this to anybody else. If he does, then you send the recording to GD management. Gunnar may think it's inconclusive, but it is not clear that management will. You let Gunnar know that. Deal?"

Karen was all for us going to Kekoa's for lunch; she wanted to give Manoa a big hug and thank you. I put her off until later in the week. "Maybe after David gives you a thumb's up."

MOTHER RECOUNTED HER activities for the day and claimed that once again she'd not been followed by the black SUV. "I think you should stop worrying about black SUVs," she said.

I almost had. I'd seen a few black SUVs, but none of them appeared to be tailing us, nor was one behind us now, although a white van seemed to be pacing us.

"This morning, you were upset about the notes."

"I don't think they are related to the SUV tailing you."

"I don't see how you can think that."

"Call it Mother's intuition." She then changed the topic to a discussion of Tahitian dance vs. Hawaiian hula. The old subject change shuffle: I wondered what she was up to.

Because Mom was beat and wanted to chill, we agreed to do Chinese takeout. I was trying to think of a place we could hit on the way home when Kealoha called.

"I have to see you," he said. "This evening."

"It's not very convenient; I have a family member visiting me this week. We have plans."

"You must come," he replied. "Kimo told me what you said about Kevin and his passion. I could not believe that my friend had been deceiving me. Now he has confessed everything."

"Kevin Ortiz is the killer?"

"You must come and hear him yourself."

Mom, catching half the conversation, deduced Kealoha's request and interrupted. "They sicken of the calm who know the storm."

"Huh?"

"Dorothy Parker. Go for the excitement. I'm not tired anymore. Let's go."

Kealoha wanted us to meet him and Kevin at Lo'i Kalo Labs Why there, he wouldn't say.

Taking the Likelike Highway to the windward side near rush hour, between three and eight on O'ahu, was like a slow drive through a parking lot, but the cool breeze streaming in our windows as we climbed the Ko'olaus was wonderful and my spirits rose with the elevation and the prospect of an end to the case.

Like Kealoha, Kevin wouldn't have had any difficulty stealing the explosives, but if he wasn't passionate about the protest movement, why had he killed Walker? Or was he part of a conspiracy at HuliHuli construction to kill Walker because of their losses on his projects? Or had he heard the voices of his ancestors demanding all *haoles* be driven into the sea?

My mother, perhaps sensing my mood, remained quiet.

At the lab we were escorted back to Tam's office where Kealoha and Kevin were already seated, each drinking a soda.

Introductions were completed, extra chairs were brought in and offers of more sodas were refused. Tam had barely taken his seat when Kealoha turned to Kevin. "Tell them," he said.

Kevin, his large frame hunched over, appeared to shrink from the unwanted attention. The confident demeanor I noted at our earlier encounter was not in evidence. He wrapped both hands around his soda and stared at the can while he talked. "I work construction. I'm an electrician. Mostly work for HuliHuli, but I've worked for Walker from time to time. Not electrician stuff. Just odd jobs."

Nobody said a word.

Kevin took another long swig from his can and wiped his mouth on the back of his tattooed hand.

"A couple times I acted tough with landowners who didn't want to sell. I didn't do nothing. Just, you know, kinda warned them. Once Walker even paid me to get a petition signed to ask the county government to buy a parcel he had and use it for ball fields. Nothing illegal in that."

"Akakoui State Park," I said, remembering Marla's story.

Kevin nodded.

"Tell them about Loʻi Kalo Labs," Kealoha said.

"Walker contacted me six months ago. Gave me $500 up front to join a protest movement against the labs. He made the same deal with Sam Abbott. Sam did odd jobs for Walker, too. Walker told us he'd pay us $100 a month to work with the movement and that if we could get the lab to close down, it would be worth $2,500 each."

"He suggested that we plant rumors that the lab was unsafe, that the genetically modified taro would contaminate native Hawaiian taro. We sent letter to the newspapers, and to national groups that are against genetically altering food suggesting they might want to join the Kūlohelohe protests."

"We had to tell some mainland groups to stay away, that this was a local issue." Kealoha directed his statement toward me.

"A few months ago, Walker suggested that we try to recruit guys with tempers to the movement."

"Did Walker suggest violence?" I asked.

"No, but we knew what he meant."

"The spray painting, the called-in threats, the attempted break-in, that was you."

Kevin squirmed. "Might have been."

I glanced at Tam, wondering why we were meeting in his office and what he made of all this.

Kealoha stepped in again. "Your visit with Mr. Tam."

Kevin drained his soda, but kept the can in his hands. He glanced at Tam before returning his gaze to his hands. "Well, me and Sam, we'd done this protest thing for eight months, and had been paid for three. I asked Mr. Walker for the money he owed us, said I needed the cash. He said he didn't have the money on hand, but if we'd continue, he'd pay me $150 a month, and the reward for shutting down the lab'd be $5,000. But he never did pay us."

"So you killed him for it," I said.

"No way. I didn't do it, and I dunno who did."

Tam spoke. "Mr. Ortiz approached me this afternoon and said that if I paid him and his friend $2,000, they'd stop protesting. I asked him how much it would cost to pay everyone off. Not that I was planning to do so, but I was curious as to what he would say."

"And?" I said.

"He told me that most of the protestors weren't in it for the money. Of course I wondered what he meant by that. I said there was no way I'd pay him not to protest; one more protester here and there makes no difference. Nevertheless, I offered him two hundred dollars to explain the money comment."

Tam paused in his narrative and turned toward Kevin who shrugged. "It was better than nothing," he said.

"After he told me about Walker," Tam said, "I called Kealoha. I wanted to know if he was aware of Walker's game."

"You seem pretty calm about this," I said to Tam. "Did you already know Walker was helping the protestors?"

"How could I know that?"

"I didn't ask that. I asked whether you knew."

Tam sat back in his chair, crossed his arms, and glared at me.

"When you met with Stacey and me, you told me that the protest movement wasn't going to go on much longer. Why would you say that unless you thought Walker was behind the protests? Unless you thought Walker had plotted this whole sequence of events, just to get your land? You were having financial trouble and you discovered Walker was surveying the land for a housing development. He was going to make millions while you lost everything."

"At first Walker said he wanted to help me find a way to save Hawaiian taro, that investing in my lab was a way to give back to the people of Hawai'i. Then he starts pressuring me about the business results being poor and suggests maybe I should sell out before I lost everything. When the surveyors came, I thought they were doing a boundary survey, but they told me they were conducting a full topographical survey." Tam paused as if expecting a reaction.

I didn't understand, and said so.

"A boundary survey is done for sales purposes," Mom interjected, "or for refinancing. A topographical survey typically precedes site development and is used for locating new roads and sewers, among other things."

Now where did she learn that?

"I admit I confronted Walker about the survey. The weasel denied everything, but I didn't believe him. I yelled at him, called him a few names. He said if I sold everything to him immediately he might, just might, let me have a deal on one of the new houses."

"So you killed him."

"No!" His shout hurt my ears. He lowered his voice. "The guy was a low life, but I didn't kill him."

"Do you have an alibi for the time Walker was murdered?"

Tam's silence was all I needed.

"I think you did kill him. You thought up the idea of a bomb and were smart enough to know that using fertilizer from your own farm would leave a signature. Somehow you got explosives from a HART construction site; I've heard there's practically no site security. In any case, you knew Walker was a big golfer so it was trivial to find out his golf plans and plant the device. Were you standing across the street with the detonator when you blew him into a thousand pieces?"

Tam glared, his body tense and jaw clenched.

"He did it? You can prove it?" Kealoha was on the edge of his chair.

"Emma doesn't have to prove anything." My mother chimed in. "She just needs to tell the police what she knows and let them do the work. I think we've been here long enough." With that, Mom stood up and strode toward the door.

What else was there to do? Exit, stage left.

THIRTY-FIVE

"I came. I saw. I conquered."
Julius Caesar

DEEP IN OUR own thoughts, we each went to our vehicles and drove off like rats leaving a sinking sampan. Mom was uncharacteristically quiet as I crept along the dark roads leading to the Likelike Highway. I was glad I'd been there before and had a general idea of the way out.

Another car, well behind me, was exhibiting similar caution. It was with relief that I turned onto the well-lit, well-traveled Likelike and pointed the car toward Honolulu. Up and *ovahs*, *brah*, and I'd be headed home. I tuned to Hawaiian 105 and heard Nathan Aweau sing about Kaneʻohe and the beauty of the Koʻolaus. They were stunning in daylight. But at night, they were dark, looming shapes where, I remembered with a shudder, many Hawaiian warriors had fallen to their deaths at the onslaught of Kamehameha's army.

"Sweetie, I know you have more experience in these things, but I am not entirely sure it's a good idea to directly accuse someone of murder," Mom said. "Not unless you have the police on speed dial."

"It's done all the time on TV."

"That's your guide? How to solve murders in an hour, with far too many commercials for Viagra and constipation?"

"I can't help it, Mom. What I'm thinking just blurts right out at high speed. Like projectile vomiting."

253

"A disturbing, if accurate, description. Your directness is one of your more endearing and maddening attributes. I'm not telling you to change, just to think about the fallout."

"Uh-huh," I said, half-listening. A truck or SUV was now tailgating me, its glaring lights reflecting off my mirror and nearly blinding me, the jerk. I was already driving eight miles per hour over the speed limit.

"Just go around, will you?" I said to the other driver.

As if hearing me, the driver pulled into the left lane and started to pass. Suddenly he veered toward me and banged into the 4Runner. *Aloha 'ino*. Keoni's paint job on the Toyota was less than nine months old.

I heard a sudden intake of breath from my mother as the Toyota swayed alarmingly. We slipped off the edge of the road and back onto pavement as the front tires found the entrance ramp for the H-3. I twisted the wheel and sped up the ramp, muttering *hele hele hele* under my breath. Behind me I heard the squeal of brakes as the other vehicle stopped. A glance in my side mirror showed my assailant backing up in order to turn onto the ramp.

I stomped on the accelerator and roared onto the interstate, merging into the right lane. Perhaps the other vehicle just wanted to pass me in a crazed rush for the leeward side. Dream on, Emma.

"What the by-our-lady are you doing?" Mom was seemingly unaware of what was transpiring behind us.

I knew that yell: I remembered it from my days as a student driver, but I didn't answer. I was too busy checking my rearview mirror and wondering what I was going to do if he caught up with me. His vehicle was much bigger than my 4Runner and thus had all the advantages of momentum; mass times velocity if I recall. Force, too, since that's change in momentum over time, and I didn't have much time. My assailant was gaining on me.

"Emma!" Mom sounded angry, not scared.

I glanced down: I was doing seventy-five.

"Sorry. The guy who tried to run us off the road is on my tail and he's going to catch us."

I was reluctant to push the 4Runner any faster; the handling characteristics already resembled those of a top-heavy stroller. The other driver had no such qualms; he must have been doing ninety and easily caught up. I was expecting another side-by-side push so I was unprepared for the ram from behind. I briefly lost control and we swerved onto the shoulder. Out of the corner of my eye I was aware of a too-small guardrail and blackness beyond.

Time does slow down during terror-filled moments of one's life. I would have been better served in this apparent disconnect in time if I'd thought seriously about my options. But I didn't. Instead, my gray matter was busy thinking about how the H-3 had been built almost entirely as a viaduct, rising over the trees as it made its way through the culturally and environmentally sensitive Haiku Valley. The guardrails had been designed and painted for minimal environmental impact. Not that I cared, I just wanted to know if the eco-friendly guardrails would keep a speeding 4Runner from going over the edge.

"Jesus-meek-and-humble," I said as I struggled to regain control, wrenching the Toyota back onto the interstate without tipping it over.

"He's trying to kill us." I stated the obvious in a near panic.

Mom had turned around in her seat and was staring at our pursuer.

"That can't be Corey," she said, her voice trembling.

"Who?"

"Corey, Keoni's friend. Keoni asked him to follow you when one of us wasn't around. He drives a black SUV."

I positioned the 4Runner in the middle of the road, giving me more room to maneuver if rear-bumped. Our pursuer moved first to one side and then the next, whether to pass or bump off center I didn't know.

Mom's words about Keoni's friend gradually penetrated my consciousness. "Who is 'us', er, are 'us?' And don't I have enough problems with stalkers without you or your 'us' recruiting one?"

"Stacey, Keoni, and I are 'us.' Corey was to stay near you when one of us wasn't around, in case of trouble. He was stalking you in a good cause."

"There's trouble now." I threw the wheel to the left, cutting off a passing attempt by my follower. I was prepared for the rear bump and sped up just before he hit us, lessening the impact and keeping the Toyota under control, barely.

We entered the tunnel under the Ko'olaus and my pursuer backed off slightly. Were I to crash here, there was every chance the 4Runner would rebound off the tunnel walls and take out the other vehicle, too.

"Can we get off this road?"

"No exits until Pearl Harbor except over the guardrail," I said.

"We must have been followed from the lab."

"Tam. It can only be Tam. I'm sorry, Mom." I'd been incredibly stupid, shooting my mouth off. Fear threatened to overwhelm me. Fear that I'd gone too far this time. Fear that my investigative zeal was going to kill my mother. Fear that my father, upon losing his daughter and wife, would be terribly, terribly alone.

"I love you, Mom."

"Step on it, Emma," she said flatly. There was no tremor in her voice. I stood on the accelerator: eighty, eighty-five, ninety and the truck fell behind for a few moments. There were a few other cars on the road and we swayed alarmingly as we whipped by. Angry horns followed our progress. Mom had a tight grip on her seat, watching our pursuer as I reached ninety-three, and the limits of my ability to control the Toyota. "I can't go faster or we'll crash," I said.

"He's gaining on us. Hold this speed," she said. I heard the click of her seatbelt and saw, out of the corner of my eye, that she was reclining the seat and clambering into the back.

"What are you doing?"

"Put down the back window. I'm going to pepper spray him when he gets close."

"But Mom ..." I momentarily lost focus and the Toyota drifted to the side of the road as we emerged from the tunnel. I gently guided it back to the center; any sudden movements now and we'd be a short paragraph in the *Honolulu Star-Advertiser*. Even my best efforts couldn't stop the back and forth swing of the 4Runner and I could hear my mother muttering as she was thrown around in the back. She might even have thrown in a swear word or two.

"Mom?"

"Don't worry about me. Focus on the road and put down the back window."

Glances in the rearview mirror revealed approaching lights and the outline of my mother crouched at the window. What she thought pepper spray would accomplish, I didn't know.

"Whatever you hear, don't look back," Mom yelled. So I didn't. I stared at the road and drove. Then it came, the squeal of brakes, prolonged tires screeching, and a crash. I heard nothing more but the rushing of the wind through the open window and my mother's calm voice.

"You can slow down, dear. We're quite all right. Oh, and please close the window. It's a bit chilly. For Hawai'i, that is."

I took my foot off the accelerator and let the 4Runner coast until we were five miles an hour under the speed limit. I could hear Mom making her way forward, crawling into her seat, adjusting it, and putting her seatbelt on with a reassuring click. My hands were still clenched on the steering wheel. I was afraid if I looked at her, I'd lose all focus and we'd crash.

The welcome sight of the lights of Pearl Harbor unfolded before us.

"I could use one of your father's gin and tonics right now," Mom said. "But I think a drink will have to wait until after a visit with the police; I don't want to be interviewed with booze on my breath. Do you know where there is a police station?"

I nodded.

"Can you make it there?"

I nodded, again.

"Good, because I don't think I could drive right now."

"But you were calm and—"

"'A hero is no braver than an ordinary man, but he is braver five minutes longer.' Ralph Waldo Emerson. My five minutes is up. I think I only lasted about ninety seconds, tops."

"How did you—"

"The pepper spray. I suppose I forgot to tell you that it also included a red dye, to make it easy for the police to track an assailant. I sprayed it when he got close. I expect that he wasn't able to see with the dye on the windshield. He panicked, hit the brakes, and slid into the guardrail. I don't think the he went over the side. He may be alive, although honestly, I don't care one way or the other."

"Thanks, Mom."

We remained in stunned silence for a moment, until I added, "Though really, red dye is so last year. Couldn't you have used a nice coral?"

At that, we both broke up, in a combination of silliness and relief. She reached over and patted my hand on the steering wheel. "We make a great team, kiddo."

Maika'i nō.

THIRTY-SIX

"'Ike aku, 'ike mai, kōkua aku kōkua mai; pela
iho la ka nohana 'ohana." (Recognize others,
be recognized, help others, be helped; such is
the 'ohana relationship.)

Hawaiian Proverb

ONCE OFF THE H-3 and headed in the direction of Waikīkī we
called Uncle Kimo, gave him the gist of what happened, and asked
him to tell Detective Karratti about the accident. Uncle Kimo suggested that hypothetically speaking, should we happen to be in
possession of any self-defense gizmos prohibited in Hawai'i—I'm
not quite sure how he knew unless the Mom to Keoni to Kimo coconut wireless was working overtime—we'd best stop at the apartment and dispose of said contraband before going to the police. So
we did and hid our weapons, all except for the empty canister of
pepper spray, which I chucked into a dumpster behind a restaurant
on Lewers Street.

At my request, Karratti and Uncle Kimo met us at the Waikīkī
substation, conveniently located on Kalākaua Avenue at Kūhio
Beach, a primo location between the Queens and Canoes surf
breaks. Karratti was slightly built and slightly stooped—hard to
believe he had played football—and more than slightly impatient.
"What took you so long?" was his greeting, without even an "*E,
howzit sistah?*" greeting.

Mom smiled brightly. "My fault. I was so darn jittery that I
asked Emma to drive me back to her apartment so I could refresh

my makeup. A touch-up to my eyeliner, a little blush and lip-gloss always soothes me. Don't know why though I swear, knowing I look good makes me feel ever so much better." Another revelation about my mother! She could act. At least, she could play a ditz. She missed a few "and I'm likes" and "then he goes," and her hair was too short to toss with an accompanying eye roll, but otherwise, nobody would take her for a Ph.D. in comparative literature. Maybe a BA in, like, psychology. Totally.

"Well, you're here now. I'd like to get your statement."

Karratti didn't bother to separate us for questioning, but took us into a small conference room. From time to time I heard a surfer plunking a board into the surf lockers just outside the police station and it was all I could do not to bolt out the door, snatch a board, and catch one of the juicy rights at Queens under the moonlight.

Uncle Kimo invited himself into the room as our lawyer. I suspect if we were hit with any charges—reckless driving, failure to indicate lane change, passenger not using seat belt, unauthorized use of pepper spray on an inanimate object even if the object richly deserved it—his experience with native Hawaiian rights would be of little use. Nevertheless, Uncle Kimo's presence was a comfort.

Karratti began by asking me what I had done that might cause someone to run me off the road. Assuming that Uncle had already explained my investigative role, I launched into the story of my visit to Lo'i Kalo Labs and Kevin's revelations. Karratti interrupted frequently for clarification. By the time I got to my deductions about Raymond Tam and accusation of murder, Karratti had ceased asking questions and limited his comments to an occasional "I see." His stiffening posture and folded arms told me he was not happy with my answers and the look of alarm on Uncle's face confirmed I was in deep *kimchi*.

I gave, I thought, a succinct account of the mad car chase. I didn't think I needed to say anything about hitting ninety-three miles per hour since the H-3 was rife with surveillance cameras and the police could calculate our speed themselves. When I concluded, leaving out the part where we had stashed the self-defense gizmos, the room was momentarily silent, except for Karratti's loud breathing: a volcano venting steam prior to a catastrophic eruption.

"Is Mr. Tam dead?" Mother was the first to speak.

Karratti turned toward her. "Tam? The driver of the car was Tony Perello. He's been taken to the hospital under guard."

"Perello?" I was stunned. "Are you sure?" Stupid question, Emma. Stupid. Not like a *haole* guy on the hottie side could possibly be confused with a geezer guy of Asian extraction.

Karratti nodded. "Can you think of any reason Mr. Perello would want to kill you?"

I shook my head, my thoughts jumbled. "I didn't even send him a note."

"A note?"

I barely heard him as I continued to think out loud. "Unless … he could be in league with Carmen. She got a note."

"What note?"

"She must have called Perello, but how did she know I wrote it? I was so careful not to mail it anyplace conspicuous. I didn't see any surveillance cameras, not that Carmen would have access to the video, or be able to—"

"WHAT NOTE?" Karratti's bellow startled me out of my nervous Emma-nations.

"Ah, well, you see, I wasn't making a lot of progress in the investigation. So a few days ago, I sent notes to some suspects—okay, maybe all of them, except the Yakuza ones because I didn't have an address for them—saying that this was the last chance to surrender because I knew everything and planned to tell the police. The letters were anonymous, of course."

I'd never see someone with such a deep tan turn as bright red as an *'i'iwi* (scarlet honeycreeper). The rest of the interview was *'olu'olu 'ole*—not pleasant, not at all. Karratti screamed at all of us: at me for waving a red flag in front of a murderer (he increased the pitch when I pointed out that that was the point—how else was I supposed to find out whodunnit?). He yelled at Mom for raising a child without a lick of common sense when it came to self-preservation. He screamed most vociferously at Kimo for dragging a rank amateur into police business. When I opened my mouth to point out that a rank amateur had solved his case, so there, too, Mom must have read my mind; she kicked me under the table.

When we emerged from the police station, battered and bruised—well, I was bruised from Mom's kick—Uncle Kimo proposed taking us somewhere to for dinner. "No," Mom said. "You can take us someplace for drinks and offer us food to wash down the alcohol." The Mai Tai Bar at the Royal Hawaiian was close, and the bartender had a heavy hand. *Kupaianaha.*

Uncle Kimo and Mom got on famously over drinks and by the time the entrées arrived, I was famished, and a bit dizzy from the alcohol. It was all I could do to shovel food in and grunt occasionally. I vaguely remember singing a chorus of "Wai O Ke Aniani" with the band. Mom and I might even have been coaxed into a hula lesson. It must have been the "Hukilau Song" because hula lessons at tourist venues are always to the "Hukilau Song." I didn't need a lesson on pulling a fish net in to music, because I had already caught a very, very big fish today. So there, Detective Karratti.

Later, Mom and I wove our way down Kalākaua dodging street musicians, mimes, and hordes of tourists enjoying the perfect ending to a perfect day in Paradise. By silent agreement, we went straight to bed. Fortunately, I was too tired to dream that night, but later, dreams of losing my mother would haunt me almost every night.

The next morning I was so mentally fuzzy that not even multiple shots of distilled caffeine could get my neurons to fire in any semblance of order. Mom drove me to work and said she planned to visit a spa for a nice massage and a mani-pedi, after, that is, she took a drive on the H-3 in the daylight to enjoy the scenery and admire the guardrails. The lovely, lovely guardrails.

We didn't hear anything from Uncle Kimo or Karratti that day, and speculated endlessly about what might be happening.

Mother suggested that I might want to call Raymond Tam and apologize for my behavior. I declined.

"The only way he'll forgive me is if I give him Stacey's address and telephone number, and she'd never forgive me if I did. She might just call the convent and tell them I've been the one giving out their phone number to oversexed males."

The following afternoon, Uncle Kimo called. He and Karratti were back on speaking terms, and he'd learned that Perello—who must have "saltwater for brains" according to Uncle—had hidden explosives in the wall-mounted sharks in his apartment. (I suggested to Mom that we move the ninja stars and stun gun we'd stashed behind the Japanese prints in the bedroom.)

Informed by Karratti that complete honesty might get him a more lenient sentence, Perello immediately confessed and fingered Carmen as the instigator, no surprise. She was after the millions from the insurance policy she'd taken out on Walker several years previously in one of his earlier sashays with bankruptcy. Carmen had feared that Walker was running out of money again and that her support payments would decline right along with her lifestyle. She couldn't face the loss of her home, the private school and elaborate summer camps for the girls, or the new car she leased each year. (I could add, "and Botox and dermal fillers are like, sooooo expensive.") Since Greg was worth more dead than alive, Carmen promised $80,000 to Perello to kill Greg and had given him a $5,000 down payment—the monetary part of the down payment, that is. Meow.

My ferreting around had made Carmen nervous and she told Perello to try to scare me off; he was the author of the grammatically incorrect menacing notes left on the 4Runner. When Carmen received the "I know everything" letter, she assumed I was the author and ordered Perello to find a way to stop my snooping. I'm grateful he didn't choose to blow me up.

Mom extended her visit for a few days, claiming she needed a real vacation after nailing the perp. I thought she might need a few days in remedial English, having lapsed into murder mystery-ese.

As for me, I returned to surfing before work, happy that I could spend more time in the water now I no longer had to hike miles to my car. Manoa greeted me warmly each day and kept guys in the lineup from dropping in on me with just a raised eyebrow. Okay, perhaps a flex of his heavily tattooed and *nui loa* biceps. He had heard the story of my adventure from his cousin's aunt's brother-in-law's niece who was, but-of-course, dating Karratti. The only secrets in Hawai'i are the *kaona:* the hidden meanings in the music.

The day before Mom left, the police found Carmen on the island of Hawai'i, trying to board a plane to the mainland under an assumed name. She denied everything, of course. Perello, bless his murderous heart, insisted that Carmen be made to pay him the money she still owed him because, after all, he had carried out his end of the deal and he needed the money for a good lawyer. Also, to mount a shark he'd recently speared.

That evening, Mom put forth an alarming suggestion. "We—that is, Stacey, Keoni, and I—concur that you need our help on your investigations, so you're going to get it. We want to know about any cases you take on."

I was speechless.

"Though really, dear, please try not to start a murder investigation in the next few months: I want to have time with my new grandchild. Maybe this summer we could look into who killed Blubber Boy."

"Who?"

"Blubber Boy, the surfer you found under your car at the beach last summer."

"Ah, Wave Hog."

"Right. I never did understand why you didn't look into that; you were on a roll, just coming off solving the murder of your boss."

Is this the same woman who freaked when I told her Padmanabh had been killed?

"And after all, you have informants in the surfing community."

"They are 'surf bros,' Mom. We don't usually discuss which surfers have been killed recently."

"Nonetheless, Stacey and Keoni and I all agree that it's a nice, close-to-home murder case where we can pitch in. In the meantime, I'd like to pick up a few more self-defense items, like the combo mace-and-pepper-spray gun in pink with a 25-foot range and an LED for those hard-to-make night shots. Would you like one for your birthday? It's small enough to fit in your purse; I checked."

If you can't beat 'em, join 'em.

"I bet if you order online, you can get a set of pink handcuffs to match."

GLOSSARY

(All words are Hawaiian unless otherwise noted)

'ahi poke – raw yellow fin tuna with spices

'ahi – yellow fin tuna

a hui hou – until we meet again

akamai – clever

'alaea – Hawaiian sea salt

aloha – hello, goodbye, love

aloha 'ino – alas, what a pity

a'ole mea – nothing

aloha pumehana iā 'oukou – warm *aloha* to you all

a'ole loa – not at all, certainly not

'apapane – type of Hawaiian honeycreeper

auwē – alas

auwē, Hōkūle'a te vahine o ke kai – oh, Hōkūle'a, woman of the sea

auwē, noho'i e – alas

'awapuhi – wild ginger

beaucoup – (French) many

broke da mout – (Hawaiian pidgin) delicious

char siu – (Chinese) a type of barbecued pork in Cantonese cuisine

corpus delicti – (Latin) body of crime

da kine – (Hawaiian pidgin) type, kind, good

de rigueur – (French) fashionable, all the rage

e luana 'oe – enjoy

'ewa – place name for area west of Honolulu

grindz – (Hawaiian pidgin) food

ha'a – war chant

hala – pandanus

hale – house

hale'aina – restaurant

hana lepo – make a mess

haole – white person, foreigner

267

hapa – person of mixed blood
hapa-haole – part white and part Hawaiian
hau – sea hibiscus
haupia – coconut custard
Hawai'i nei – here in Hawai'i
he'e – octopus
he'e nalu pua'a – wave hog
he 'ike ana hou – a fresh look
hele – come or go
he nohea 'oe i ku'u maka – you are lovely indeed
hoaloha – friend
honi – to kiss
honu – green sea turtle
ho'olei – to put a *lei* on someone
ho'omā'ona – eat up
ho'oponopono – to make things right
hula – Hawaiian dance
hūpō – stupid
'i'iwi – scarlet honeycreeper
ilio – dog
imu – underground oven
i mua – forward
'iole – rat, rodent
Kahiki – Tahiti
kahiko wale nō – old, indeed
kalo – taro
kālua – to bake in a ground oven
ka lumi ho'opau pilikia – bathroom
kama'āina – native-born
kanaka maoli – true native
kānaka Hawai'i – the people of Hawai'i
kāne– man
kāne nui loa – very big man
kaona – hidden meaning in Hawaiian poetry or music
kaukau – (Hawaiian pidgin) food

kau mau hoa maikaʻi – your good friends
ke Akua – God
keiki – child, children
keʻokeʻo – white
ke ʻōlelo paʻa nei au – I promise
Kepanī – Japanese
kīkā – guitar, cigar
kimchi – Korean pickled or fermented cabbage
kine – (Hawaiian pidgin) type, kind. Also *da kine*
koa – acacia koa, a native Hawaiian hardwood
kōkua – help
kuʻekuʻe wāwae wahī – ankle wrap
kukui – candlenut tree
kulikuli – noisy
kūlohelohe – natural, unprocessed
kupaianaha – amazing
kupuna – ancestor, grandparent
kuʻu pua nani – my beautiful flower
lānai – porch, veranda
lau hala – woven pandanus leaves
lei – necklace, typically of flowers
lei o mano – a shark tooth-encrusted Hawaiian weapon
liʻiliʻi – little
lilikoʻi – passion fruit
loʻi kalo – taro field
lomi – salmon or fish, usually raw, worked with the fingers
lomilomi – type of Hawaiian massage
lūʻau – taro tops, Hawaiian feast
mahalo, e ke Akua – thank you, God
mahalo no ka lei lani – thank you for the beautiful *lei*
mahiki – Bermuda grass
mahimahi – dolphin fish, wahoo
maikaʻi nō – good
maile – a Pacific island vine, often used in a *lei*
makai – seaward

make – to die, death

makemake au i kope – I want coffee

makuahine – mother

malahini – newcomer

mālama – preserve, protect, care for

mana – spiritual power

manapua – Hawaiian contraction for "*mea 'ono o ka pua'a*" or "delicious pig thing"

mauka – mountain, toward the mountains

mauna – toward the sea

mea ho'okani pila akamai – skillful musician

mea hūpō – fools

moai – carved monolithic stone figures

mo' bettah – (Hawaiian pidgin) even better

mu'umu'u – Hawaiian loose dress

nā mele – songs

niele – nosy

nigiri – (Japanese) a type of sushi with raw fish slice atop oblong, compacted rice

niho mano – shark teeth

niu – coconut

nohea – handsome

nō ka 'oi – the best

nui loa – very large

'ohana – family

'okina – separation, glottal stop

'ōkole – rear end, buttocks

'ōkolehao – a drink made from *ti* root

'olu'olu 'ole – not pleasant

'ono – delicious

'ōpū nui – big stomach

pakalolo – marijuana

papale – hat

pau – finished, ended, done

pau hana – end of work

pehea 'oe – how are you

pehea 'oe i keia ahiahi – how are you this morning

pia – beer

pīkake – jasmine, peacock

pilikia – trouble, problem

pipikaula – Hawaiian beef jerky

poi – Hawaiian food staple made from taro

poke – raw fish

pōloli loa – very hungry

pua melia – plumeria

pūpū – hors d'oeuvre

pupule – crazy

quelle surprise – (French) what a surprise

rident stolidi verba latina – (Latin) only fools laugh at the Latin language

sic utere tuo ut alienum non laedas – (Latin) use [what is] yours so as not to harm [what is] of others

slippahs – (Hawaiian pidgin) flip-flops

ti – cordyline terminalis, member of the lily family

'ulu – breadfruit

ulua – giant trevally

wahine – woman, female

welina – a greeting similar to *aloha*

wikiwiki – quick, quickly